Gently Daniel dropped a hand to her shoulder. Lizzie felt her breath catch in her throat as she anticipated his next move.

Slowly, so slowly, Daniel ran his fingers along the neckline of her dress, and she knew she'd scream if he didn't delve deeper. Lizzie knew what they were doing was wrong, but she also knew that if Daniel stopped she would shatter from pure frustration.

Daniel stopped. Lizzie moaned, trying to pull him closer again, not caring if she was behaving like a common street walker. She wanted Daniel. Her body was screaming out in need of him.

She looked up with unfocused eyes and saw the confusion on his face. Of everything she'd expected to see there, confusion hadn't been part of it.

Lizzie wondered once again what he saw when he looked at her. She knew he couldn't truly be attracted to her, but when he kissed her it seemed so real, so passionate, she couldn't believe he didn't feel some spark of desire. Surely even the most consummate of actors couldn't fake what they had just shared?

Author Note

I started to write *An Earl in Want of a Wife* when I was heavily pregnant, and when I was planning this book my mind was taken up with all things to do with children. In this day and age in our society it does not much matter if your parents are married or not when you're born, but with motherhood looming I got to thinking about families in Regency England. I realised that illegitimacy had far-reaching consequences for those living a couple of hundred years ago, and a man with an illegitimate child would have had many difficult decisions to make. With all this in my mind Daniel, a gentleman agonising over such decisions, was born.

As Daniel's character developed I realised he needed a very special woman to help him overcome not only the harsh judgements of society but also his own sometimes misguided ideas about fatherhood. Lizzie is that woman. She is the quintessential ugly duckling, but throughout the book she blossoms into a confident young woman. When writing *An Earl in Want of a Wife* I was infused with the sentimentality of pregnancy, and I wanted her to find her happy ending just as I would my own child.

AN EARL
IN WANT OF A WIFE

Laura Martin

This is a work of fiction. Names, characters, places, locations and incidents are purely fictional and bear no relationship to any real life individuals, living or dead, or to any actual places, business establishments, locations, events or incidents. Any resemblance is entirely coincidental.

First published in Great Britain 2016
By Mills & Boon, an imprint of HarperCollins*Publishers*
1 London Bridge Street, London, SE1 9GF

Large Print edition 2016

© 2016 Laura Martin

ISBN: 978-0-263-26304-6

Our policy is to use papers that are natural, renewable and recyclable products and made from wood grown in sustainable forests. The logging and manufacturing processes conform to the legal environmental regulations of the country of origin.

Printed and bound in Great Britain
by CPI Antony Rowe, Chippenham, Wiltshire

Laura Martin writes historical romances with an adventurous undercurrent. When not writing she spends her time working as a doctor in Cambridgeshire, where she lives with her husband. In her spare moments Laura loves to lose herself in a book, and has been known to read cover to cover in a single day when the story is particularly gripping. She also loves to travel, especially visiting historical sites and far-flung shores.

Books by Laura Martin

Mills & Boon Historical Romance

The Pirate Hunter
Secrets Behind Locked Doors
Under a Desert Moon
An Earl in Want of a Wife

Visit the Author Profile page
at millsandboon.co.uk.

For Jack, my constant companion.
Your smile melts my heart.

And for Luke.
Every day with you is even better than the last.

Chapter One

Lizzie peered out of the carriage window and tried to calm her racing pulse. Never before in her life had she felt so alone. Before boarding the boat bound for London she'd heard so much about the city, but now she was here she couldn't quite believe how busy and crowded it was. Momentarily she longed for the rolling hills just outside Bombay, but then silently reprimanded herself. She hadn't been happy there, not truly. This was the opportunity she'd been waiting for her entire life.

As the carriage slowed Lizzie let the curtain fall back into place and tried to put herself into the role she was to play for the next few weeks. For at least a fortnight she was no longer to be Miss Elizabeth Eastway, orphaned daughter of a penniless second son. Instead she would play the role of Miss Amelia Eastway, cherished only child and heiress to a substantial fortune. She found herself smiling ruefully, knowing Amelia was the only person in the world who could have persuaded her to go along with such a ruse. If anyone else had asked, she would have laughed and shook her head, then proceeded to bury it in whatever book it was she was reading, but Amelia was different. Amelia was the sister she'd never had, her only champion and friend in a world that did not favour penniless orphans. Lizzie knew she would jump in the path of a crazed horse to save Amelia, so when her cousin had asked her to swap identities for a couple of weeks she could hardly say no.

Of course, Amelia hadn't thought the whole thing through. Lizzie knew by agreeing to swap identities with her cousin it would be she who suffered in the long-term. She didn't have a large dowry or a substantial inheritance; people would forgive Amelia, but penniless Lizzie would be ruined. If her cousin had realised that, Lizzie knew she wouldn't have asked, but as always Amelia hadn't even stopped to consider the consequences. In Lizzie's mind she didn't have much to lose, so when Amelia asked, she agreed. It wasn't as though she ever expected to make a good marriage or start a family, so Lizzie kept telling herself she wasn't sacrificing that much for her beloved cousin.

The carriage rolled to a stop and Lizzie took a second to compose herself, trying to mimic the sunny smile that came so easily to Amelia's face. She had to be cheerful and outgoing these next few weeks; there was no one to hide behind, no one to take the focus off her. All her life Lizzie had been kept in the shadows and she'd rather got used to it there. Now she was being pushed into the light and she just hoped she didn't let her cousin down.

A footman opened her door and Lizzie allowed him to help her down. She stared up in awe of the mansion they'd stopped across the street from and had to remind herself not to gawp.

'If you'd just follow me, miss,' the footman said, indicating they were to cross the road and ascend the steps to the very house she was in awe of.

Lizzie nodded, stepping out on to the street.

Immediately she heard a man shout and a horse let out a snort. Spinning to her left, Lizzie cowered backwards. The beast was almost upon her, rearing up, hooves flying through the air towards her face. Lizzie stumbled and lost her balance, landing with a jarring thud on the dusty street. She wished she could close her eyes, wished she could look away, but it was as though she were entranced. As if in slow motion she saw the rider pull on the reins, trying desperately to bring the beast under control, but Lizzie knew it was too late. The horse would trample her and there was nothing she or the rider could do about it.

With an almighty shout the rider threw himself off the horse and used the momentum to push the beast to one side. The horse's hooves met the ground just inches from Lizzie's head and she shuddered at the sound of the impact.

For a long few seconds the entire street was silent, as if digesting the near tragedy. Then the horse whinnied and the spell was broken. Half a dozen people rushed towards her and the rider, but he motioned for them to stay back. Slowly he rose from the ground, limping slightly from where he had landed on one leg, and approached his horse. Lizzie watched as he soothed the beast, stroking its mane and speaking quietly in a gentle tone. After handing the reins to a young lad he turned back to Lizzie.

Lizzie swallowed and tried to meet his stare, but she could tell he was furious. Slowly he walked towards her and she felt at a distinct disadvantage sitting on the dusty ground, her skirts tangled between her legs and her body still shaking from fear.

He stopped when he was almost directly above her, his body blocking out the sun. Lizzie swallowed and offered a weak smile.

'What were you thinking?' he asked in clipped tones.

Lizzie opened her mouth to answer but found no sound would come out. She motioned vaguely with one hand.

The rider stared at her for what felt like an eternity, then offered his hand.

Lizzie reached up and took it, and allowed him to effortlessly pull her to her feet.

Now she was standing Lizzie felt a little more at ease, but only a little. He still held her hand in his own, so their bodies were quite close together and for the first time Lizzie was able to make out his features. She gulped. Trust her to be almost trampled to death by the most handsome man in London.

As she studied him Lizzie felt his eyes roaming over her features. Immediately she stiffened. Lizzie knew she wasn't a hideous crone, but she also knew she wasn't what society deemed to be attractive. Her hair was just a little too brown, her skin had a few too many freckles, and where men seemed to admire petite women Lizzie could look most men in the eye without straining. Many she even had a good view of their bald spots.

It had happened so many times that she could see this man's thoughts as he looked her over. Within two seconds he had dismissed her.

'Be more careful in future,' he said with authority.

Lizzie found herself nodding despite his imperious tone. She wished she had mastered Amelia's haughty look. Her cousin could slay a man merely by raising an eyebrow. Lizzie supposed it came with confidence and probably being a stunning petite blonde didn't hurt, either.

She watched as he strode back to his horse, athletically mounted the beast and moved off. Their whole encounter couldn't have lasted for more than a minute, but it had been enough to crush any confidence Lizzie had summoned to face the world as Miss Amelia Eastway.

The footman appeared back at her side.

'Are you harmed, miss?' he asked, his face ashen.

Lizzie smiled at him kindly, knowing he would likely get the blame for her clumsiness.

'Not at all,' she said with a false bravado. 'Just a little shaken.'

Carefully they crossed the road and ascended the steps. As they reached the top the front door opened and Lizzie was ushered inside.

'My dear Amelia, what on earth happened?' A woman in her midforties rushed forward to greet her.

Lizzie supposed this was Amelia's aunt Mathilda. And the young woman standing in the corner with a smug grin on her face was probably her odious cousin Harriet.

Lizzie felt the colour start to rise in her cheeks as she began to mumble something about falling over, then she realised this would never do. She was meant to be Miss Amelia Eastway, the sort of young woman other people admired. She needed to start acting the part.

'It was most harrowing,' she said, pressing her fingers to her temple. 'I was crossing the street and I was almost trampled by a careless rider.'

Aunt Mathilda rushed to her side and took her hand.

'What an awful ordeal for you, my dear, why don't you come and sit down?'

Lizzie allowed the older woman to lead her into a drawing room, but as she left the hall she caught a glimpse of the expression on Harriet's face. Lizzie knew then that Harriet had seen the whole episode and knew that Lizzie's carelessness was to blame.

'You must be exhausted after such a long journey.'

'It was only an hour from the dock.'

'Mother meant from India,' Harriet said as she followed them into the room.

'Oh, of course,' Lizzie mumbled.

'Although I never understand why people insist that travelling wearies them. It's not as though you have to sail the ship yourself.'

Lizzie thought of the endless days of nausea and

disequilibrium, the nights she'd spent staring at the rocking ceiling and wishing it were all over. Even now, hours after disembarking, she still felt a little wobbly.

'Have you ever been on a long sea voyage?' she asked sweetly.

Harriet shook her head.

'No, I didn't think so.'

Lizzie perched on the edge of an uncomfortable armchair and watched as the young woman's eyes narrowed to slits, and realised she'd just made a big mistake. Her life for the next couple of weeks would be hard enough without making an enemy in the place that was supposed to be her sanctuary.

Either Aunt Mathilda didn't notice the animosity between the two girls, or she deliberately ignored it.

'I can't believe my dear little niece Amelia is here sitting in my drawing room,' Aunt Mathilda said. 'The last time I saw you, you were a lovely little thing with pigtails and a gap between your front teeth.'

Lizzie smiled serenely, trying to quell the sickness in her stomach. No doubt Aunt Mathilda was remembering the sweet little blonde-haired girl and wondering when she had turned into this tall brunette. Luckily Amelia's father had settled in India fourteen years ago and Amelia hadn't seen her aunt since. Hopefully the older woman would just assume time had changed her sister's daughter beyond recognition.

'We've got such a busy week planned, my dear,' Aunt Mathilda said as she rang the bell for a maid. 'We've got dress fittings and shopping trips galore, and at the end of the week you shall make your début.'

Lizzie's eyes widened.

'So soon?' she managed to ask, her voice breaking a little with the surprise. Amelia had assured her it would be weeks before she was meant to make her début. The plan had always been for Lizzie to step into her shoes for a fortnight at the most, and that fortnight would be spent settling into London life, going shopping and strolling round the parks. Neither of them had ever expected Lizzie would actually have to go out in public as Miss Amelia Eastway.

'Your father was quite insistent,' Aunt Mathilda said softly. 'He instructed that you make your début as soon as possible.'

Of course it was all Uncle Robert's doing. Even Lizzie had to admit Amelia had become a handful in the past few months, although she, of course, knew the reason behind this rebellion. Amelia's father had sent his daughter to London so she would find a husband and settle down, and by extension not be his problem any longer. It made sense that he had wanted Amelia to be out husband-hunting as soon as possible—it meant less time for her to cause mischief.

Lizzie knew she couldn't be introduced to London society as Amelia, but right now she couldn't think of a good reason to give Aunt Mathilda, so instead she just smiled and nodded. She would have to feign an illness, or invent some family tragedy that required a period of mourning. Anything that would push back the début until Amelia returned. Her cousin had promised she would not leave Lizzie alone in London for more than a week, two at the most, and flighty though Amelia was she normally kept her promises. Amelia simply wanted to have a few days of freedom to find the young officer she was enamoured with before being introduced to society. Lizzie had no doubt they would both get into trouble for this ruse, but she was certain Aunt Mathilda would want to keep any hint of the scandal quiet and that would only be possible if she hadn't been presented to London as the season's most eligible heiress.

'But let's not get ahead of ourselves,' Aunt Mathilda said. 'You've had a long and tiring journey and I'm sure you just want to settle in and rest.

I will have one of the maids bring some light refreshments to your room.'

'Thank you,' Lizzie said and stood. She smiled at
her aunt and cousin and exited, but instinct made
her pause outside the door, just out of sight.

'It's a good job she's rich,' Harriet said quietly.

Lizzie heard Aunt Mathilda tut at her daughter,
but no reprimand was forthcoming.

'Don't tell me you're not thinking the same,
Mother. She's hardly beautiful and she's one of the
most awkward people I've ever seen.'

'Don't complain, Harriet, you'll have enough to
contend with when the gentlemen hear how much
her dowry is. We want you to make a good match
as well, remember.'

'It's so unfair,' the younger woman said. 'She'll
get to marry someone titled and be a great lady, all
because her father has made money in trade. She
doesn't deserve it. Not after what her father did to
us.'

Lizzie realised she didn't want to hear any more.
Quietly she slipped away, following a maid upstairs
and trying to fight the tears that were forming in
her eyes.

Chapter Two

Daniel was in a foul mood and he knew he only had himself to blame. He was standing on the perimeter of the Prestons' ballroom trying to look inconspicuous. And failing quite spectacularly. Already the eligible young women were beginning to flutter their eyelashes in his direction and, even worse, their mothers were looking at him with undisguised interest. He hadn't attended a society event like this in years; in fact, he could count the number he'd shown his face at on one hand.

Which meant all the young ladies of marriageable age were immediately intrigued, and convinced he must be there to search for a wife.

Daniel groaned. He was there to look for a wife. As little as he wanted his current lifestyle to change, a visit to his accountant that afternoon had put things into perspective. He needed money, and he needed it soon. Hence his presence at the Prestons' ball this evening, and his need to be sociable and personable.

'What on earth brings you here, Blackburn?' A familiar voice broke into Daniel's thoughts.

Daniel turned and smiled his first genuine smile all evening. The night wouldn't be such a disaster with Fletcher by his side.

'I'd have thought that was obvious,' Daniel said, keeping his expression impassive. 'I'm here for the scintillating company.'

Fletcher moved to Daniel's side and perused the ballroom.

'You're creating quite the stir. I've heard the name Lord Burwell mentioned at least a dozen times and I've only been here five minutes.'

Daniel knew he should be pleased, he should want every eligible young woman with a good dowry thrown at him that evening, but he couldn't quite conjure up the enthusiasm.

Fletcher looked at him appraisingly. 'You're looking for a wife,' he said in a matter-of-fact tone after a few seconds.

'Good God, is it that obvious?' Daniel asked, hoping he wasn't coming off as desperate.

'There are only three reasons a man comes to these events,' Fletcher explained. 'And seeing as you don't have any female relatives to escort and you don't need to do any social climbing, it must be to look for a wife.'

Daniel nodded glumly. Fletcher was right, of course, he was there to look for a wife and he felt rather shocked by the fact. Just yesterday he had been a bachelor, firm in his conviction that he would never marry, happy to flirt with any woman who crossed his path, but unwilling to settle down. The problem was now he had no choice—he had to marry. The idea of finding a young woman with a good fortune and marrying her to acquire that fortune didn't sit well with him. In fact, he felt rather disgusted with himself that he was about to become one of the fortune hunters he so despised in society, but he really had no other option. He kept telling himself his future wife would be well-treated, she'd gain a title and an old family name, but he felt bad that she wouldn't be loved. For one thing Daniel was sure of was that he was never going to risk his heart again. He'd loved once and the experience had left him emotionally battered. He wouldn't allow that to happen a second time.

'There's no need to look so down, old chap. We'll have you dancing with the most interesting and beautiful before the evening's out.'

Daniel found himself scowling. He didn't want a beautiful wife, or one that was particularly interesting. He wanted someone kind and quiet, who would let him continue with his current lifestyle and not interfere. Plus, of course, she needed to be wealthy. He found himself wondering when he had become so cynical, but deep down he knew. You couldn't have your heart broken and come out unscathed, and Daniel had certainly had his heart trampled on.

'I need someone rich,' he said bluntly.

Fletcher looked at him appraisingly but didn't comment.

'Then we have a shortlist. There are three very wealthy young women in attendance tonight.'

'How do you know all this?' Daniel asked.

'When you have four sisters out in society it's hard not to know everything about their competition. Including the size of their dowries.'

'Who are the three?' Daniel asked, hating having to be so direct, but knowing it would be better to get directly down to business. Then he wouldn't have to attend so many of these events.

'First up is Miss Priscilla Dethridge, daughter to the very successful banker Mr James Dethridge.' Fletcher motioned discreetly to a young woman in her early twenties. She was pretty enough and seemed to be having a lovely time on the arm of a young gentleman Daniel didn't know.

'Then there's Miss Trumping. No one knows how

her father made his money, probably wasn't strictly legal, but she does have the advantage of being very attractive.'

Daniel looked over at the stunning young woman Fletcher was indicating. She was beautiful, there was no denying it, and she was surrounded by far too many men.

'And the last?' Daniel asked.

'Miss Amelia Eastway.' Fletcher was scanning the room looking for the young lady in question. 'Father is Colonel Eastway, an army man settled in India, very successful trading business. She'll be an extremely rich young woman when he meets his maker.'

Daniel waited patiently for Fletcher to locate her and perhaps even introduce him.

'I can't seem to see her.' Fletcher shrugged. 'She is quite an unassuming young thing. Not unattractive exactly, just rather normal.'

Daniel smiled. She sounded perfect. Or at least perfect for him. Wealthy, available and not someone he was going to lose his head over. Although all three qualities were necessary, he rather thought the last was the most important. Daniel was certain he never wanted to lose control like that again and Miss Amelia Eastway sounded like the perfect young woman to save him financially and allow him to carry on with life as normal.

'And now I need to go and do my duty,' Fletcher said with a sigh that Daniel didn't quite believe. His friend was quite dedicated to his family, whatever he'd have the world think.

Once again Daniel was left alone on the perimeter of the ballroom. He could sense the curiosity of the female guests almost reaching a peak and knew if he wasn't careful he would find himself trapped into dancing with some young woman or another. He grimaced. All he wanted was an introduction to the eligible Miss Eastway, to murmur something charming as he kissed her hand and to make his escape. Desperate though he might be, Daniel was sensible enough to know he would not make much more progress than that tonight, but he at least wanted to make the acquaintance of the woman he was going to marry.

He scanned the ballroom for someone who met Fletcher's description of Miss Eastway with little success. There were no plain-looking women surrounded by fortune hunters that he could see. He felt a stab of panic as he wondered whether she had already been claimed and let his eyes wander to the open doors leading to the terrace. Surely even a naïve young woman new to London society wouldn't allow herself to be led outside by an un-scrupulous suitor.

Telling himself he was just being a gentleman, checking on a lady's safety, he strode across the ball-room, resolutely not looking at anyone in his path. In truth, he felt a bubble of irritation. If the innocent Miss Eastway had gone and got herself compromised, it would ruin all his plans.

He stopped short as a young woman stepped into his path.

'Lord Burwell,' she purred, dipping into a curtsy and looking up at him with a coquettish smile.

'Mrs Winter.' Daniel took her hand and brought it to his lips.

'It has been far too long,' the widow said.

Daniel couldn't help but smile. He and the charming Mrs Winter had been bumping into each other for six months now. Each time they shared a drink and a few words and then moved on, but there was a certain spark in her eyes that told Daniel he wouldn't need to do much more than smile and she would come to him willingly.

'I've missed our scintillating chats,' Mrs Winter said, her hand curling around Daniel's upper arm possessively.

They walked a few steps together, Daniel always keeping one eye on the door to the terrace in case someone matching Amelia Eastway's description came through the opening.

'I heard the most scandalous rumour about you,' she said, dropping her voice to a loud whisper.

'I'm sure it's not true.'

'It was involving you and a pretty little actress called Victoria.'

Daniel felt a grin tugging at the corners of his lips. Victoria was a sweet little thing who just seemed to enjoy Daniel's company and demanded nothing more.

'And my dear friend Mrs Highton has been dropping the most obvious of hints. I do hope you don't favour her over me.'

Daniel grimaced. This was why nothing had happened between him and Mrs Winter; he got the impression that she could become rather possessive. Daniel had never wanted a long-term mistress, instead preferring short liaisons with women who did not make a fuss if he called things off.

'How could I prefer anyone to you?' Daniel asked, turning towards the young widow with his most dazzling smile.

That seemed to placate her a little and Daniel took the opportunity to escape. He wasn't in the mood for flirtation tonight. His decision to marry was sitting heavily on him and he wanted to find his possible future wife, introduce himself and return home before he could talk himself out of it.

He reached the terrace doors in less than a minute and slipped out into the cool summer's night. The outdoor space was illuminated by candles dotted along the stone balustrade, but there were plenty of dark corners a young woman with little experience could find herself lured to by a man with less than noble intentions. Daniel wondered what to do next—he'd expected to come outside to find someone who fitted Miss Eastway's description and had planned to whisk her gallantly away from danger. Now he was here even he knew that plan was foolish. Firstly, the people who slipped outside normally didn't want to be disturbed, and secondly, he couldn't very well rescue a damsel in distress if he couldn't see her.

Daniel almost gave up and returned to the ballroom, but compared to the cramped, stifling atmosphere inside, the summer's evening was lovely and cool. He thought he might sit for a moment or two before returning to find the woman he was going to marry.

Quietly he slipped down the stone stairs into the garden proper and seated himself on a little bench looking out into the garden. Not for the first time he wished he was back on his estate in Cambridgeshire, strolling about his own garden with a glass of whisky in his hand. Or even at his club in London, sitting quietly with a newspaper or discussing the day's events with his friends. Balls and ballrooms didn't suit him. He wondered not for the first time if there shouldn't be an easier, more pleasurable way of finding oneself a spouse, but knew in today's society things were unlikely to change any time soon.

Daniel was just about to get up from his bench when he heard the doors to the ballroom open on the terrace above him. For a few seconds the music swelled and pulsed, then it was quiet as whoever had slipped outside closed the door. Daniel waited for the whispers of two illicit lovers and wondered if he should clear his throat to let them know they were not alone.

No whispers came, just the unmistakable swish of silk as someone started to descend the stairs towards him.

Daniel didn't want to startle the woman, but equally he didn't want to be caught in a deserted garden with some empty-headed young thing. He stood, coughed quietly, then approached the steps.

In the darkness Daniel heard a cry of surprise before he saw something moving towards him at great speed. He tried to jump backwards, out of the way of the careening object, but his reflexes weren't quite quick enough. Something warm and soft crashed into him and knocked the breath from his lungs. Unable to keep his balance Daniel toppled backwards, taking whatever it was with him. They landed together with a quiet groan.

For a few seconds Daniel was too stunned to move. It was obvious now the object that had come hurtling down the stairs towards him was a woman. A rather stunned young woman if her silence was anything to go by.

Slowly he became aware of her body pressed up against his. One of her legs was nestled between his thighs and her chest was pressed closely to his. Her face must have been cradled into his neck as he could feel her soft breath tickling his skin. She was trembling, he realised, and too shocked to move.

Gently he rolled her over and sat up, being careful not to move suddenly.

'Are you hurt?' he asked, thinking himself rather foolish. After all, who could fall down quite so many steps and not be hurt?

'Erm…yes…no. I don't know.'

Daniel found himself smiling. She was conscious at least and sounded rather charmingly befuddled.

'Let me check you over,' he said, in a voice that invited no argument.

It was dark outside, too dark to make out much of

the young woman's features, but Daniel's eyes had become accustomed to the blackness and he could at least see her outline. Gently he reached over and took one hand in his.

He heard a sharp intake of breath as he traced the lines of her arms with his fingers, checking for any broken bones. He did the same with her legs, but when he was just reaching her knees it seemed she had regained at least some of her wits and pulled sharply away. Daniel sighed—he was just starting to enjoy himself.

'I'm sure I'm fine,' the young woman said in a voice that wasn't in the least bit convincing. 'What about you?'

'Me?' Daniel asked. 'Oh, I'm used to cushioning the falls of fair maidens,' he said with a grin. 'But that was certainly the most pleasant introduction I've had all evening.' Daniel pictured the young woman's cheeks turning pink and silently reprimanded himself; sometimes he couldn't help his flirtatious side. 'There's a bench just over here. Let's see if you can make it over.'

Daniel thought he saw her nod her head in the darkness and stood, leaning down to assist her up. He felt her totter a little and slipped an arm around her waist to steady her. She was slender, but Daniel could feel the flare of her hips beneath her dress and felt the first stirrings of desire. Reluctantly he pushed them away. This was most likely a well-bred young lady who he couldn't dally with. And, he reminded himself sternly, he was here for one purpose only: to find a wealthy wife, no matter how much the idea galled him.

Together they hobbled over to the bench and sat down.

'What happened?' he asked gently, not letting go of the woman's hand.

She sighed. 'You'll think me foolish.' There was a modicum of humour in her voice and Daniel found himself smiling. The whole situation was farcical really, and most young women would be in hysterics, but this one was taking it all in her stride.

'I wanted to escape...' She paused, then corrected herself. 'No, I needed to escape. If I spent one more second in that ballroom, I would have screamed.'

'Surely it wasn't so bad that you had to throw yourself down the steps?'

Although he couldn't see her expression Daniel rather thought she'd smiled.

'Almost.' She sighed. 'I'm sorry, I'm sure I've ruined your...' Instead of finishing the sentence she waved a hand in his general direction. 'Whatever it is men wear to these balls.'

Daniel found himself leaning in a little closer, trying to make out what his mystery woman looked like. He knew she was tall, with a slender waist and delightfully curvy hips, but he wished he could catch a glimpse of her facial features.

'I just wanted some peace and quiet, just for a few minutes. When you coughed you startled me and I tripped.'

'I wanted you to know you weren't alone.'

Daniel felt himself drawn to this woman and started to gently trace his thumb backwards and forwards across her hand. He knew it was wrong and he knew he should send her back inside immediately. If they were found in this position, outside and alone together, there would be a terrible scandal, but he couldn't quite bring himself to send her on her way just yet.

'Why did you want to escape the ball so much?' Daniel asked. 'A lovely young woman like you must be the centre of attention.'

He could tell she grimaced even in the darkness. 'I feel like an antique up for auction.'

Daniel laughed, he couldn't help himself.

'Not that I think I'm any kind of prize, quite the opposite,' she rushed to reassure him. 'It's just when you know people are only interested because of money…' She let her sentence trail off.

Daniel suddenly felt a little guilty. All evening he

hadn't thought of anything but securing himself a wealthy wife. He hadn't considered what his potential spouse's feelings would be on the matter, hadn't even thought of her as a real person. That must be what this young lady felt like, an object up for auction. Daniel pushed his qualms aside. He would treat his wife well, give her anything she asked for, and all he needed in return was for her to save him financially. It wasn't even as though he'd squander all her money gambling like most husbands; her fortune would be going to a good cause.

'We should get you back inside before you're missed,' Daniel said reluctantly. He didn't know why he was so loath to let her go, he was certainly enjoying himself more than he'd expected to at a ball, but he knew she had to return to the ballroom before someone noticed she was gone.

'I am sorry I fell on you,' the woman repeated.

Daniel stood and offered her his arm. She stood up rather too abruptly and he found himself face-to-face with her. Even in the darkness Daniel could make out the curve of her lips and suddenly he had an overwhelming urge to kiss her.

Without thinking of the consequences Daniel lowered his lips to hers, feeling the sharp intake of breath as she realised what he was about to do. He half expected her to push him away and storm off, but for a few seconds she stood frozen, as if too stunned to react. Then he felt her body melt into his.

It was the first time she'd been kissed, Daniel was sure of it, but her lips were full and inviting and Daniel knew he wouldn't be able to pull away. He breathed in her scent and pulled her closer to him, revelling in the small moan that escaped from her lips as they kissed.

Suddenly she stiffened and Daniel knew the moment was over. Even though he'd met this woman only a few minutes previously he knew she wouldn't become hysterical, just that she'd come to her senses. Slowly he pulled away, keeping one hand resting gently on her waist.

'That…I mean… Well.'

Normally Daniel would have prided himself at rendering a woman speechless, but already he was beginning to feel like a churl. He'd just seduced an innocent young woman he had no intention of marrying. It went against everything he believed in, every code of honour he lived his life by.

'That was unforgivable of me,' he said softly. 'I just couldn't help myself. I wouldn't have been able to resist kissing you even if there was a sword to my heart.'

'I should go,' she said, pulling away. Almost immediately she stumbled and Daniel sprang forward, steadying her so she didn't lose her feet.

'Can I at least know your name?' he asked quietly.

It seemed like an eternity before she answered and Daniel had the absurd feeling that she might give him a false name.

'Amelia,' she said eventually. 'Amelia Eastway.'

Daniel felt the bottom drop out of his world as Amelia slipped from his grasp and started to ascend the steps back to the terrace.

'May I call on you tomorrow?' he called after her.

He wasn't entirely sure, but he thought he saw her nod her head before she disappeared into the darkness completely.

Chapter Three

Lizzie was a bundle of nerves. It didn't help that she hadn't slept much at all. Every time she'd closed her eyes she'd been back in the Prestons' garden being seduced by a mystery man. She didn't even know his name. Even now she could feel the faint tingle of desire as she remembered his hands on her waist and his lips brushing her own.

She wondered if he would call on her, as he'd said he would. She didn't know if she even wanted him to. She was torn. Half of her wanted to meet this man who had kissed her so passionately the night before, but the other half wanted to hold on to the dream. If he saw her in the light of day, Lizzie knew he'd realise he'd made a mistake. Perhaps it would be better if their dalliance was kept as something magical, something Lizzie could hold on to for the rest of her life. It wasn't as though he would desire her once he actually met her properly and maybe it would be better if she didn't actually see the disappointment in his face as he looked at her in the daylight.

'Look, Amelia,' Aunt Mathilda said as she entered the room, 'these have just arrived for you.'

She was carrying a beautiful bouquet of flowers, tied with a red ribbon. Lizzie found herself smiling, wondering if they were from her mystery gentleman the night before. She hadn't even found out his name, she realised.

She took the card from Aunt Mathilda and felt her smile falter slightly as she read it. No, these certainly weren't from her mystery gentleman. The card was signed Mr Anthony Green and Lizzie found it hard not to shudder as she remembered their encounter the night before. She'd been introduced to many eligible gentlemen, both young and old. Most had been pleasant, although she suspected had been more interested in putting a face to the dowry than actually making her acquaintance. Mr Anthony Green had been repulsive. Not in looks—in fact, he was quite a handsome man in his early thirties—but in manner. He'd lingered over her hand just a little too long and gone out of his way to touch her upper arm at any opportunity. That in itself, of course, didn't make him repulsive, but she'd found that he had spent more time ogling the fine jewels that hung around her neck than actually looking at her. And he'd spoken of her fortune and her dowry to her face. It might have been Lizzie's first night out in society, but even she knew dowries were something that were whispered about behind closed doors. Mr Green had made it perfectly clear that all he was interested in was her money, and that he didn't even think it was worth trying to disguise the fact.

Aunt Mathilda arranged the flowers on the windowsill and looked at them approvingly.

'I'm sure you'll be receiving many more bouquets, my dear, and hopefully a few gentlemen callers this afternoon.'

Lizzie saw Harriet's eyes narrow at the idea of her receiving a call from an eligible gentleman, but Lizzie tried to ignore it. She wasn't sure why Harriet disliked her so much on first sight, but she wasn't going to provoke the situation.

'I'm sure you're glad you were sufficiently recovered from your illness to make your début now,' Harriet said snidely.

Lizzie had tried to feign an illness to delay her coming out, hoping that Aunt Mathilda might let her stay hidden in her house until Amelia returned. She'd complained of a headache, fever and light-headedness, and had even gone as far as to hold the teapot to her cheeks before Aunt Mathilda came to check on her, but the older woman had sat down beside her, taken her hand and told her not to worry. She had seen through Lizzie's ruse and put it down to Lizzie feeling nervous about making her début, so Lizzie had found herself hustled into her beautiful dress and into the carriage before she could even begin to think of another excuse to delay.

The door to the drawing room opened quietly and the butler, an elderly man with an unflappable demeanour, stepped inside.

'The Earl of Burwell to see Miss Amelia Eastway,' Tippings announced.

Immediately all three women stiffened. Certainly they had been expecting calls from gentlemen of the *ton*, but an earl was in quite another league.

Aunt Mathilda quickly crossed the room to Lizzie's side.

'You know the Earl of Burwell?' she asked, her face drained of colour.

Even Harriet looked a little impressed.

Lizzie couldn't answer. Had she met the Earl of Burwell? If so, he hadn't stuck in her mind and she rather thought an earl should do.

Unless, of course, he was her mystery gentleman. Lizzie suddenly felt sick. Had she been kissed by an earl in the Prestons' garden? Surely not. Surely that was something a girl would know. He'd seemed so nice, so normal, not earl-like at all. She felt her face flush at the idea of him seeing her in the light of day and wondered if she had time to escape. Maybe feign a swoon.

The door opened once again and a man stepped inside. Out of habit Lizzie found herself standing and dropping into a little bob of a curtsy as a greeting. Only then did she have the courage to raise up her eyes and look at the man she might or might not have kissed the night before.

Her mouth fell open and her eyes widened. Whomever she had expected to be standing in front of her it wasn't this man.

'You,' she said before she could stop her mouth forming the words.

Lizzie could see this man was equally as surprised.

A thousand thoughts ran through Lizzie's mind at once, not a single one coherent or helpful. Aunt Mathilda looked between Lizzie and the earl, but ever the polite hostess she invited him to sit without any further enquiry.

'It is delightful to see you again, Miss Eastway,' the earl said, sounding rather too composed for Lizzie's liking.

The pieces started to fall into place and Lizzie wondered how she had not recognised his voice the night before. The Earl of Burwell was certainly her mystery gentleman, but it was not the first time they'd met. He was also the gentleman who had saved Lizzie from nearly being trampled to death by his horse, the man who had dismissed her with a single glance.

Lizzie wanted to curl up and disappear. She wondered how disappointed he was when he saw her, when he realised last night was not the first time they'd set eyes on each other.

'It's a beautiful afternoon,' Aunt Mathilda said, trying to break some of the tension in the room.

'It is indeed,' the earl said.

'How did you and Miss Eastway meet?' Harriet asked and Lizzie remembered the smirk on her cousin's face as she had witnessed Lizzie's humiliation on her arrival to London.

The Earl of Burwell turned to face Harriet and looked at her appraisingly. His gaze was superior and a little haughty, and Lizzie was surprised Harriet didn't squirm under the intensity of it.

'We were formally introduced last night,' he said eventually. 'And I enjoyed our conversation so much I decided I wanted to see Miss Eastway again today.'

Although Lizzie knew that wasn't quite the whole truth she was glad he'd silenced Harriet's mocking before it had started.

'How absolutely delightful,' Aunt Mathilda said. 'Now, Harriet, why don't I show you that thing I was talking about earlier?'

Harriet looked blank but allowed her mother to usher her out of the room. Aunt Mathilda pulled the door behind her but left a chink between the wood and the frame for propriety's sake.

Lizzie knew she would have to turn and face the earl, but she was finding it hard to summon the courage. She didn't want to see the disappointment on his face, she didn't want to hear him utter some made-up excuse to escape as soon as possible. For she knew he would be disappointed. Last night he hadn't known who she was, she was sure of that. He hadn't realised she was the woman who had caused so much havoc in the street just a week before. That woman he had dismissed without a second look, but last night he had treated her as though she were the most desirable woman on earth.

Lizzie's heart started to sink. Maybe it had all been engineered, maybe her perfect fairy-tale moment had actually been nothing more than a fortune hunter making a naïve young girl feel attractive. She glanced briefly at the earl. He didn't look like a fortune hunter, but she knew they came in all shapes and sizes.

'I should apologise for last night,' he said as he caught Lizzie's eye.

She waited for him to actually apologise, but he was not forthcoming.

'But I find myself unable to regret my actions.'

'Why?' The word was out before Lizzie could stop it. She berated herself immediately. She needed to get control of her tongue.

'Why?' he asked, raising an eyebrow.

'Why did you kiss me?' she whispered.

He regarded her silently for a minute, then looked away. She wondered if he were concocting a lie, trying to find something flattering to say.

'It was rather magical last night, wasn't it?' he said eventually. 'The warm summer's evening, the faint echo of the music from the ballroom. Then a charming young woman comes and crashes into me and I just couldn't resist.'

Lizzie found herself nodding. It had been rather magical. Not the part where she'd fallen down the stairs, or winded him so badly he hadn't been able to breathe for a few moments, but afterwards. The caring way he'd helped her up, the feel of his touch on her skin and the moments they'd spent sitting on the bench side by side.

Then they'd stood up and Lizzie had felt him

move towards her and she'd known she was about to be kissed.

'It was not gentlemanly,' he said seriously, but then broke out into a smile. 'But I don't regret it.'

She tried to believe him, tried to believe that sitting here he was not regretting the moment from the night before, but she wasn't sure she could. Self-consciously Lizzie brushed a strand of hair away from her face. Ordinary brown hair, framing an ordinary face with just a few too many freckles.

With a glance at the door the earl stood and moved towards Lizzie. She found herself staring up at him, trying to control her breathing.

'I really did enjoy our time together last night,' he said, sitting himself down beside her.

Lizzie found herself nodding again. She'd enjoyed it, too.

'And I really would like to get to know you a little more.' His voice was low and a little seductive and Lizzie knew hundreds of women had fallen prey to him before.

She wanted to ask him why, wanted him to confess he was only interested in her for her supposed dowry, but she found her words had deserted her. His body was just that little bit too close, his thigh pressing against hers, and Lizzie knew she wouldn't be able to construct a coherent sentence.

'I think last night might have been the start of something special,' he said.

Lizzie made a small murmur of agreement, even though she wasn't sure she agreed. She felt mesmerised by him, completely under his spell, and even though her mind was screaming out that it wasn't her that he wanted, it was Amelia, Lizzie found at this moment she didn't really care.

She felt him studying her, his eyes flicking from her mouth to her cheeks to her hair, but always back to her mouth. Involuntarily she felt her lips part ever so slightly and she realised she wanted him to kiss her. Right then it didn't matter why he was doing it, just that she wanted him to. She wanted to be lost once again in the oblivion of a kiss, wanted to feel the explosions within her body as his lips met hers.

Slowly, as if building the anticipation, the earl lowered his lips to hers. He started out gently, barely touching her. Lizzie felt the tension mounting and a soft moan escape her lips. She wanted more, needed more.

As if responding to her innermost thoughts he pressed his lips more firmly on to hers and deftly flicked his tongue inside her mouth. Lizzie's eyes closed and she was lost. She didn't care why he was kissing her; all she wanted was for it not to end.

She felt her body melting into his and relished his

touch as he looped an arm around the back of her head, pulling her closer towards him. She wanted his hands all over her body, wanted him to touch her in places no one else had ever even seen.

Just as she felt the kiss couldn't get any better suddenly the earl pulled away. He was smiling, but Lizzie could tell something was wrong. She wondered if she'd inadvertently done something terrible, something that would make him want to run from the room.

Suddenly Lizzie felt very self-conscious and raised a hand to cover the lips he had been so thoroughly kissing just moments before.

'I'm sorry,' he murmured. 'I just couldn't seem to help myself.' He sounded a little puzzled and Lizzie could see a flicker of confusion in his eyes.

'You are just so tempting,' he said, tracing a pattern on the back of her hand.

Immediately Lizzie crashed back to reality. She knew that was a lie. She straightened up, pulling away, and gave him a forced little smile.

'I'm sure my aunt will be back in a few minutes,' she said pointedly.

The earl looked confused, as if no one had ever rejected him before, but took the hint and moved back across the room to the chair he'd been sitting in before. An uncomfortable silence followed and

Lizzie found herself blinking the tears away from her eyes. This was cruel and unnecessary. Up until very recently she'd been quite content with her lot. She'd known she wasn't a great beauty. Combining that with her lack of fortune, she'd never expected to make a good marital match. In fact, she'd been quite convinced she would never be a wife, just a spinster all her life. Now here she was being utterly seduced by a handsome and charming man, knowing all along it wasn't her that he wanted at all.

Chapter Four

Daniel wasn't quite sure what had just happened. He *knew* he'd just kissed the young woman sitting across the room from him. He just didn't know how to classify his reaction.

He'd been thrown when he realised he'd met Miss Amelia Eastway before last night. He'd hardly taken any notice of the unassuming young woman who had stepped in front of his horse. She'd seemed so ordinary, so normal. Not like the woman in the garden. She had been intriguing and almost mystical. Daniel had found himself drawn to her, attracted and aroused despite his years of experience.

Then when he'd found out the woman who he'd kissed was the very one he was meant to be pursuing, his world had almost fallen apart. He didn't want to desire his future wife. Desire complicated everything. Desire made a man lose all sense of reason and preceded bad decisions. Over the past four years Daniel had become a master at keeping his desire in check. That wasn't to say he'd been celibate, just that he hadn't let his desire overshadow his common sense.

It was the shock, he realised. He hadn't expected to recognise his mystery woman in the daylight, he hadn't even considered that they might have met before. He'd looked her over appraisingly and found rather an ordinary young woman sitting in front of him. Not someone who made his pulse race and his temperature rise. He'd felt comfortable, reassured. She wasn't the irresistible vixen he'd thought the night before, she was just an average young woman with no particular distinguishing features.

He'd planned to kiss her, of course. He needed to marry her and he needed to do it soon. After their kiss the night before Daniel knew she was an innocent and he knew that his charm was legendary with women all over London. He was hopeful that Amelia would enjoy his attention and flirtation.

And then it had happened. He'd moved closer, leant in to begin his seduction, and he felt as though he'd been punched in the gut. He couldn't quite put his finger on why he felt this way, just that he needed to kiss Amelia Eastway, not so she would have to become his wife and save him from financial ruin, but because it was the only thing that would keep him going.

He wasn't sure if it was the delicate curve of her lips or the charming set of freckles that covered her nose, he just knew he had to kiss her. And far from being completely in control, as he had planned, Daniel had felt rather wonderfully at sea. He'd kissed her as though he hadn't kissed a woman in years, allowing himself to pull her body towards him, run his hands over her skin. He'd lost himself in that kiss and that was worrying him.

He glanced back across at Amelia and wondered if she had somehow sensed all of this. She'd wanted him, Daniel was experienced enough to recognise the signs: her pupils had dilated, her breathing had become just a little shallow and her lips had parted. She'd kissed him as passionately as the night before, but now she was regretting it. Something had changed. It was as though a shutter had come down over her face and now they were sitting apart like complete strangers, not a couple who had kissed twice in the space of twenty-four hours.

Daniel knew he had to do something to salvage the situation. Whatever his current internal conflict Miss Amelia Eastway was still the solution to all his problems. He needed to court her and marry her before the month was out. He would have to push aside any doubts he had. When he looked at her objectively he knew he should be able to resist her. He would just have to learn to control his urges and no doubt soon enough their relationship would slip into easy companionship rather than one fuelled with desire.

'Would you care to join me for a stroll in the park?' Daniel asked.

Amelia looked at him as though he had grown two heads. He wondered if he had uttered the sentence in Latin or some other foreign tongue.

Eventually she sighed and nodded her head. 'That would be most delightful,' she said, sounding anything but delighted.

Daniel felt himself bristle. Again he wondered what had happened to bring about this change in her feelings for him so abruptly. One minute she'd been melting in his arms, responding to his kiss, the next she was forcing herself to take a stroll with him.

'Maybe your aunt would be so kind as to find a chaperon?' he enquired. 'Although I'd much rather be alone together. Such wonderful things happen when we're alone,' he murmured.

Amelia seemed to soften towards him slightly.

'I'm sure she will.'

She made no effort to go and sort this out and Daniel felt his mood darken further. Most young women would be swooning at the thought of strolling through the park on the arm of an earl for all society to see.

'Would you like to go and ask her?' he suggested.

'Of course, my lord.'

'Daniel, please,' he said, thinking it was ridiculous having her call him by his title when already they were quite intimate. 'Since we already know each other so well.'

He watched as she rose and walked out of the room. Despite having fallen down stairs into him, and nearly having been trampled by his horse, Miss Eastway seemed to move with a fluid kind of grace when she was on her feet. He found himself watching the soft sway of her hips as she left the room and once again felt the first stirrings of desire deep within his body.

Daniel took a deep breath and closed his eyes. He would not desire Amelia Eastway. Although deep down he knew desire wasn't something you could easily keep in check, equally he knew he was a man of the world, not some green boy of twenty. He had control over his emotions and he would not lose his head over a woman even if she had charmingly kissable lips.

He'd have to kiss her again, of course, but next time he would be completely in control.

He rose as Amelia re-entered the room and saw with dismay that she was accompanied by her cousin. Daniel had spent less than five minutes in the young girl's company, but he knew she was spiteful and jealous.

'Harriet would like to accompany us,' Amelia said, her lack of enthusiasm obvious in her tone.

'That would be delightful,' Daniel said. 'I just hope our discussion on ancient literature does not bore you too much.'

Daniel saw the flicker of a smile cross Amelia's lips. Harriet's eyes narrowed as she tried to work out if Daniel was being serious. He kept a neutral expression on his face, hoping all the time she would change her mind and stay at home. He wasn't likely going to make much progress with Amelia if her cousin was present and annoying her.

'Harriet, I need your help this afternoon,' Aunt Mathilda said as she glided back into the room. 'I'll send one of the maids out to chaperon you, Amelia.'

Daniel wondered if Harriet would argue, she looked as though she wanted to, but in the end she kept her mouth shut.

Within minutes Daniel was strolling towards Hyde Park with Amelia on his arm. He realised she felt right beside him, her strides matched his own and the weight of her hand resting on his arm was comforting. He felt quite comfortable with her, despite the odd moment of madness where he seemed to want to ravish her. If he could only overcome those, he thought Amelia would make a very good wife. She was quiet and unassuming and he didn't think she'd protest too much when he continued with his current lifestyle.

'I understand you've only recently arrived in London,' he said, thinking a little bit of small talk would help break down the barrier between them.

She looked wistfully into the distance for a moment before replying. 'I've lived in India all my life, or at least for as long as I can remember.'

'Do you miss it?'

She nodded. 'When I was there all I could think about was getting away, coming to London, but now I've left it behind I miss the rolling green hills and the days filled with sunshine.'

Daniel wondered what her upbringing had been like. From his subtle enquiries he'd found out she'd been raised the only child of the very wealthy Colonel Eastway. She'd always been destined to marry well, but to look at her you wouldn't believe it. She seemed rather overwhelmed by the sudden attention and he had the impression that she hadn't expected to be courted this soon.

'Do you wish you were back there?' he asked softly.

She considered for a moment, then turned to him with a smile. 'No. As much as I like to reminisce, it was time for me to leave, time for me to start the next chapter of my life.'

'As a débutante in London.'

He saw her grimace out of the corner of his eye.

'Something like that,' she said vaguely.

They'd reached the entrance to the park and walked in through the archway. Daniel found he was enjoying himself more than he'd imagined. When he'd realised he was going to have to marry he'd been a little disgruntled to say the least. He didn't want his life to change, he was quite content running his estates, spending time in London and making sure he didn't make any lasting connections. The idea of having to marry was bad enough, although Daniel was a pragmatist and knew where his priorities lay, but he'd dreaded having to find and court a wife. He'd imagined some air-headed young miss that he'd have to listen ramble on about nothing. Amelia Eastway was not like that at all. In fact, he was rather enjoying himself.

Chapter Five

Lizzie slowly felt herself relaxing. She didn't know what game Daniel was playing, but she'd decided she was having none of it. She was going to be courteous and polite, but she would not allow him to kiss her again. That would be madness.

Walking along, her hand in the crook of his arm, Lizzie felt almost content. He was attentive and seemed to want to listen to what she had to say. Lizzie could almost convince herself she was having a good time. Just as long as he didn't look at her intensely with his piercing blue eyes and shift towards her, Lizzie knew she could keep up a mundane conversation. She tried not to think what would happen if he attempted to kiss her again. She liked to think she was a strong young woman who knew her own mind, but twice she'd been utterly seduced by his kiss and she wasn't sure how she would resist if he turned to her again.

Luckily they were out in public, in full view of the world. He wouldn't try anything whilst they were strolling through the park. Then Lizzie wondered if she could rely on that. For some reason he had decided to court her and she doubted it was because he found her wildly irresistible. Even if their meeting the night before hadn't been engineered, Lizzie thought there was something driving Daniel today and her first guess was her dowry. Or at least Amelia's dowry. She sighed. This was all getting to be a bit of a mess and she'd only been out in society for one day. She wished Amelia would return and sort it all out, but she hadn't heard from her cousin since they'd disembarked the ship from India together, her cousin hopping into the first carriage she'd seen on the London dockside, and she doubted Amelia would make an appearance anytime soon. She would just have to deal with this debacle herself.

She felt a bit sorry for the earl. Not that he was the sort of man who invited pity, but he was thinking he was courting an heiress with a substantial dowry, where instead he was wasting his time on a penniless orphan. She wondered whether he would switch his affections to Amelia when she returned, and found herself feeling more than a little put out at the thought.

They stopped walking as they reached the Serpentine and Daniel led her over to a bench.

'Sometimes I come here to think,' Daniel said quietly.

Lizzie regarded their surroundings with surprise. There was no denying Hyde Park was beautiful with its myriad of waterways and copses of trees, but Daniel hadn't exactly picked the most secluded spot for his contemplations. They were sitting on a bench right next to the Serpentine, in a place where all the children gathered to feed the ducks. In the early-afternoon sunshine the children were whooping and shouting in delight as they threw bread to the obliging creatures.

She glanced sideways and saw him looking wistfully at a group of small boys out with their nanny. One of the boys was only about three or four years old and tottered after his older siblings, trying to keep up with their games.

Lizzie wondered momentarily whether this was all part of his plan, to bring her to Hyde Park and let her see how much he liked children, but then she dismissed the idea. She could tell this wasn't all engineered. This truly was where he came to sit and think about the world.

'I guess it's because I miss the countryside when I'm in London,' Daniel said with a shrug.

'Do you spend much time here?'

He shook his head. 'I prefer the country to be honest, but I find myself in London more and more.'

Lizzie wondered what his country estate was like. She'd left England before her third birthday and hadn't been back since. Her home was the dry heat and lush green valleys near Bombay, but she doubted the English countryside was anything like that.

'But enough about me,' Daniel said with a grin, 'I want to know more about you.'

Lizzie shrugged and looked down at her hands. 'I'm sure you know the basics.'

'I don't want to know the basics,' Daniel said, leaning in closer, 'I want to know something the rest of society doesn't. Something that the masses will never know when they talk about you.'

His smile was infectious and Lizzie felt herself beginning to properly enjoy herself. She rather suspected the earl was known to be flirtatious in nature, but right now she didn't care. She was sitting on a bench with a handsome man, enjoying herself.

Lizzie thought for a moment, wanting to select something suitably vague for the earl so there was no chance he would work out she wasn't who she claimed to be.

'When I was twelve I was bitten by a crocodile.'

Daniel burst out laughing. 'You're joking?'

Lizzie shook her head.

'Well, you must be the only débutante that can make that claim. Truly unique. Now you have to tell me more, I'm intrigued.'

'I was walking down by the river near our home. As usual, I had my head in a book and wasn't really looking where I was going.' Lizzie shuddered as she remembered the moment she'd realised she had stumbled into the path of a rather large crocodile. 'For about thirty seconds it just looked at me with those terrifying little eyes and then it lunged.'

She had thought she was about to die.

'Luckily it was just a warning shot, a quick nip and then the crocodile backed off. I had some pretty deep teeth marks, but I didn't lose my foot as many do.'

'Even without an entire leg you would still light up any ballroom. In fact...' Daniel paused, raised his hand close to his eye and positioned it so it obscured one leg from his view '...being the first one-legged débutante would probably make you the most interesting person to have graced society for decades.'

'Your turn,' Lizzie said. She was really beginning to warm to Daniel. She knew she shouldn't allow him to flirt with her quite so openly, but it was nice being the centre of someone's attention.

'An interesting fact about me,' Daniel mused.

'Something hardly anyone else knows.'

'I've been shot.'

Lizzie's eyes widened and she quickly glanced over his body, wondering where exactly he had been shot. She felt a little distracted by his broad shoulders and muscular arms, but quickly pulled herself together.

'You have to tell me more,' she said.

'It was a duel. I was second for a good friend of mine. We were young and foolish at the time.'

'And someone shot you?' Lizzie asked, thoroughly intrigued.

'It's nowhere near as glamorous as it sounds.' Daniel leaned in closer and dropped his voice. 'In fact, it's really rather painful.'

Daniel edged closer to her and Lizzie didn't protest. Sitting here by the Serpentine with Daniel felt right somehow, as if this was what her entire life had been leading up to.

'The man who was aiming at my friend had terrible eyesight, he might as well have closed his eyes and fired. The shot missed its intended target and clipped me instead.'

Daniel must have seen how Lizzie's eyes were roving over his body, trying to figure out where he had been hit.

'When we're somewhere less public I'll show you the scar.'

Lizzie's eyes widened and for a moment she hoped it was somewhere on his chest or abdomen. She desperately wanted to peel back his crisp white shirt and run her fingers over the muscles beneath. At the thought of doing something so intimate she felt the blood rush to her cheeks and she coughed to try to cover her embarrassment.

'Now it's your turn again,' Daniel said with a smile that Lizzie knew would set any woman's heart racing.

Suddenly there was a shout and a commotion over by the Serpentine. Immediately Daniel was on his feet, rushing towards the water, with Lizzie following quickly behind.

The small boy they'd been watching only minutes before had tumbled into the murky waters and was now thrashing about. It was obvious he couldn't swim and it was too deep for him to touch the bottom. His petrified nanny was trying to reach him from the bank, but his thrashing was just causing him to get further and further away.

Lizzie watched as Daniel shrugged off his jacket, kicked off his boots and jumped into the dirty water. He touched the bottom easily, the water coming up to his waist, and he quickly waded out to where the boy was thrashing. Firmly he grabbed him and lifted him clear of the water, saying something soothing that Lizzie couldn't quite hear. She was reminded of their first meeting when she had almost been trampled by his horse and the way he'd soothed the petrified beast then.

Daniel's words must have done the trick as the boy calmed down and allowed himself to be carried to the bank and back into his nanny's arms.

Lizzie could only look on as Daniel pulled himself out of the water, clothes stuck to his muscular legs and torso. His shirt was almost see-through and it outlined the contours of his chest and abdomen in quite a scandalous way. Lizzie felt the heat rising in her body and forced herself to look away, worried that otherwise she would become mesmerised. He smiled at her and shrugged, as if this kind of thing happened every day, then turned his attention back to the boy. Quickly he checked he wasn't injured and then left him to be hustled home by his nanny.

'That was remarkable,' Lizzie said as Daniel made his way back towards her.

'I couldn't just sit by and let him drown.'

Lizzie shook her head in agreement but knew that not many gentlemen would actually jump into the Serpentine to rescue a strange boy.

'You must be frozen.'

Daniel shrugged again, but Lizzie could tell the wet clothes were making him uncomfortable already.

'Perhaps we could begin to head back,' he suggested.

Lizzie nodded, motioned to the maid who was sitting a couple of benches away, and they started to walk back through the park.

'I won't take your arm,' Daniel said with a smile.

Lizzie found herself smiling back. There was something quite irresistible about the man walking next to her. He might have an agenda and he might be pursuing her for all the wrong reasons, but she couldn't quite find it in herself to dislike him.

They walked in a companionable silence back through the park for a few minutes, gaining odd looks from other members of society who were out taking their afternoon strolls. Daniel nodded in greeting to many but didn't stop to engage them in conversation. Lizzie supposed he must be feeling rather cold now. Even in the pleasant afternoon sunshine walking around dripping wet couldn't be very good for your health.

'I'm sorry we've had to cut our outing short,' Daniel said, looking down at Lizzie with a smile.

Despite all her reservations Lizzie was sorry, too. She'd been enjoying herself. She'd almost been able

to forget it wasn't she that Daniel was really courting, but Amelia. She'd enjoyed his lively conversation and she'd enjoyed the small insights he'd given
her into his life.

'Maybe we could do this again sometime soon,'
he suggested.

Lizzie found herself nodding, even though she
knew she shouldn't encourage him. It would be so
much easier if she never saw him again, if he disappeared from her life and she never had to reveal
that she wasn't Amelia Eastway, but her penniless
cousin. Even though she knew this Lizzie found
herself agreeing with him.

'That would be lovely.'

She glanced up at his face and found him smiling at her, and just for a second she thought she saw
a flicker of desire. She almost laughed. No matter what had happened in the Prestons' garden she
knew Daniel didn't really desire her. She'd seen the
quick way he'd dismissed her on their first meeting
and she knew she wasn't the sort of woman men
fantasised about.

'Please don't feel you have to escort me home,'
Lizzie said as they neared the edge of the park. 'You
must get back to your house and get out of those
wet things.'

Daniel considered a moment, as if weighing up his gentlemanly duty against his discomfort.

'Only if you promise to let me call on you again tomorrow,' he said with a devilish smile.

'People will talk,' Lizzie warned him.

'People will always talk. By this evening there'll be ten different versions of what happened down by the Serpentine, each more ludicrous than the last.'

Lizzie knew it was true. Already half of society would know that she had spent the afternoon with the Earl of Burwell. She cringed a little. This would make it all that much worse when she had to reveal her true identity to the world.

'Either you agree to my calling on you tomorrow, or I'll insist on walking you home now. You'll be responsible if I catch a fever and spend weeks delirious and at death's door.' He said it with a grin on his face and Lizzie knew she wasn't going to be able to resist.

'I would very much welcome you calling on me tomorrow, my lord.'

'I told you to call me Daniel.'

'Daniel.' Lizzie uttered his name quietly, nothing more than a whisper between her lips. It seemed too intimate, too informal, but she felt a wicked little chill down her spine as she said it.

'And I shall call you Amelia,' he murmured in her ear.

It was enough to force Lizzie back to reality. For a moment she'd allowed herself to live the fantasy, to believe that it was her Daniel wanted, but just the mention of Amelia's name made all those dreams come crashing down.

She pulled away slightly but forced herself to smile, even though she feared it would look like a grimace on her face.

Daniel looked at her intently for a few seconds, then turned away, as if he sensed she needed a moment of privacy to compose herself.

'Lord Burwell, whatever has happened to you?'

Lizzie turned to see an attractive young woman gliding towards them. The newcomer looked Lizzie up and down and then turned her full attention to Daniel.

'Mrs Winter,' Daniel said. 'I took a little dip in the Serpentine.'

Lizzie recognised the woman and realised she must have been at the Prestons' ball the night before.

'You must look after yourself, Lord Burwell, you would be sorely missed if anything were to happen to you.'

Lizzie didn't miss the suggestion that Mrs Winter would be the one missing him.

'Please excuse us, Mrs Winter, Lord Burwell needs to get out of these wet clothes,' Lizzie said. Immediately she knew she had made a mistake. The older woman turned to her and gave her an icy glare, before catching herself and replacing the expression with a sweet smile.

'Of course. Take care, my lord. And if you catch a cold and need someone to nurse you back to health, don't hesitate to ask.'

Daniel said farewell and they continued on, Lizzie feeling rather inferior to the attractive Mrs Winter. They were just nearing the entrance of the park when Lizzie noticed Daniel freeze beside her. One moment he was walking along, seeming like the carefree peer of the realm he'd been all morning, the next he was just frozen. She stopped beside him and waited for him to move. Five seconds passed, then ten. She followed his gaze, trying to figure out what was going on.

His eyes were fixed on a young woman and a small boy about thirty feet away. The woman was pulling the boy along behind her impatiently and the boy was dragging his feet.

'Daniel?' Lizzie asked, wondering what exactly about the scene had caused him to turn so white.

He didn't answer, didn't even acknowledge that she'd spoken. To Lizzie it seemed as though he was so lost in his own world that he hadn't even heard her.

The woman and boy were drawing closer and Lizzie wondered whether there would be some sort of confrontation.

Lizzie knew the exact moment the woman noticed them. Daniel stiffened beside her, his eyes met this woman's and his expression deepened into a frown. The woman stopped in her tracks and looked at them for a few seconds, before smiling sweetly and continuing on her way. Daniel followed them with his eyes for a long minute until they disappeared out of view.

No one had uttered a single word during the confrontation, but Lizzie felt as though she'd just witnessed something monumental.

'Daniel?' she repeated.

This time she got a response. Daniel took her elbow in his hand and guided her quickly from the park. He didn't say a single word to her and Lizzie felt too stunned by this sudden change in character that she didn't know what to say herself.

They exited the park and walked briskly down the street, Lizzie having to stumble to keep up with Daniel in his frenzied state.

'Who was that?' she managed to ask as they reached the corner.

He didn't answer her, didn't even acknowledge that she'd asked him a question.

'Daniel?'

'Will you be able to find your way home from here?' he asked stiffly.

Lizzie nodded, stunned at the change in the man who could laugh off ruining his clothes jumping into the Serpentine, but would not even look at her after this latest confrontation.

'I will call on you tomorrow.'

Again Lizzie nodded, unsure what else she could say. Open-mouthed, she watched as he hailed a passing hackney carriage and jumped in. He didn't even look at her as it pulled away, let alone bid her goodbye. She stood there motionless for a good minute after the carriage had pulled away, unsure what had just happened. Daniel had changed completely and it had been just as he'd seen that woman.

Shaken and confused Lizzie roused herself and began the walk home, wondering whether tomorrow she would get any answers from him.

Chapter Six

Daniel felt sick. No, he felt more than sick. He felt as though his whole world had collapsed. Up until that point the whole afternoon had been a success. Amelia seemed receptive to his advances, and even if she withdrew every so often, that was something that could be easily overcome.

He'd found her a pleasant companion, they'd talked easily during their walk around the park and he'd managed to convince himself that the desire he'd felt the evening before and when he'd kissed her in the drawing room had been anomalies. When he looked at her in the light of day he could see she wasn't a seasoned temptress. She was just a normal young woman who shouldn't drive him mad with desire. And if his pulse raced a little when he glanced at her lips, then he could put it down to the memory of their kiss and nothing more.

He'd even not minded his little dip in the Serpentine. Of course, he'd had no choice, he couldn't have let the young boy drown, but he knew Amelia had seen his act as heroic and that could never hurt a man's chances.

Everything had been going swimmingly well... until he'd seen them.

Daniel ran a hand through his hair and tried to focus on something other than his rage. At this moment he was close to losing control and he hated not being in control. He breathed in deeply through his nose and watched the world pass by as the hackney carriage weaved through the busy streets.

He'd last seen his son four months ago when Annabelle had shown up at his estate, demanding more money. He'd been heartbroken. Already the boy was growing up so fast he barely looked like the young lad he'd seen six months earlier. Daniel knew he'd missed his son's first steps, his first words, and he would miss a whole world of firsts as time went on. The knowledge that he wasn't the one there, watching his son grow up, broke his heart.

If only there was another way, but he knew there wasn't.

Then today, in the park, Daniel knew that Annabelle had engineered that little meeting. She'd done it to let him know she was in town, to remind him of his promise and let him know she wasn't afraid of the consequences if he didn't pay up.

Daniel closed his eyes and pictured the little boy she'd been dragging behind her. His son, Edward. He had beautiful dark hair and piercing blue eyes, skin like porcelain and full lips. And he hadn't even once glanced at Daniel. That was what hurt the most. Throughout the whole encounter Edward had been looking around at the park. He hadn't taken one little bit of notice of the man whose heart was breaking just watching him.

Daniel ran a hand through his hair and made himself relax back into the seat of the carriage. There was nothing to be done about it. He'd made his bed four years ago when he'd invited Annabelle into his life. He'd been convinced she was the woman of his dreams, convinced that she loved him the way he'd loved her. It hadn't been long before he'd found out differently, that he'd found out that he was just the latest in a long line of conquests for Annabelle. She'd swept into his life when he was grief-stricken and vulnerable, and then like a seasoned con artist she had become his entire world, slowly cutting him off from his old friends, his old life. When he had found out the truth about Annabelle, the fact that she was already married, he had been devastated. His pride had been irreversibly damaged when he'd realised he'd been tricked into loving her, and his heart broken, but he'd known he would recover eventually. He was a young man with a full life ahead of him, he would get over the betrayal once she was out of his life.

The problem was she hadn't left his life, not really. A year after he'd thrown her out she'd turned back up with a baby in tow. Daniel had laughed at first, telling her he wouldn't believe a word she said and that there was no way this baby was his. Although from her very first words Daniel had begun to doubt himself. When they had been together Annabelle had told him she couldn't get pregnant, couldn't have children, so he had never insisted that they use protection.

Then he'd looked down at the baby and he'd known the truth. Just one glance and he'd known irrefutably that the child was his. The bond was immediate and unbreakable, and Annabelle had looked on with glee.

His world had crumbled. Of all the things that could have happened to him this was the very worst. He didn't care that Annabelle had tricked him into loving her. He didn't care that he was now much more jaded and untrusting. But he did care that he had fathered an illegitimate child.

His whole world had come crashing down. He

knew first-hand what tragedy haunted illegitimate children. He'd seen the suffering and the contempt and he knew it was the very last thing he would wish upon anyone, let alone his own son.

He'd tried to take the child, but Annabelle had refused. And then the blackmail had started.

Daniel watched as the carriage pulled up outside his town house. In a daze he stumbled out on to the pavement, paid the driver and made his way up the steps. Once safely ensconced in his study, he reached for the whisky and started to drink. He wanted to drink to forget and he wanted to drink to numb the pain.

After two glasses of whisky Daniel started to feel a little more in control. He poured one final glass, then set down the decanter and regarded it for a second. Later he could get drunk, later he could lose himself in the oblivion of alcohol, but right now he needed his wits about him.

Annabelle was only here for one reason. Despite all his pleas and his following of her terms she never let him see his son other than when she wanted something. Then it was just a brief encounter like today in the park. Daniel longed to sit the boy on his knee, to read him a story, or perhaps take him for his first riding lesson, but he knew all of that was impossible. He was destined to be in the background for ever, never knowing his son's personality, his likes and dislikes, never knowing what made him laugh and what made him cry.

Annabelle was here for money. Again. Every few months she turned up and demanded even more. Sometimes she came alone, sometimes she brought Edward with her, allowing Daniel just a fleeting glimpse of his son, but always the demand was the same. Pay up or the whole world gets to know Edward is illegitimate. Including Edward himself. Daniel knew he couldn't have that on his conscience. He needed the boy to grow up happy, to grow up thinking he had lost his father in the war. Better to have a hero for a father than to be illegitimate. Daniel couldn't bear his son's heart breaking as other children tormented him for that. He knew what the consequences could be and he wasn't about to risk that with his own son.

The problem was he didn't have any money. Annabelle had bled him dry over the past few years, demanding more and more. He knew it would never stop, but he couldn't see any other way out. Hence his need for a wealthy wife. A good-sized dowry would keep Annabelle at bay for years to come and when that ran out, well, maybe then his son would be old enough and strong enough to learn the truth, to be able to withstand the jibes from society and still hold his head up high.

Taking a gulp of the whisky, Daniel relished the burning sensation in his throat and wondered how long it would take Amelia to agree to marry him. Maybe a couple of weeks if he worked fast, but then it would still be even longer until the wedding. He could apply for a special licence, but doing so would raise suspicion. He sighed. One thing Annabelle wasn't was patient. Now she had turned up in London he expected to hear her demands within the next day or two, then he would have a matter of weeks to raise the money. If he didn't, then she would threaten to reveal the truth to Edward and to the world.

Daniel really needed Amelia's dowry. He grimaced and wondered when he had become quite so cynical. When he had been a young lad setting off for Cambridge he'd felt as though the whole world was at his feet. He was heir to an earldom, about to commence on a great life adventure and was surrounded by friends. He'd been convinced one day he'd fall in love with a beautiful woman and have a lovely family. Never did he think he'd have to marry for money. How different life had turned out to be.

He hated the fact that he was going to have to marry Amelia under false pretences. Whatever his faults he had always prided himself on never deceiving women. Over the years he had enjoyed many short liaisons, but he had always made it clear from the start these encounters were not going to be lasting relationships. Already he was deceiving Amelia, courting her with the express intention of getting her to marry him. He hated the idea that he was going to have to marry and give up his old lifestyle, but he hated the idea of not being entirely truthful about his motivations to Amelia more. He was turning into one of the fortune hunters he'd always despised.

Refusing to let himself become too melancholy, Daniel tossed back the rest of the glass of whisky and firmly set the decanter down on the table beside him. He needed a plan. In fact, he needed two plans. He needed a plan to make Amelia agree to marry him in record time and he needed a plan to raise a little bit of money to keep Annabelle at bay in the meantime.

He grimaced. He knew exactly where he could raise a little bit of money, but it meant renewing an acquaintance with a man he'd hoped never to see again. He wondered whether the man would agree to see him—they'd not parted well all those years ago. Daniel distinctly remembered telling Ernest Hathaway never to speak to him again.

He doubted Hathaway would agree to meet him,

so he'd have to be far more underhand. Maybe if he recruited his old friend Fletcher to his cause he could help. Fletcher wouldn't have to know all the details, all the sordid ins and outs, but he would be able to persuade Hathaway to be at a particular place at a particular time and to hear what Daniel had to say. If nothing else Fletcher was a persuasive man.

Daniel allowed himself to relax a little. Maybe things would work out all right in the end. He would continue his pursuit of Amelia tomorrow and he would sort out some money to keep Annabelle at bay in the meantime.

His thoughts went back to Amelia and he wondered if he'd ruined his chances with her by acting so strangely. He'd have to come up with some sort of story to satisfy her curiosity. Amelia might be a quiet wallflower, but she wasn't stupid. Her eyes shone with intelligence when they conversed and she had noticed something was wrong from the very start.

Maybe he could make her forget with a few illicit kisses. He knew she responded to his touch and his kiss, and if he was honest with himself he enjoyed kissing Amelia more than he'd enjoyed anything in years.

At the thought of kissing her Daniel felt the first stirrings of desire and frowned with agitation. He didn't want to desire his future wife. He'd desired one woman, let his heart rule over his head, and look where that had got him. Amelia was perfect for him because she wasn't head-spinningly beautiful. She was just nice and average.

He thought of the little freckles across her nose and the curve of her lip when she smiled and repeated to himself that he would not be attracted to her. He refused to desire his future wife. They would have a comfortable companionship and nothing more.

Standing, Daniel repeated to himself that he didn't desire Amelia. He was far too in control for any nonsense like that.

Chapter Seven

Lizzie forced herself to step away from the window and sit back down in her chair.

'No sign of the earl today, then?' Harriet asked mildly.

Lizzie forced a smile on to her face. 'He said he would call today. I'm sure he'll be here later.' She was sure of no such thing after their parting yesterday. She'd never seen a man change in character so quickly.

'I'm surprised he didn't walk you home yesterday afternoon,' Harriet said.

'He had some business to attend to.'

'Still…' She let the word hang in the air.

Lizzie picked up a piece of embroidery she was meant to be working on and started stabbing at it with the needle. She had never been very good at sewing or embroidery, she much preferred to be out and about in the fresh air, but it gave her hands something to do and stopped her reaching across the room and strangling Harriet.

Lizzie had spent half the night tossing and turning in bed, trying to work out why Daniel had become so agitated in the park. She wondered if the woman was one of his former mistresses, someone he had used for pleasure, then abandoned when he had grown tired.

'The earl has quite a reputation, you know,' Harriet said after a couple of minutes.

Lizzie knew she shouldn't rise to the bait, but she desperately wanted to know more about Daniel. She wanted to know what motivated him and what secrets lay buried in his past.

'Oh?' she said, trying not to sound too interested.

Harriet glanced over her shoulder to check her mother wasn't about to enter the room before continuing.

'He's quite the rake. Rumour has it that once he had four mistresses at one time. And he's dated an opera singer.'

Lizzie smiled serenely. 'Well, I suppose everyone has to have a past.'

Maybe that woman was the opera singer. The quick look Lizzie had got of her had shown her to be very pretty, but seeing a former mistress didn't explain why Daniel had become quite so withdrawn.

'He's known to be very selective in his choice of woman, apparently only the most beautiful will do.'

Lizzie felt her heart starting to sink. She couldn't help but picture the beautiful Mrs Winter they had met in the park and realised she was probably more Daniel's normal type of woman.

'He'd never shown any interest in settling down before,' Harriet continued, 'but I suppose even earls can become short of funds.'

Lizzie couldn't even bring herself to answer. She knew Harriet was just saying these things to be cruel, but whatever her motivation there was certainly some truth in her words. Why else would Daniel be interested in a nobody like her? He was titled, handsome and charming. He could have his pick of fawning young ladies, or he could just as easily continue having illicit affairs with more experienced women. The only reason he'd ever be interested in her was her dowry. Or at least Amelia's dowry.

She stabbed her needle once again into the piece of fabric and watched as the colours blurred before her eyes as the tears started to form. Just once she wanted something of her own. She wanted someone to be interested in her, not just pretending so they could get closer to Amelia. All her life she had been second best, often ignored completely when her cousin was around. From a young age her uncle had made it clear she was nothing more than a burden, someone no man would want to marry. For a few moments Lizzie had indulged in a sweet dream that Daniel might like her for who she was, but deep down Lizzie knew it wouldn't be so.

Blinking away the tears, Lizzie looked up as the butler entered the room.

'The Earl of Burwell,' he announced.

Daniel strode in, looking his normal composed self. There was no trace of the haunted and shaken man she'd glimpsed yesterday.

'Miss Hunter,' Daniel said, addressing Harriet, but not really looking at her. 'And, Amelia, it's lovely to see you again.'

Lizzie suppressed a smile as Harriet's eyes narrowed at the familiarity.

'Thank you for calling on me again.'

'I can't think of anywhere I'd rather be.'

Lizzie didn't bother pointing out he hadn't been able to get away from her fast enough yesterday afternoon. She smiled serenely at the compliment and wondered how they could get rid of Harriet so she could find out what had upset him so much. The idea of being alone with him sent a shiver down her spine. She told herself she was just curious, she just wanted to know what about the woman and small boy had spooked him, but if she examined her feelings hard enough there was also a desire to see if he would kiss her again. Although she knew their liaison was built on lies and it wasn't really her that he wanted, Lizzie couldn't help but want Daniel to kiss her one last time. For his lips to meet hers and for her to feel that tightening of desire deep inside her. To forget that she was plain old Lizzie Eastway and become a woman a man like Daniel could want.

'I'm afraid I've been a little presumptuous,' Daniel said with a wide smile.

Lizzie marvelled at how relaxed he seemed—there was no trace of the harrowed man she'd seen yesterday.

'I thought it would be the perfect afternoon to go for a ride.'

Lizzie found herself nodding. She missed the freedom of racing along the mud tracks surrounding her uncle's home just outside Bombay, she missed feeling the warm breeze on her face and seeing the scenery whip by. She'd always much preferred being outside to indoors. Back home her perfect afternoon had been trotting off on her own on horseback with a book tucked under her arm. She'd ride for a while, then find a spot to sit and read for hours on end until the light was fading. Amelia never had understood how Lizzie could spend so long in her own company, but for Lizzie it had been a welcome escape from a home where she didn't really belong.

'I've instructed my groom to be waiting in Hyde Park with two horses. If you would like, we can spend the afternoon on horseback.'

Lizzie stood and smoothed down her skirt. It sounded like a wonderful way to spend the afternoon and if they were riding they would be alone, which gave her the opportunity to find out exactly what secrets Daniel was hiding.

'I'll go and change,' she said, hurrying from the room.

Twenty minutes later they were strolling through one of the entrances to Hyde Park. Lizzie noted that Daniel was careful enough to avoid the spot where they'd seen the woman and small boy the day before, as if by not reminding Lizzie of it he could pretend the encounter hadn't happened.

'What beautiful horses,' Lizzie said as they approached Daniel's groom.

One was the huge black beast that had nearly trampled Lizzie the week before. The other was a slightly more docile-looking chestnut mare.

'Will you let me assist you up?' Daniel asked.

Lizzie nodded, feeling her heart start to race as he moved behind her. She positioned herself to mount the chestnut mare and glanced back over her shoulder. Daniel was close, almost as close as he'd been during their encounter in the Prestons' garden. She could feel his breath on the nape of her neck and it sent delicious shivers down her spine. She could imagine him wrapping his arms around her waist, pulling her back against his body and lowering his lips to her skin.

Lizzie swallowed and tried to regain control. She wasn't even sure if she liked him and here she was fantasising about him being entirely inappropriate in a public park.

'Are you ready?' His voice was low and seductive in her ear.

She managed to nod before she started to pull herself up on to the horse. His hands looped under her leg and boosted her the rest of the way, lifting her as effortlessly as if she were a rag doll.

Seated on the horse, Lizzie took a moment to regain control. Now Daniel wasn't quite so close she felt as though she were in charge of her brain once again.

'Shall we set off?' Daniel asked as he pulled himself up on to his horse.

Lizzie nodded and nudged her horse forward, concentrating on finding her equilibrium for a few seconds before falling into step beside Daniel.

They rode slowly at first. This part of the park was busy and Daniel had to greet most of the people they passed. It gave Lizzie the opportunity to watch him and try to figure him out. Daniel was still very much a mystery to her. She'd seen so many sides to him she didn't feel as though she knew the real man.

After about ten minutes the crowds started to thin out. Lizzie knew now was her opportunity to ask him what had upset him so much the previous day. If she left it much longer, it would be difficult to bring up.

'Daniel,' she said, still wondering how to phrase her question.

He turned to her with a lazy smile and for a few seconds Lizzie forgot entirely what she was meant to be saying.

'Yesterday, just before we left the park, something upset you.'

Daniel nodded, the smile remaining on his face, but Lizzie could tell underneath he was frozen.

'What happened?'

There was silence for well over a minute and Lizzie had almost convinced herself that he wasn't going to answer her question.

'I am sorry about how I left you yesterday,' Daniel said. 'It was rude and ungentlemanly. I hope you can forgive me.'

Lizzie nodded, she'd forgiven him already, but it wasn't his apology she wanted, it was an explanation.

'Something upset you. Was it that woman who walked past?'

His whole body stiffened and Lizzie knew she was right. He'd known the woman who'd not even stopped to speak to him. She wondered again if it was an old lover and felt an immediate pang of jealousy. Lizzie tried to shake it away, Daniel wasn't hers to be jealous over.

'It was nothing,' he said eventually. 'A case of mistaken identity. I thought she was someone I once knew. I was wrong.' It was said with such finality that Lizzie knew he would say no more on the matter.

They lapsed into silence. Daniel's evasive answer had reminded Lizzie that she didn't really know anything about the earl. He was charming and attentive towards her, but she had to keep telling herself it was because he thought she was someone else. In reality she didn't know this man at all. It might feel as though she'd known him for ever when he covered her lips with his own, but for him that was probably just another part of this charade.

It was clear Daniel was not going to tell her who his mystery woman was, and for a moment Lizzie wondered if he might still be seeing her. Surely he wouldn't be courting her and carrying on with a mistress at the same time. Lizzie knew a lot of married men kept mistresses, but she didn't want to believe Daniel would be kissing her by day and sleeping with another woman at night. With a shake of her head Lizzie dismissed the thought. She might not know the earl well, but she was almost certain that he wouldn't be so cold and disrespectful. Which still left the question of who the woman was.

'I wanted to ask you a favour,' Daniel said as they rode, his expression serious. 'I want you to educate me about India. I find I'm most ignorant on the subject. Did you know before yesterday I didn't even know they had crocodiles in that part of the world?'

Daniel grinned and Lizzie couldn't help but smile. His good mood was infectious and very effective at distracting her from thinking about his potential mistresses.

'What do you want to know?'

'All the interesting stuff,' he said. 'I'm your avid pupil.'

Lizzie thought a moment before saying anything more.

'The cow is the sacred animal of India, at least to the millions of Hindu people who live there.'

'The cow? Really?'

'Trust me, we found out the hard way just how sacred they are.'

'You have to explain.'

'My cousin was very popular with the army officers,' Lizzie said, knowing that was a bit of an understatement. 'She happened to mention one day that she was fed up of eating curry and wished she could have a lovely meal of roast beef and potatoes.'

'Ah.'

'Some of the more eager young officers took it on themselves to provide the freshest beef possible, enraging the locals. There was nearly a rebellion.'

Daniel turned to her with a smile. 'At least she didn't say she wanted an elephant steak for lunch.'

Lizzie felt herself smiling, too. There was something about Daniel's easygoing manner that made her relax. She knew she shouldn't encourage him, but he made their time together so enjoyable. Lizzie couldn't remember the last time anyone had wanted to know anything about her life and Daniel's attention and good-humoured observations meant she was having a lovely time on their outing.

'I took the liberty of laying out a picnic,' Daniel said after a few minutes of riding in silence. They were just reaching the top of a small hill and there were wonderful views over the rest of the park. Lizzie could see a blanket and a hamper on the grass ahead of them. She glanced around, knowing he must have had a member of his staff set out the picnic, but not able to see anyone in the vicinity.

'We should be quite alone for a while, not many people venture this far into the park,' he said. He gave her a salacious wink that was so over the top Lizzie couldn't help but laugh. Daniel might have a reputation as being a flirt, but he also knew how to poke fun at that reputation and laugh at himself. It was rather an attractive quality.

They stopped beside the blanket and Daniel quickly dismounted. Before Lizzie could even begin to get off her horse she felt his strong hands around her waist, lifting her to the ground. Even though there were at least three layers between his skin and hers Lizzie felt the heat from his hands as if he were touching her bare skin. They were close, almost chest to chest, and Lizzie knew if she tilted her head back she would see that smouldering look in his eyes. Then she'd be lost, unable to control what happened next.

Slowly she tilted her chin back. Daniel's eyes met hers and there was an intensity there that Lizzie had never seen before. One of his hands moved from her waist to her face, tracing the soft skin of her cheek with his fingers. The other hand stayed possessively on her waist.

Lizzie knew there was nothing she could do to stop him. She wanted this so much. Even though she knew their whole brief relationship was built upon lies, she didn't care. She wanted him to kiss her, she wanted him to lay her down and cover her body with his own. She wanted to feel desired and to know she was the one who drove him crazy.

Her heart was pounding in her chest as he continued to trace the contours of her face with his fingers. She felt herself stepping even closer, wanting to feel his body pressed up against hers. Lizzie didn't know why he wasn't kissing her, the anticipation was driving her crazy.

With a deep groan he dipped his head and covered her lips with his. Lizzie felt her body relaxing into his and for the first time she let her instincts take over. Her hands came up and laced through his hair, pulling him closer to her. She trailed her fingers down his neck and felt him shiver as she traced circles on his skin.

Gently Daniel dropped a hand to her shoulder. Lizzie felt her breath catch in her throat as she anticipated his next move. Slowly, so slowly Lizzie thought she might scream from frustration, Daniel ran his fingers along the neckline of her dress. He paused just for a second, then dipped his fingers inside the thin material. Lizzie felt the coil of desire deep inside her and silently begged Daniel to continue. His fingers were inching over her breast and she knew she'd scream if he didn't delve even deeper. Lizzie knew what they were doing was wrong, but she also knew if Daniel stopped she would shatter from pure frustration.

Daniel stopped. Lizzie moaned, trying to pull him closer again, not caring if she was behaving like a common streetwalker. She wanted Daniel, her body was screaming out in need of him.

She looked up at him with unfocused eyes and saw the confusion on his face. Of everything she'd expected to see there confusion wasn't part of it.

Daniel grasped her by the upper arms and studied her face, as if trying to work out who she was.

Lizzie looked back, wondering once again what he saw when he looked at her. She knew he couldn't truly be attracted to her, but when he kissed her it seemed so real, so passionate, she couldn't believe he didn't feel some spark of desire. Surely even the most consummate of actors couldn't fake what they had just shared.

She had nearly summoned the courage to ask him when Daniel quickly dropped his hands and stepped back. Lizzie followed his gaze and saw they had company. She felt the colour rise in her cheeks as she wondered how much the man had seen. Trying to act as though nothing had just happened, Lizzie turned to face the newcomer. As she turned she noticed the dark expression on Daniel's face and wondered what side of the earl she was about to witness next.

Chapter Eight

He must be sick, it was the only explanation. Daniel had always planned on kissing Amelia again, but in his imagination he'd been cool and in control, not breathless with anticipation like a green boy.

He shook his head. Something was wrong with him, that was for sure, but now wasn't the right time to figure out what. Later in the privacy of his study he could analyse what exactly was going on, but right now they had company. Decidedly unfriendly company.

Daniel forced a smile on his face as the newcomer stopped his horse in front of them. He wondered how much this man had seen and cursed himself for not choosing somewhere more private for his and Amelia's liaison. He'd thought the park would seem romantic to her, with the views across London, but he'd known there was a risk of passers-by happening upon them. Not that this man was a simple passer-by. Daniel groaned quietly as the man slowed his horse, and wondered how the newcomer had found them, for it could not be mere coincidence that Ernest Hathaway had come upon them.

'Burwell,' Hathaway said, looking down at Daniel.

'Hathaway,' Daniel greeted him in clipped tones.

'Won't you introduce me to your lovely companion?'

Daniel gritted his teeth. He didn't want Amelia to be introduced to this man. Hathaway was untrustworthy and selfish and looked out only for himself.

'Miss Amelia Eastway, this is Mr Ernest Hathaway.'

Amelia inclined her head in greeting. Her eyes were wide with curiosity and silently Daniel cursed. This was going to be something else he had to explain his way out of.

'Ah, the famous Miss Eastway. Your arrival in London has caused quite a stir.'

Amelia's eyes narrowed. 'I'm sure you must be exaggerating,' she said mildly.

Despite most of his mind being focused on Hathaway, Daniel felt a bubble of annoyance at her words. Although he'd known her only a short while Daniel knew Amelia sold herself short. Indeed, she might not be what society classically thought of as stunning, but his own reaction to her was enough for him to know she was attractive in her own way. Shaking his head, he turned back to Hathaway.

'Not at all, all of society can't help but talk about London's most eligible *heiress*,' said Hathaway. The emphasis was entirely on the word *heiress*, making it clear this was the only reason the *ton* thought Amelia gossip-worthy. Daniel glanced sideways and saw two faint spots of colour appear on Amelia's cheeks; she'd understood Hathaway's message and the implied insult. He almost reached up to pluck Hathaway from his horse and punch him, but managed to keep his temper in check. He needed the man and punching him, no matter how tempting, would not help his cause.

'Can we help you at all?' Daniel said, trying to make his voice as polite as possible. 'We were just about to sit down for some refreshments.' Daniel motioned to the blanket and the hamper, hoping Hathaway would take the hint and leave them alone. He might need to speak to the man, but there was no way he was going to do it in front of Amelia.

'That's a most gracious offer,' Hathaway said, swinging himself to the ground and walking towards the small picnic that was laid out.

Daniel's eyes narrowed. He knew Hathaway had deliberately misconstrued his meaning. There was no way he'd ever invite the slimy man to sit with them. Over the years Daniel's and Hathaway's paths had crossed numerous times and each encounter had left the two men disliking each other more than the last.

'I spoke to Fletcher,' Hathaway said casually. 'He said you wanted to discuss some business.'

Daniel felt like punching Hathaway. He had asked Fletcher to set up the meeting, not really expecting Hathaway to agree to it. What he certainly hadn't been expecting was an ambush like this whilst he was out with Amelia. He cast a glance sideways at Amelia and wondered how he was going to get out of this situation. The last thing he needed to do was discuss his business with Hathaway in front of the woman he was meant to be courting.

Hathaway waited until Amelia had sat down on one edge of the blanket, then proceeded to sit himself. Knowing Hathaway had trapped him in a very awkward situation, Daniel sat and waited for the disaster to begin.

'I'd heard rumours Burwell was courting you, Miss Eastway. How delighted I am to find out it is true.'

Daniel knew Hathaway was anything but delighted.

'You have known the earl a long time?' Amelia asked.

'Oh, we go back years. We were at school together.'

Amelia smiled, but Daniel noticed it didn't quite meet her eyes. She was astute, he realised, and hardly missed a thing. She had definitely picked up on the fact that Daniel and Hathaway were not friends, despite their long acquaintance.

'How lovely,' Amelia murmured.

'Although of course I was closer to Burwell's brother at the time.'

Daniel froze. He felt the blood drain from his face and for a moment the world around him seemed to stop.

'I didn't know you have a brother,' Amelia was saying as everything came back into focus.

'I don't,' Daniel said curtly. 'He died.'

He could see the shock on Amelia's face, but he didn't have it in him to sugar-coat the words. Rupert's death had torn him apart and still, over a decade on, he hadn't forgiven himself for what had happened.

'So tragic, to die so young,' Hathaway said, his voice laced with sympathy.

Daniel suppressed the urge to strangle the man. Hathaway wasn't responsible for his brother's death, but he certainly hadn't helped to prevent it.

'Such a shame nothing could be done to prevent it,' the man continued.

Daniel felt burning fury rise up inside him. He would have done anything to change what had happened to his brother, he'd have moved heaven and earth to stop his tragic death, but the truth of the matter was Rupert was dead. He had died years ago and every day since Daniel had regretted not having done more to keep him alive. Hathaway knew this and was trying to stir up the guilt and regret Daniel still felt so keenly.

'I'm so sorry,' Amelia said, reaching and covering his hand with her own.

Daniel barely felt her touch. His mind was back in his childhood, in his teenage years—the years when he could have helped Rupert. If only his father had accepted Rupert as a true son, or his mother had allowed him to even occasionally set foot in the house. For years he had resented his parents for the part they played in rejecting Rupert, but there was no one he blamed more than himself. He'd been there at school, term after term, as Rupert had shrunk into himself. No amount of blaming his cold, unfeeling mother or his father, who was trying to please everyone, would change the fact that Daniel himself could have made a difference.

'It must be awful to lose a brother,' Amelia said quietly.

Daniel pulled himself back to the present and focused on Amelia, trying to block out Hathaway's presence altogether.

'It is,' Daniel said simply.

'Especially if you're close,' Hathaway supplied.

Daniel ignored the comment. He and Rupert hadn't been close, despite being less than a year apart in age. They'd shared classes at school and had even started at Cambridge together. They should have been inseparable. And maybe if Daniel had spent a little more time with the boy who had shared his blood he would have been alive today. Daniel knew this and wished every day that the outcome had been different.

'I know I'm affected by the loss of my parents still,' Amelia said quietly. Daniel glanced at her quickly and saw her eyes widen as if she'd said something she shouldn't. 'The loss of my mother,' Amelia said quickly. 'My mother died many years ago now.'

Daniel knew she was reaching out to him, sympathising, but he couldn't deal with her sympathy right now. He wished they would change the subject, wished they would talk about almost anything else, but he knew even if the topic of conversation did change he'd still never be able to outrun his guilt.

'What happened?' Amelia asked gently.

Daniel froze. He didn't know how to answer the question. It wasn't that he was ashamed of the way his brother had died, but more that he was ashamed he hadn't done anything to stop it.

Hathaway was looking at him with barely concealed amusement in his eyes. He was enjoying Daniel's torment.

'My brother was very unhappy. He took his own life.'

To Amelia's credit she did not gasp or twitter on incessantly as most people did. Some of the colour drained from her face, but otherwise outwardly she did not react to his statement.

'I'm sorry,' she said simply and reached out and took his hand in hers.

Daniel felt oddly comforted by the gesture. Normally he hated sympathy from people on the subject of his brother's death, but he didn't feel as though Amelia was judging him. In fact, the frown she directed towards Hathaway showed she'd picked up on his character flaws pretty quickly.

'Mr Hathaway,' she said sweetly, 'was there something you wanted to discuss with the earl?'

Hathaway looked a little surprised to be addressed so directly.

'Of course,' Hathaway said with a predator's smile. 'I think *you* wished to discuss a loan, Burwell.'

Daniel groaned inwardly. Amelia was learning so

many of his secrets this afternoon. He wouldn't be surprised if she ran for the hills immediately.

'We could discuss the matter later, maybe at the club.' Both Daniel and Hathaway frequented the same gentlemen's club, although normally Daniel made a point to avoid Hathaway at all costs.

'I'm not sure when I'll be free again,' Hathaway said, examining his fingernails nonchalantly. 'If you want the loan, we'd better discuss it now.'

Daniel glanced at Amelia, who was looking resolutely down at the blanket. He knew the implied conclusion of this discussion wasn't lost on her. He needed money and he needed it so desperately that he would borrow it off a man he despised. Amelia would, of course, assume that he was pursuing her for the same reason.

She was a sensible young woman and Daniel knew that deep down she was aware that many of her suitors' interest in her was because of her dowry. However, most people did not come out and say it directly.

'I'm willing to loan you up to two hundred pounds at a good rate of interest—what are friends for after all?'

'And the rate?' Daniel ground out.

'Twenty per cent.'

It wasn't as extortionate as Daniel had expected.

He supposed Hathaway's humiliation of him in front of Amelia was payment enough.

'How long for?'

Hathaway eyed Amelia for a couple of seconds.

'Two months should be long enough for you to get your affairs in order.'

Amelia recoiled involuntarily as if she'd been slapped in the face. The implication couldn't have been more clear: it should take Daniel only two months to finalise his marriage to Amelia and be in possession of her dowry.

Seeing he had caused the desired effect, Hathaway stood.

'Think on it, Burwell, send word to me if you decide to accept my offer and I'll get you the funds within the week.'

Daniel wished he could punch the man. Amelia looked devastated and all he could do was sit by and watch.

'It was delightful to make your acquaintance, Miss Eastway, especially after I've heard so much about you.'

Amelia managed a short nod of acknowledgement.

Hathaway mounted his horse and rode off without another word. Daniel and Amelia sat in silence for a whole minute, the gap between them seeming to widen with every passing second. Daniel wished he could reach out and take her hand, whisper something in her ear that would bring back the closeness they'd shared just moments before Hathaway had arrived. He hated the desolate look in Amelia's eyes. Although it was true he was pursuing Amelia for her dowry and the fortune she would bring to the marriage, he hadn't wanted her to end up feeling so unwanted and unattractive. He liked her, probably more than he should, and the last thing he wanted was for her to be hurt.

'Thank you for this afternoon,' Amelia said abruptly, standing before Daniel even realised what was happening. 'But I think I will return home now.'

He watched open-mouthed as she strode across to her horse and mounted easily without any help.

'Amelia,' he called after her, knowing he had to stop her or everything was lost.

She ignored him and spurred her horse forward into a canter. He cursed loudly before jogging over to his horse and swinging up on to his back. He needed to catch her, to try to smooth over the mess Hathaway had caused, otherwise he would lose her and Annabelle would ruin his son's future.

Chapter Nine

Lizzie felt the tears stinging her eyes as she galloped through the park. She couldn't believe she'd allowed herself to get hurt. She'd let Daniel draw her in and convince her that maybe he was just a little attracted to her. How could a man kiss a woman the way he had kissed her and not be even a little attracted to her? She thought back to Harriet's words earlier that afternoon and realised Amelia's cousin was telling the truth. Daniel was a rake, a man so practised in the art of seduction he could make any woman fall for him with a single kiss whilst not feeling a thing himself. He could even make the most unattractive woman feel beautiful and desired.

She raised a hand and swiped the tears that fell down her cheeks. She would not cry over him. Lizzie had known deep down that the only reason Daniel was courting her was because of Amelia's dowry. She'd repeated it to herself several times each hour, but still a small part of her had hoped. It wasn't as though they could ever be together anyway—after her lies about who she was Lizzie knew she'd be hounded out of London society, but for a moment it had felt wonderful to feel desired. Then to have that man come and reveal Daniel's crippling debts—and they must be crippling if he was willing to turn to someone like that for money—had been humiliating for both of them. Hathaway had even gone so far as to calculate when Amelia's dowry would be available if Lizzie and Daniel married. That had been the final blow.

Lizzie shook her head and tried to regain control of her emotions. Normally she was good at hiding when she was upset. For years in India she had been a burden to her uncle and he had let her know at every opportunity. There was one memory that was seared in Lizzie's mind so clearly it never really left her. A dressmaker had come to the house to measure her and Amelia for a new dress and she'd brought some samples with her. Both Lizzie and Amelia had been very excited teenagers, trying on the dresses and parading round. Amelia, of course, told her she looked stunning. Lizzie could always rely on her cousin for a compliment even if no one else ever thought to give her one. Her uncle had entered the room, in a foul mood for some reason, and on seeing Lizzie he had snorted. He'd instructed the dressmaker not to bother with a new dress for Lizzie as nothing was going to improve the disaster that she was becoming. Lizzie had swallowed back her tears and smiled when Amelia had later said she would help alter one of her new dresses for Lizzie.

So if she could hold her head up high to her uncle back then, why was she blubbering like a fool now?

'Amelia.' The shout came from some distance away and Lizzie turned to look behind her.

Daniel was gaining on her, riding like a man possessed. Lizzie rolled her eyes. He was no doubt wanting to ensure nothing was going to get in the way of him getting his hands on her precious dowry. She urged her horse to travel faster. Trees whipped past on her right and Lizzie knew it wouldn't be long before they were back in the more popular part of Hyde Park. If she could just reach there before Daniel caught up with her, she would be saved having to talk to him. She didn't want to exchange another word with him ever again and she certainly didn't want to listen to his lies about how he found her attractive. His silence when Hathaway had insulted her had been confirmation enough of his views.

Lizzie glanced back over her shoulder once again, wanting to see if Daniel had gained on her. Just as she was turning back to face forward a branch from a tree came out of nowhere. Lizzie ducked instinctively and managed to avoid the branch, but the sudden movement put her off balance. She pulled desperately on the horse's reins, trying to slow down as she felt herself lose her seat and start to topple. Arms flailing, Lizzie knew falling was inevitable and forced her body to go limp as she toppled from the horse. She rolled as she hit the ground, the breath forced from her lungs, and when she finally stopped moving she stayed curled in a ball, too frightened to move.

'Amelia!' Lizzie heard Daniel shout as he raced towards her. She didn't look up, instead concentrating on trying to breathe.

'Dear God,' he exhaled as he pulled his horse up beside her.

Lizzie heard him dismount and immediately felt his arms embracing her. Momentarily she forgot she was angry with this man and she allowed herself to melt into his body.

'Amelia, can you hear me?' he asked, his voice panicked.

Lizzie managed to nod, not having found her voice yet.

'What hurts?'

Everything hurt. Everything from the top of her

head down to the bottom of her feet hurt and she felt bloodied and bruised.

'Everything,' she managed to mutter after a few seconds.

Lizzie felt Daniel slowly sit her up and rest her body against his.

'Do you know who I am?' he asked slowly.

Lizzie nodded. 'The earl,' she said, not wanting to use his given name.

Daniel didn't seem to notice, instead he just seemed pleased she was at least a little orientated.

Slowly he moved round so he was facing Lizzie. They were both still sitting on the ground, but now Daniel was holding her round the waist whilst looking at her face.

Lizzie allowed her eyes to flutter open and raised a hand to her head. It didn't seem to have any large dents in it.

'Keep still,' Daniel instructed. Lizzie felt a pang of annoyance that he was telling her what to do, but had to concede it was good advice.

Slowly she watched as he raised his hands to her head and started to run his fingers over her scalp. His touch was gentle and Lizzie felt herself relaxing a little.

'Ouch,' she muttered as he found a sensitive spot.

'You've got quite a bump.'

Lizzie raised her own hand and traced the egg-sized bump that was forming on the back of her head. She would likely have a headache for days.

Daniel moved on, inspecting each part of her body much the way he had in the Prestons' garden when she had hurtled down the steps and landed on top of him. Gently he ran his fingers over her arms, satisfying himself there weren't any breaks, then he moved on to her body. He grasped her around the waist and slowly moved his hands upwards, squeezing as he went as if checking for broken ribs. Lizzie felt bruised and tender, but there was no sharp stab of pain.

As his hands moved higher Lizzie felt her breathing getting shallower. She hated him, hated him so much she never wanted to see him again, but she still couldn't stop her body responding to his touch. With each stroke of his fingers or squeeze of his hand she felt every nerve ending in her body come alive and begin firing. She yearned for his touch and at the same time wanted to push him away for ever.

Daniel's hands lingered on her waist for a few seconds and Lizzie knew he was trying to meet her gaze. She looked resolutely off into the distance, refusing to be sucked in by him.

'I need to check your legs,' Daniel said quietly.

Lizzie's eyes snapped upwards and met his. Already he was moving away from her and taking her left ankle in his hand. Carefully he encircled her lower leg with his hands and started to move his touch upwards. Lizzie didn't think anyone had ever touched her legs before him. It was intimate, maybe even more intimate than when his hand had dipped into the neckline of her dress earlier, and she knew she should pull away.

This was the man who had kissed her as though she were the most attractive woman on earth, then let his acquaintance insult her so openly. He'd not denied it was her supposed fortune he was after and Lizzie had to keep reminding herself he was a seasoned seducer.

Daniel moved his hands to her right ankle and immediately Lizzie let out a strangled cry.

'Does that hurt?'

She nodded, biting back a sarcastic comment.

He examined her carefully, probing gently with his fingers and stroking the length of her calf with his hand.

'I don't think it's broken,' he said eventually. 'Probably just sprained.'

Lizzie nodded, wondering if a sprain could be this painful.

'We should get you home.'

'If you would be so kind as to assist me on to my

horse, I'm sure I can find my own way back,' Lizzie said, her words stilted and her tone formal.

Daniel looked at her as though she were crazy.

'You want me to abandon an injured lady in the middle of Hyde Park?'

Lizzie nodded.

'Amelia,' he said, his voice strained with emotion. 'What happened—'

'Don't,' Lizzie interrupted him. 'Please don't say anything.'

He looked as though he was going to protest, he even opened his mouth to start his explanation, but must have thought better of it.

'I will not let you ride home alone,' he said eventually.

He rose to his feet and offered her his hand. Reluctantly Lizzie took it. Always the pragmatist, she knew realistically she wasn't going to be able to mount a horse without his help.

As she stood Lizzie felt a bolt of pain shoot through her ankle and she bit back a scream. Daniel must have seen the pained expression on her face and heard the sharp intake of breath for as soon as she was upright he swept her into his arms.

Lizzie started to protest but was silenced with a single look from Daniel.

Silently he walked over to his horse and carefully set her down.

'Stay here.' It was an order and, given his tone of voice, one Lizzie didn't dare disobey. She stood where he'd set her, balancing on her one good foot whilst she watched him fetch the horse she'd been riding and carefully tie its reins to his own. Then he pulled himself up on to his horse's back and effortlessly swung her up in front of him. It had all happened so quickly Lizzie didn't have time to protest. One moment she was standing on one foot, the next she was nestled between his thighs with his arm wrapped round her waist.

'I'm perfectly capable of riding,' she mumbled, knowing it was pointless to argue. Daniel had a determined look about him and she doubted anything less than divine intervention would convince him to let her ride on her own.

He urged his horse forward into a comfortable walk and despite herself Lizzie felt herself relaxing back into his chest.

'Amelia,' Daniel said once they had started to move, 'I need to apologise.'

Lizzie didn't disagree, but she didn't want to hear it. Either he was going to admit he was just courting her for a dowry she didn't even possess, or he was going to lie to her. She didn't want to hear what he had to say in either scenario.

'Hathaway was inexcusably rude and I'm afraid I wasn't much better. I shouldn't have allowed him to speak to you like that.'

Lizzie held herself completely still, wondering what his next words would be.

'I was shaken by having the memory of my brother's death raked up, but that is no excuse.'

He sighed and not for the first time Lizzie sensed Daniel was a troubled man. He put on a good show, but underneath the smiles and easy conversation there was so much more going on.

'I only hope you give me the chance to make it up to you.'

Lizzie wanted to shout at him, force him to admit why he was really courting her. She wished the truth was out in the open, that he would tell her he was only interested in her for her dowry, then she would be able to start putting him out of her mind. It would be better all round than continuing this charade, and she would be able to go back to being plain old Lizzie Eastway, the girl who was always second best.

Chapter Ten

Daniel knew he'd made a mess of things. Actually that was an understatement; courting Amelia had turned into a complete disaster. For years he had prided himself on his ability to seduce a woman with a single look, a single compliment, and now it really mattered that not only had he not complimented Amelia, he'd allowed her to be most grievously insulted while he stood by, mute.

He'd been completely thrown by Hathaway's presence, but that wasn't any kind of excuse. In truth, he'd been thrown before the man had even turned up. It had all started with that damn kiss. Once again Daniel had planned to further his courtship of Amelia with a kiss. In his mind it was to be something of passion and romance, something she could not help but fall for. She'd responded to him, there was no denying it, but once again he'd also lost control. Far from being rational and clear-headed, he'd felt the heat rise up inside him and his desire had taken over.

After Annabelle he had sworn never to let a woman get under his skin. But there was something about Amelia, something that reared its head whenever he kissed her—hell, whenever he got close to her—that made him lose control.

Daniel was brought out of his musings by a sharp knock on the door. Seconds later his butler was easing himself into the room.

'You have a visitor, sir.'

Daniel frowned. He wasn't expecting anyone. Maybe it would be Hathaway, come to rescind his offer of a loan from earlier. Daniel hadn't exactly jumped at the man's offer, even though he needed the money badly.

'A lady.'

Ah. Annabelle. Of course. Daniel should have known it wouldn't be long before she was knocking at his door, demanding money for her silence.

'Show her in.'

The last person he wanted to see right now was his ex-lover, but he knew if he made some excuse Annabelle would only make him suffer for it. She'd turned up at his club once before and at the house of one of his mistresses another time. Knowing his luck, Daniel thought this time she would choose

Amelia as her target. It would be better all round if he just gritted his teeth and dealt with her now.

'So lovely to see you yesterday, Daniel,' Annabelle said as she sailed into the room and delicately perched on the edge of a chair. She was a beautiful woman, but she was always arranging herself to show off her best side, fussing and preening, which Daniel now saw detracted from her beauty.

'Where's Edward?'

'Our son is safe, he's with a friend of mine.'

Daniel tried not to let his disappointment show. Annabelle hardly ever actually let him see his son, just catch glimpses of him as he had done the day before.

'Bringing up a child is a very expensive business,' Annabelle said, smoothing down her skirt, then looking up at Daniel and fluttering her eyelashes.

Daniel couldn't believe he had once been in love with this woman. She was cruel and manipulative, and he'd been completely besotted.

'You want more money.'

'For our son, of course. Otherwise I might let it slip that his father wasn't a war hero, now sadly deceased.'

Daniel grimaced. No matter how much he despised Annabelle he couldn't let her reveal the truth to his son. He couldn't let Edward grow up to be an outcast like Rupert had been, teased because he was the illegitimate son of an earl.

'How much?' Daniel asked, knowing there was no point quibbling.

'Just the usual amount. Twenty pounds a month, so two hundred and forty pounds for the year.'

It was extortionate, more than most titled gentlemen had as their yearly income. Annabelle had bled him dry over the years, but Daniel knew he would continue to pay.

'I want to see Edward.'

'I don't think that's wise. He might start asking who this strange man is.'

Daniel hated the thought that he was a stranger to his son.

'You've got a week to raise the money. I'll come back to collect it. Just remember what will happen if you don't pay.'

Annabelle stood and walked round the desk, leant over and gave Daniel a peck on the cheek.

'We could have been so happy,' she whispered in his ear.

'I think I owe you an apology.' Daniel raised his head to see Fletcher approaching his table.

Daniel had been sitting in his club for the best part

of an hour nursing a whisky. His frown had stopped any passing acquaintances from approaching him, but it did not deter Fletcher.

'I asked Hathaway to meet with you. I didn't realise he would actively seek you out.'

Daniel nodded, grimacing as he remembered the expression on Amelia's face as Hathaway had insulted her.

'I take it Miss Eastway was present.'

'She was.'

'Did Hathaway actually bring up business whilst she was there?'

Daniel raked a hand through his hair. 'He brought up the subject of a loan, after telling Miss Eastway about my brother and insinuating I was only interested in her for her money.'

Even easygoing Fletcher couldn't find anything to say for a moment or two. Instead he motioned for another glass of whisky for them both.

'What happened?' he asked eventually.

Daniel didn't say anything about his brother. Fletcher had been his friend since school, so he knew most of the sordid details. He knew the guilt Daniel carried around over Rupert's death and in part he shared some of that guilt.

They'd all been at Eton together. Daniel and Fletcher had hit it off immediately, been friends from the very first day. Hathaway was already a slimy little toad and the two boys had gone out of their way to avoid him. Rupert had begun the term late, only two weeks, but it was enough to make him noticeable. Boys were notoriously unforgiving at that age and immediately they wanted to find out what had caused the delay.

When Rupert had arrived Daniel hadn't known how to act. It wasn't the first time he'd laid eyes on his illegitimate half-brother, but it was the first time they'd ever been close enough to interact. They had circled each other warily for a few days, neither wanting to be the one to make the first move.

And then everything had changed. Somehow Hathaway had found out that Rupert was illegitimate. Boys whispered about him as he walked from class to class, the few friends he had managed to distance themselves. It didn't matter that his father was bothering to send him to Eton despite being illegitimate. He was ostracised, made an outcast. Daniel could have done something. If he'd extended the hand of friendship, then others would have followed, but he'd been too wrapped up in his own life to even notice.

By the time they left Eton and started at Cambridge Rupert had turned into a recluse, leaving his lodgings only to attend lectures. Older, slightly wiser and certainly more aware of his half-brother's misery, Daniel had tried to reach out a few times, but when Rupert rejected him he all too easily gave up.

Then Rupert had killed himself. On the last day of the winter term he'd been found hanging in his room. He'd left a note, but even without it Daniel didn't need a dead man's accusations to know the truth: he could have prevented his brother's death. If he'd persevered, if he'd tried just a little harder to reach out to him, maybe Rupert would still be alive.

'It wasn't your fault,' Fletcher said softly after a couple of minutes, knowing his friend was thinking of his brother.

Daniel shook his head and took a gulp of whisky. He knew his guilt would never ease.

'Hathaway agreed to lend me the money, but he all but said the only reason I'm pursuing Miss Eastway is because of her fortune.'

Fletcher shrugged. 'Well, it is, isn't it?'

Daniel considered. When he'd asked Fletcher to point out Amelia in the Prestons' ballroom all he could think about was her dowry and the means to pay Annabelle to shield his son against the truth of his birth. Then he'd encountered her in the garden and he'd felt the stab of desire he hadn't felt in years. At each subsequent meeting he'd realised that he actually liked Amelia. She was quiet and thoughtful, but a sharp intelligence hid behind her unassuming manner. He found he enjoyed talking to her and the hours they spent together passed quite pleasurably.

He actually enjoyed the company of the woman he was hoping to marry, which would be fantastic if he didn't desire her so damn much.

Most of the time he could think rationally. When they were walking in the park or riding side by side he could look at her and see the modest, gentle woman the rest of the world saw. There was just that small percentage of the time, normally when Amelia was standing close to him, when his heart started pounding in his chest and he knew he had to have her. He wanted to run his hands over her entire body, kiss her in all her most intimate places and make her his. He wanted to lay her down and make love to her until neither of them knew where one body stopped and the next began.

'Ah,' Fletcher said, 'I see.'

Daniel knew he hadn't said a word, but with four sisters Fletcher was unusually sensitive and astute.

'What?' Daniel asked.

'You feel something for her.'

Daniel didn't bother to deny it. He did feel something for Amelia. He wasn't going to claim it was love or anything as noble. He liked the girl, but more than that he desired her.

'Most people would be happy to feel something for their future spouse.'

Daniel knew it was true. Most *ton* marriages were marriages of convenience, much like the one he'd planned to have. The match was made either for money or for a title and an alliance. Many married couples thought themselves lucky if they didn't completely despise each other.

'It complicates things,' Daniel said.

Fletcher regarded him for a few moments and Daniel knew his friend was considering whether to say anything more.

'We've all had women who have got under our skin,' he said eventually. 'The trick is not to let them control the rest of your life.' With that his friend stood, clapped him on the shoulder and walked away. Unfortunately a much-less-welcome companion soon approached his table.

'Burwell, twice in one day. What an unexpected pleasure.'

Daniel took a few seconds to compose himself before raising his head to look at Hathaway. The man irritated him and had been unforgivably rude to Amelia, but Daniel knew he needed his old acquaintance to lend him the money to get Annabelle off his back.

'Hathaway,' Daniel said, his voice low and not much more than a growl.

'So delightful to meet the future Lady Burwell earlier. Isn't she a quiet little thing?'

'Miss Eastway is a charming young woman.'

'With a charmingly large dowry.'

Daniel felt the muscles in his hand clench as he formed a fist, but forced himself to relax. He hadn't let Hathaway goad him when they had been at school or university together and he wasn't going to start now.

'Thank you for the offer of a loan. I will send a man to collect it in a few days.'

For a moment Daniel thought Hathaway might stay, that he might want to bait Daniel further, but luckily his old acquaintance didn't seem in the mood for taunting him tonight. After a few seconds of being ignored by Daniel, Hathaway picked up his drink and moved on.

Daniel nursed his whisky for a few more minutes before gulping down the last of it and standing to leave. He needed some fresh air and he needed to clear his head.

Daniel thought back to the conversation he'd had with Fletcher earlier in the evening. He knew his old friend was right; most men would be ecstatic to desire the woman they were courting, but Daniel wished he felt nothing beyond mild affection for Amelia. He had experienced gut-wrenching passion before, he'd let it cloud his judgement and overtake his life, and now he wasn't the only one paying for it. It was because of desire that he could never truly know his son and it was because of desire that one day that boy he loved so much would probably find out he was illegitimate and have his world shattered.

The past few years had forced Daniel to become a pragmatist, and as he walked he strived to take his emotions out of the equation. The facts remained: he was broke, he needed money to pay off Annabelle.

There were really only two problems. The first was the way Daniel seemed to lose his head whenever Amelia's body brushed up against his and the second was the fact that after this afternoon she probably never wanted to see him ever again.

Daniel had been walking absentmindedly for about half an hour when he realised his subconscious had brought him to the house Amelia was staying in with her aunt. He glanced up at the windows, wondering which of them belonged to Amelia's room. It was far too late to call on her, despite Daniel wanting to try to move on from their disastrous afternoon out in the park. He was just about to turn away when he saw a flicker of orange in one of the windows. Frowning, he stared for a minute before realising what it was.

Chapter Eleven

After her disastrous afternoon Lizzie had fled straight to her room on arriving home. She hadn't wanted to answer Aunt Mathilda's questions on how things were going with *the dear earl* and she hadn't wanted to endure Harriet's snide comments. All she did want to do was bury her face in her pillow and cry.

On reaching her room Lizzie allowed herself to sob for five minutes before sitting up and wiping her eyes. Whilst she was growing up there had been hundreds of occasions that had made Lizzie want to shut herself away from the rest of the world and cry until she had no more tears, but she'd learnt to control her sadness. No one comforted her then and no one was going to comfort her now.

As she had many times Lizzie wondered how different things would have been if her parents were still alive. They had died in a coach accident when

Lizzie had been very young—all she could really remember was her mother's warm smile and her father's hearty laugh. She couldn't imagine having a mother, someone who would love her unconditionally, who would wipe away her tears and tell her she was worth so much more. Lizzie could never imagine being the centre of someone's world.

She shook her head. She probably wouldn't ever be the centre of someone's world. For odd moments she had fooled herself about Daniel when he looked at her with his wolfish eyes and claimed her with a kiss that was so searing and possessive she had dared to hope he might want her as he wanted no other. She had dared to hope he might be the one who could love her unconditionally.

It had all been nothing more than an illusion. What made it hurt even more was the attraction Lizzie felt for Daniel. She knew nothing could come of their liaison, she knew that once her identity was revealed she would be hounded from London society, but that didn't stop her heart racing whenever he smiled at her or her skin tingling when he touched her. He was a good-looking man and a seasoned charmer, but it was something more than that. When he touched her it was as if all the jumbled pieces of Lizzie's life fell into place.

She'd been fooling herself, wanting something that

was so far out of her reach, and now it was time to accept reality and move on. When Amelia returned and revealed her identity, Lizzie would have to disappear. Her cousin would beg her to stay, of course, and normally Lizzie would do anything for Amelia, but this time she had tasted how her life could have been if she had been born Amelia's sister rather than her penniless cousin. She couldn't go back to being poor, insignificant Lizzie who no one took any notice of. She would leave London, leave the country and seek out a life for herself elsewhere.

Deep down Lizzie knew in reality it wouldn't be the *ton* in general she would be running from, but rather a very specific dashing earl with smouldering eyes.

A knock at her door gave her a moment's panic, but she took a moment to straighten her dress and wipe her eyes before answering.

'Come in.'

Rosie, a young maid who had been assigned to help Lizzie dress and do her hair whilst she was living with Aunt Mathilda, opened the door and dropped into a little neat curtsy.

'Begging your pardon for disturbing you, miss, but a letter came for you when you were out.'

Lizzie's eyes widened with anticipation. It would

be from Amelia surely. Lizzie still hadn't heard a thing from her cousin since they had parted at the dock. She was becoming increasingly worried about Amelia. In the time they had spent together on their voyage Lizzie had tried to talk her cousin out of her foolish plan so many times. She'd tried to explain the scandal that would ensue if anyone found out Amelia had run off to meet a man, but as usual her cousin had just laughed off her concerns.

Lizzie was beginning to wish she had made Amelia realise that it wasn't only her reputation she was risking, but Lizzie's, too. At the time she had agreed to Amelia's reckless plan because she never expected to want to marry, never expected to find someone who wanted to marry her. Now she was getting so worried about her cousin she would use any tactic, including guilt over ruining Lizzie's reputation, to keep her cousin from disappearing.

'I'm sure it could have waited until morning, miss, it was just…' The young maid tailed off.

'Yes?' Lizzie asked kindly.

'It was just that Miss Harriet was poking around it and I was afraid she might read something she shouldn't,' Rosie said, dropping her voice.

'Thank you, Rosie, you are very astute.'

The maid looked confused at the compliment but

curtsied again, handed over the letter and backed out of the room.

Lizzie turned the envelope over in her hands and immediately felt disappointment. The handwriting was nothing like her cousin's. The two girls had taken all their lessons together, so Lizzie could recognise Amelia's hurried scrawl easily.

Instead the letters were neat and carefully spaced; it was her uncle's handwriting.

Although the letter was addressed to Amelia, Lizzie slid her finger under the seal and opened it. She needed to know what was so important he'd sent a letter so soon after their departure. For this to have got to London so quickly he must have sent it mere days after they had left India.

Sinking down on her bed to read it, Lizzie felt her eyes widen with shock and her skin start to prickle with dread.

Dear Amelia,
I hope this letter finds you well and that you are closer to securing a suitable husband.

Her uncle, the colonel, always did get straight to the point.

I will not waste time with pleasantries, instead I send instructions.

The colonel didn't waste time with pleasantries in person, so Lizzie wasn't surprised he was as direct in his correspondence.

I trust as instructed you will focus on finding a husband with all possible haste. I sent your cousin Elizabeth with you so you would have company on the voyage and for your arrival in London. However, her place is not in London society with you.

At the mention of her name Lizzie sat up straighter and started to read faster.

I have often despaired of what to do with your cousin once you are married, but now I have found a pleasing solution and would like her to return to India as soon as possible.

Lizzie closed her eyes and took a moment to steady herself before she found out what fate her uncle had in store for her.

I had assumed Elizabeth would remain a spinster. She is a plain girl who lacks the necessary attributes to marry well, but I have found a man willing to be her husband.

She gasped in shock. Not at her uncle calling her plain—he'd always made it clear she was much inferior to Amelia or any other girl of the same age—but at the idea of him wanting to marry her off. She'd always assumed Amelia would marry someone rich and she'd become her cousin's companion.

Taking a deep breath, Lizzie steeled herself to finish the letter.

Colonel Rocher is in need of a wife and is willing to take Elizabeth on. He is eager that the formalities should be taken care of as soon as possible. Please instruct your cousin Elizabeth to arrange passage back to India with all possible haste.
Your Father

Lizzie sat in shock for five whole minutes, reading and rereading the last section of the letter. She couldn't quite believe her life had changed so much in mere minutes.

She couldn't marry Colonel Rocher. Of all the men in India he was the very last she would ever want to marry. It wasn't because he was at least double her age, or that physically he was repulsive. Lizzie wasn't so naïve to have ever expected an attractive husband and she would certainly not turn down a man just because he didn't have rippling muscles or a winning smile. It wasn't even that he leered at every woman under the age of sixty and had wandering hands that were the stuff of legend. All that Lizzie could forgive—after all, it wasn't as though she was a prize. No, the reason she just couldn't marry Colonel Rocher was because she knew he would beat her. He had beaten his first wife and he had beaten his second. Both had often been seen sporting bruises or injuries and, far from denying hurting either of the women, he had often boasted about keeping them in line.

She'd always known she was a burden to her uncle, he'd told her often enough, but she'd always hoped that deep down he loved her just a little. Or at least cared enough that he would not send her to endure a lifetime of humiliation and pain.

Lizzie couldn't stop the image of Daniel flashing before her eyes. He was everything Colonel Rocher was not—young, attractive—and Lizzie knew instinctively he would never beat his wife. However, the main difference, the most heartbreaking difference, was that once Daniel knew her true identity he would never want her as his wife.

She refused to cry any more. This interlude with Daniel had been nothing more than a fantasy. She'd allowed herself to get swept away with it, but now her head had cleared and she saw his attention for what it really was. Lizzie knew she had to stop obsessing about the earl and instead work out what she was going to do about her future.

Of course, she would have to wait until Amelia returned, which should be any day now, but then she had to decide whether to obey her uncle and return to India or whether she was brave enough to try to survive on her own.

Lizzie knew she was far too shocked to make a rational decision, so instead she busied herself getting ready for bed, placed the letter on her bedside table and blew out her candle.

It was unbearably hot. Lizzie tossed and turned in her bed, throwing off her covers as she transitioned from a deep sleep to a light state of drowsiness. Her eyes slowly opened and at first she couldn't quite make sense of what she was seeing. There was light in the room, not the piercing clarity of sunlight, but a dull flickering. She was covered in sweat and she could feel beads of water running between her shoulder blades.

Groggily Lizzie pushed herself up into a sitting position and forced her brain to engage with her surroundings.

She tried not to scream, knowing panicking would only make things worse. The room was on fire. The curtains had already been consumed by flames and every second that passed the fire was creeping closer to her bed. Black smoke billowed as furniture caught light and the room became a blazing inferno.

For a second Lizzie was paralysed with fear, then her survival instincts kicked in. She jumped from the bed, knowing if she didn't get out of this room in the next thirty seconds she would die in it. In her haste her feet caught in her nightgown and she felt herself falling to the floor. She cursed her clumsiness but caught herself on her hands and knees and pushed back up to her feet. The pain from her injured ankle shot up her leg as she stood, but she managed to stumble on. Coughing as the smoke irritated her lungs, Lizzie felt her eyes also begin to water and the outline of the door, just a few feet away, became hazy.

She staggered forward, clutching at pieces of furniture that weren't alight to try to guide herself out of the room. It was almost impossible to see anything now and as her breathing became more and more laboured Lizzie began to feel the darkness descend. She struggled on for a few more steps, dragging red-hot air into her burning lungs. Her vision, previously obscured by smoke, now was hazy from lack of oxygen and she knew she was never going to find her way to the door.

Refusing to give up, Lizzie collapsed to her knees and dragged herself a few more paces before her strength deserted her. Just before she slipped from consciousness Daniel's face flashed before her eyes and his strong, confident voice sounded in her ears. Lizzie felt herself smile; at least she'd experienced a divinely pleasurable kiss before she'd died.

Chapter Twelve

She was smiling. The crazy woman was smiling. She was seconds from death and there was no mistaking the smile that danced over her lips as she collapsed on to her front.

Daniel surged into the room, trying to ignore the fiery heat and the black clouds of smoke that obscured almost everything. Three short strides took him to Amelia's side and without pausing he scooped her up into his arms and retreated from the room.

Even though he'd only been in the burning room for seconds he felt the strain from the smoke on his chest and his skin still prickled as if the flames were licking at it. The hallway, which had been relatively clear when he'd bounded into the house, was now filled with smoke and Daniel knew it was only a matter of minutes before the whole house was consumed by flames.

As he raced through the house he glanced down at Amelia. She was a dead weight in his arms, completely unconscious. There had been no flicker of recognition as he'd picked her up, nor any stirring since. Her face was blackened with soot and her nightgown, which he assumed was normally a standard white, was singed at the edges and grey all over. He couldn't see any obvious burns on her body, but he doubted she had escaped unscathed; no one could last more than a minute in a room that was burning at that intensity and not suffer from any permanent injury.

The thought of a burn on her lovely flawless skin made Daniel feel angry at whoever had been careless enough to allow the fire to start. No doubt a candle had been left burning or a fire left smouldering when it should have been put out. Fires didn't occur spontaneously.

Daniel reached the stairs and descended quickly. As he reached the ground floor the air was a little clearer and he felt the smoke begin to leave his lungs. He resisted the almost overwhelming urge to cough and instead pressed on towards the door.

It was less than a minute after Daniel had swept Amelia into his arms that he burst through the open door and into the night. He didn't stop walking until he was a good fifty feet from the house, well clear from the billowing black smoke that was now coming from every window. When he reached the crowd of assembled family, staff and curious onlookers he sank to his knees and placed Amelia gently on the ground.

'Amelia, Amelia!' Immediately Amelia's aunt Mathilda was at their side.

Daniel ignored the frantic older woman and quickly inspected the woman lying unconscious in front of him. The first thing he noticed with relief was that her chest was rising and falling regularly; whatever other damage she had sustained at least she was still breathing.

As he bent lower to wipe some of the grime from her face he tried to block out the crowd of curious onlookers who were surging closer. He needed to focus on Amelia. He had no idea how long she had been in the room with the fire burning around her, but he was sure she needed space and a doctor.

Decisively he stood.

'Move back,' he shouted, his voice commanding despite the croak from the smoke inhalation.

The crowd obeyed.

'I need a carriage.'

A smartly dressed man caught Daniel's eye and nodded, before disappearing at speed to find one.

'And I need someone to fetch a doctor.'

A young lad who Daniel had seen emerge from a neighbouring house stepped up.

'I'll fetch a doctor for you, sir,' he said.

Daniel reckoned this boy was a servant or stable boy for Amelia's aunt's neighbours and was grateful for his volunteering.

'Send him to Twenty-Three Burton Street.'

The boy scampered off, no doubt to find the doctor his employers used whenever they were unwell.

'I'm taking Amelia to my house to be seen to,' Daniel said, turning to Aunt Mathilda.

She nodded, not really taking in what Daniel was saying. He supposed there wasn't much more distracting than watching your family home burn to the ground.

'Is anyone else still unaccounted for?'

Aunt Mathilda looked around desperately as if she hadn't considered anyone else might be left in the house.

'Everyone is here,' the butler said, stepping forward.

Daniel appraised him and saw he was shaken but able to take charge of this crisis.

'Arrange for Mrs Hunter and Miss Hunter to follow me to my town house,' he said. 'If any of the servants are injured or suffering from the smoke, send them quickly, too. After Miss Eastway has been seen to the doctor can check them over.'

The butler nodded. 'I'll keep any healthy, uninjured men with me here to supervise things and help fight the fire.'

Already the street was alive with people hauling buckets of water ready to fight the fire. Luckily the Hunters' house was detached and had a little land surrounding it, but it took only a gentle breeze to lift some embers and the whole street could be ablaze.

Satisfied things were under control, Daniel turned his attention back to Amelia. She was still unconscious—in fact, she hadn't once even stirred—and the depth of her insensibility worried Daniel.

At that moment a carriage clattered round the corner and the crowd parted obligingly. Daniel quickly gave his address to the driver, impressed on the man how important it was that they got there with all possible haste and swept Amelia back into his arms. Carefully he stepped up into the carriage and held her tightly across his lap as they set off through the streets of London.

He only lived a ten-minute carriage ride away, but those ten minutes seemed the longest of Daniel's life. In the darkness he couldn't see Amelia and he kept laying a hand on her chest to check she was still breathing. As London sped by outside the carriage window Daniel knew there was a very real chance Amelia wouldn't make it to his house alive. He choked back the emotion that overcame him, not wanting to examine his feelings as well as cope with everything else that was occurring.

Eventually the carriage slowed to a stop and Daniel hurriedly jumped down. As he strode towards his front door he called back to the carriage driver telling him someone would come out and pay him in a few minutes.

Daniel's front door opened as he reached the top of the steps and the face of his worried, elderly butler looked at him with amazement.

'Wake the household,' Daniel instructed. 'Miss Eastway has been in a fire and is gravely injured. A doctor will be arriving shortly but I need plenty of clean water and send Mrs Greystone to my room.'

Daniel hurried up the stairs and into his bedroom, placing Amelia down on top of his four-poster bed. He'd just straightened and was about to start checking Amelia over for external injuries when he heard his very capable housekeeper bustle into the room.

'Dearie me,' she said. 'What on earth happened to this poor lamb?'

Mrs Greystone took one look at Amelia and immediately began issuing orders to the two maids who trailed behind her.

'You look a state,' she said, appraising Daniel.

He grinned for the first time that evening. Mrs Greystone had known him since he was a baby and the older woman never minced her words around her young master. In a world where most servants were too respectful to meet their employers' eye as they went about their daily chores, it was refreshing to have someone like Mrs Greystone around.

'I should send you out, but I'm guessing nothing will make you leave the room until you know this lass is all right, so go and sit down in that chair and keep out of the way.'

Daniel knew it was pointless arguing with his housekeeper. He crossed the room and sank into a high-backed chair. Immediately he felt exhausted. For the past hour his body had been filled with energy as he'd rushed to rescue Amelia and then hurry her to a place where she could be best looked after. Now he'd stopped moving he felt physically drained and mentally fatigued. All he could think about was Amelia, lying on the floor of her bedroom, the life slowly draining from her body.

He watched as Mrs Greystone supervised the maids who were bringing bowls of warmed water and towels. Gently they dabbed the soot from Amelia's face before turning to the rest of her body.

Daniel knew the curves of her body, he knew

them more than he should. From that first time he'd skimmed his hands over her hips and encircled her waist with his arm Daniel had memorised her contours. As she lay on the bed, draped in the shapeless soot-stained nightgown, Daniel wanted to run his hands over her body again. He wanted to assure himself no inch of her body went unchecked, that there were no hidden wounds and every single bit of skin was intact.

Instead Mrs Greystone turned to him and raised an eyebrow.

At first he didn't move, wondering if he could insist on staying and supervising, but even though this was his house and the women in the room were his staff, he knew they would band together to protect Amelia's virtue and privacy, despite never having met her before.

Wearily Daniel rose from the chair, pleased to hear a male voice in the hallway. The doctor must have arrived.

'Go and rest, Master Daniel,' Mrs Greystone said kindly. 'I'll send the doctor to see to your wounds once he's finished with this poor lass.'

Daniel nodded and left the room, knowing he would not be able to rest whilst Amelia lay unconscious. He passed the doctor in the doorway, who looked him up and down.

'You need to get that arm cleaned up,' the medical man said without any preamble.

Daniel glanced down at his arm, confused. Sure enough his jacket and shirtsleeve had been almost completely destroyed on the right side and a raw-looking wound was starting to blister on the skin. Daniel grimaced. Now he had noticed the burn it started to throb and hurt. Up until this point he'd been so focused on Amelia he hadn't even realised he'd been burnt.

Quickly he returned downstairs to his study and asked the butler to organise some clean water to be put in the guest room next to his own. He also informed the elderly man they were likely to have an influx of guests arriving soon, many shaken and scared by the night's events.

The butler took it all in his stride. Daniel knew the older man had served in the army for years and had never encountered a situation that fazed him.

Wearily Daniel returned upstairs, eager to be close to Amelia should he be needed. As he waited for the water to clean his wound his valet quietly entered the room with a change of clothes.

Daniel sank on to the bed. He realised his hands were shaking and his heart had started to race in his chest. Throughout the entire ordeal his head had remained clear and his body in control, but now he had rested and he knew there was nothing more he could do, his body was reacting to the shock of the evening.

He tried not to imagine what was happening in the room next door. He knew Amelia would not come through this unscathed and he only hoped her injuries were superficial ones. He didn't want to examine the steely grip of panic around his heart or what it meant. He just knew his life would never be the same if Amelia didn't make it through the next few hours.

Chapter Thirteen

Lizzie struggled to open her eyes. It was as though her eyelids were made of a heavy metal and her brain was refusing to cooperate with the rest of her body. Eventually her eyes flickered open and she frowned as she tried to take in her surroundings. Everything was blurry for a couple of seconds and her eyes stung as if she'd washed them with soap.

She let out a small groan as she remembered the fire. That was why her eyes were stinging so much and why her chest hurt with every laboured breath she took. Slowly the room came into focus and she realised she didn't recognise her surroundings at all.

It was clear she was in a man's bedroom. The muted colours and functionality hinted at good taste without being over the top. Lizzie struggled to remember arriving here, wherever here was.

The last thing she remembered was falling to her knees as she rushed to get out of her burning bedroom. Her feet had caught in her nightgown and she'd stumbled. Had she ever managed to get up again?

She wondered how she had escaped from the fiery inferno, looking around all the time for clues.

When the door opened Lizzie was fully awake and she turned her head towards it to see who entered. Even that little movement sent spasms through her chest and she began coughing, the irritation spreading from her throat to her chest in no time and causing her to wince with pain.

Daniel. Of course it would be Daniel.

He walked into the room, leaving the door ajar for propriety's sake, and frowned at her. Quickly he poured her a glass of water and held it to her lips, allowing her small sips at a time. The cool liquid soothed Lizzie's throat, but did nothing for the heaviness in her chest. It was a few minutes before the coughs subsided and she felt able to speak.

'What happened?' she asked, her voice unnaturally croaky.

Daniel didn't answer for a few seconds and Lizzie took the opportunity to look him over. He appeared tired, as if he hadn't slept at all. He was neatly turned out, but not dressed for the outside world. It must be his house they were in. She glanced down at his arm and grimaced when she saw the bandage. He was holding his injured arm across his chest, as if it pained him, but she saw no evidence of it in his face.

'What do you remember?' Daniel asked.

Lizzie closed her eyes and tried to think back, past the billowing black smoke and inferno of flames, past the panic and the feeling of certainty she'd had that she was going to die.

'I remember going to bed,' she said. She'd been reading her uncle's letter over and over again, but eventually she'd decided to sleep. She had placed the letter down on her bedside table and blown out her candle. 'Then I awoke and the room was boiling hot and filled with smoke. The curtains were on fire and it spread so quickly. I couldn't breathe.'

Lizzie tried to block out the panic that was rising with the memory. She felt Daniel's hand cover her own and immediately her racing heart started to slow and her mind cleared.

'I tried to escape, but I tripped,' she said with a shake of her head. 'I thought I was going to die.'

Lizzie glanced at Daniel again, taking in his bandaged arm and concerned expression, and realised the truth. He'd saved her. Somehow he'd battled the flames and the smoke and he'd saved her.

'You found me?' Lizzie asked quietly.

He nodded. 'I was passing the house when I saw

the fire. When you didn't emerge I went in and got you out.'

Lizzie knew there must have been much more to it than that. He would have had to push past everyone fleeing the burning house, going against every survival instinct that was screaming for him to stay well away from the fire. Then he would have had to brave the smoke and the flames and search the burning building before he came across her unconscious body. Once he'd found her, he would have had to carry her all the way outside even though the flames would have been licking at his heels and the smoke filling his lungs.

'Thank you,' Lizzie said sincerely, holding his eye. She knew what he had done deserved so much more than a 'thank you', but she also knew he was not the sort of man to seek out praise. It was enough that he had saved her. 'Did everyone…?' She trailed off, not knowing how to ask the question.

'Everyone got out alive. Some of the staff have minor injuries and smoke inhalation, but nothing that time won't heal.'

Lizzie nodded, the movement setting off another bout of coughing. Her chest felt as though it were about to explode and her throat burned.

'You were injured?' she asked when the coughing had subsided.

He shrugged. 'Just a small burn.'

Lizzie felt guilty at having been the reason he was in the burning house to start with.

'We should let the doctor know you're awake,' Daniel said. 'And your aunt.'

'Poor Aunt Mathilda, she's lost her home.'

Lizzie fell silent. She wondered for a moment how the fire had started, whether a candle had been left burning or an ember from a fire had floated on to a nearby piece of furniture. Something was nagging her, dancing around the edge of her consciousness.

'When you came and got me was the whole house burning?' Lizzie asked.

Daniel shook his head. 'No, only upstairs, your room, the couple on either side. There was smoke throughout the house, though.'

Lizzie nodded, carefully trying to keep her face composed. She tried to picture her room just before she had closed her eyes and gone to sleep. She quite clearly remembered blowing out the candle by her bed and lying in the darkness. So it couldn't have been her who started the fire.

Still something was nagging at her. Forcing herself to maintain her composure, she thought back to what she had seen when the room was on fire. She'd been panicked, more scared than she had ever been before, but she had noticed something.

Suddenly it came to her; there had been another candle in the room. It had been sitting on the small desk by the window, right next to the curtains. Lizzie knew she hadn't left it burning—in fact, she was sure she hadn't left the candle there at all.

Her thoughts were interrupted by the door opening again and Aunt Mathilda hurrying in, followed reluctantly by Harriet.

'Oh, my dear, we were so worried about you— weren't we, Harriet?'

Harriet nodded vaguely but didn't make any snide comments.

'Were you hurt?' Lizzie asked, quickly running her eyes over both women, looking for injuries.

'Thankfully, no, we got out whilst the fire was still small.' Lizzie saw Aunt Mathilda hesitate before continuing. 'I don't suppose you have any idea how the fire started, my dear?'

Lizzie shook her head. 'I remember blowing out my candle before I went to sleep.'

Aunt Mathilda nodded. 'I just don't understand how it happened.'

'Amelia said she doesn't know anything,' Harriet said in a tetchy voice.

Everyone in the room turned to Harriet in surprise. The young woman had made it no secret that she was not fond of Lizzie and her defence of her now seemed unnatural.

'Well, she did,' Harriet muttered.

'It really doesn't matter,' Aunt Mathilda insisted. 'The main thing is that you escaped largely unharmed.'

'What about your poor house?'

The older woman shrugged, but Lizzie could see the tears in her eyes.

'Please excuse me, I think I'll go and have a lie-down.'

Aunt Mathilda left the room. Harriet stayed where she was for a moment or two, staring at Lizzie, before she followed her mother out. Just as she reached the door Harriet turned back towards Lizzie.

'It looks like once again you came out on top. What a surprise. We've lost our home and the Eastways have lost nothing.'

'How strange,' Daniel murmured.

'She's had a shock. They both have. Losing your home must be awful.'

Lizzie felt the tears well up in her eyes and spill out on to her cheeks. Her hands started to shake and the spasms in her chest returned, making her cough. She knew they had all come close to dying. If Daniel hadn't rushed into the house, there was no doubt she'd be nothing more than a pile of ash.

Daniel was at her side in moments. He took her hand in one of his and stroked her hair with his other. Lizzie closed her eyes and tried to catch her breath.

'Hush,' Daniel said. 'You're safe now.'

Lizzie nodded, but still the tears kept flowing.

With her eyes still closed Lizzie felt rather than saw the moment Daniel moved to sit on the bed beside her. He scooped her into his arms and held her close to his body. Lizzie felt the warmth of his body against her skin and his touch soothed her. After a few seconds her cough subsided and a minute later the tears followed.

They sat in silence, the rise and fall of their chests following the same rhythm, Daniel's breath tickling Lizzie's neck. She felt safe here, ensconced in his arms, protected by his embrace, but even whilst she was enjoying the closeness Lizzie knew it could never last.

Daniel still thought he had rescued Miss Amelia Eastway, most eligible heiress of the season. He might find her plainness and lack of beauty acceptable whilst he thought her rich, but that concession would soon sour once he knew she was almost penniless, a charity case her uncle had taken pity on. She squeezed her eyes tighter shut and wished she could suspend time. She wanted to stay as they were right now, with Daniel's arms wrapped around her and him thinking she was so much more than she really was.

They sat in silence for ten minutes, all the while Lizzie wished again and again that she was her cousin. She wanted Amelia's life so badly, not for her money or her confidence, but she wanted to be the kind of woman Daniel could not ignore. Instead of being plain old Lizzie, eternally condemned to be overlooked by everyone, she wanted to be the woman people sat up and took notice of. Time and again at social occasions Lizzie had stood beside her cousin, watching people's eyes light up as they were introduced to Amelia and then glaze over as they turned to her. Each time that happened the words her uncle had spoken to her as a young girl always flashed back into her mind.

'You're plain, Elizabeth, plain and unappealing. Our best hope for you is for a blind man to happen along in search of a wife.'

She'd been seven at the time. A very gangly and ungainly seven-year-old. Her confidence had never recovered.

It didn't matter that every so often she saw a spark of desire flash in Daniel's eyes. She knew she would always be plain and unappealing. For years she had told herself she didn't care that she wasn't a beauty like Amelia, but that had been before she met Daniel. Now there was someone that she wanted to be desired by she did care. She cared so much it tore her apart.

There was a soft knock on the door and Daniel quickly stood up. Lizzie had to hide a smile. Despite it being his house, they still had to act with propriety.

'Doctor, thank you for returning.'

'How is the patient?' the short bespectacled man asked.

Lizzie managed to croak a short, non-committal sound.

'Hmm, I see the smoke inhalation has caused some damage to your throat,' the doctor said. 'That should recover with rest and fresh air.'

'She's coughing a lot,' Daniel supplied.

The doctor stepped closer to Lizzie, then motioned for Daniel to turn around. Daniel obliged and Lizzie breathed deeply whilst the doctor placed his ear against her back.

'Rattly, as you would expect,' he said without further explanation.

They waited as he checked her pulse, got her to stick out her tongue and inspected the back of her throat.

'No permanent damage,' the doctor declared eventually. 'But I would advise a week or two of good, clean country air.'

Daniel showed the doctor out and returned to her bedside.

'That settles it,' he said.

Lizzie looked at him questioningly.

'You can come and recuperate at my country estate. The fresh air will do you good. Your aunt can come along to chaperon you—'

Lizzie opened her mouth to object. A whole week with Daniel away from the world sounded like bliss, but she knew it would make it all that much harder to give him up.

'No argument, it's the doctor's orders.'

Chapter Fourteen

Daniel was whistling to himself as he drew his horse up outside the inn. He loved it when a plan came together. He was currently riding out to his country estate, which he much preferred to London, and in the carriage that was just rolling to a stop behind him was the woman he was going to marry. A few days in the country and he was convinced Amelia would say yes when he proposed. He'd seen her staring at him with dreamy eyes, even if she did look away rather sharply when he looked in her direction. He knew she desired him, that she replayed each kiss they'd shared over and over in her mind. Now he just had to convince her that he liked her, too.

He wasn't sure when he had warmed quite so much to the idea of having a wife, or more specifically of having Amelia as his wife. True, he still needed her money and he wasn't going to deny that was the reason he was going to propose, but somewhere along the way he had realised that being married to Amelia would have more advantages than just saving his son.

He liked her. He liked her quiet intelligence and how her gentle tone hid a quick wit. And he knew they certainly had chemistry. Their kisses were proof enough and now it took only one look at her and he was simmering with pent-up desire inside. Marrying Amelia would have the distinct advantage that he could take her to bed. And stay there for a week.

Daniel hopped down from his horse and tried to keep his desire in check. He waited for the carriage to come to a complete halt, then opened the door and prepared to assist the women down.

Amelia came shooting from the carriage as if she were being chased by rabid dogs.

'Traitor,' she hissed in his ear.

'Nice to see you, too, my sweet,' he whispered back.

Dutifully Daniel helped down Amelia's aunt and cousin before turning back to escort his future wife inside the inn.

She was already stalking through the door without a backwards glance. Daniel strolled in leisurely after her and found her fuming.

'You left me,' Amelia managed to hiss before the other two women joined him.

The first half of their journey that day, the painfully slow slog through London, Daniel had sat in the carriage with the three women. Aunt Mathilda had snoozed almost from the moment she'd sat down. Amelia, sensible girl that she was, had brought a book, but it had appeared that Harriet wasn't going to give her a single moment to read it. For the awful few hours Daniel had spent in the carriage Amelia's cousin had snipped at and goaded Amelia until the two young women were almost clawing at each other across the carriage. Daniel had decided at their lunch stop that although he very much enjoyed brushing up against Amelia he couldn't spend another minute in the carriage with her odious cousin, so he'd opted to ride for the afternoon. He'd spent a most pleasant couple of hours taking in the countryside and imagining all the things he would do to Amelia once they were married and a couple he was planning on doing before.

'Good evening, my lord,' the landlord of the coaching inn said deferentially. 'We received your message and have our finest three rooms ready for you. Shall I show you the way?'

Daniel strode after the landlord, catching Amelia's arm as he went by and pulling her along beside him. For a moment she resisted, but, sensible girl that she was, she must have realised he had the superior strength and that if she didn't budge he might do something much more embarrassing such as throw her over his shoulder. Daniel glanced sideways at her and let his mind wander through the possibilities of things he could do to Amelia after hefting her over his shoulder.

'Here is the first room, sir,' the landlord said. 'Your room is just across the hall and the room for the two young ladies is the last on the left.'

If looks could kill, Daniel would have been felled twice. Amelia and Harriet shot daggers in his direction. For a moment he thought about putting the two young women in the same room and locking the door. He had no doubt one would be dead by morning, and in his eyes Amelia was the more intelligent of the two, so she'd be sure to survive.

'Good landlord,' Amelia said, sounding like a character from a play, 'I don't suppose you have another room going free tonight?'

The landlord's face fell.

'But, my lord,' he said, turning back to Daniel, 'you only requested three rooms. I'm completely full.'

Daniel gave the poor man a reassuring smile. 'I did only request three rooms. The fault is all mine.'

He pulled Amelia close to him, momentarily distracted by the adorable way her brow crinkled when she was frowning. 'You can share with me if you'd rather,' he murmured.

Amelia sent him a withering stare. Aunt Mathilda must have sensed the content of his whisper and stepped forward.

'Harriet, you can share with me,' she announced.

The landlord looked very relieved and slinked away before anyone else could argue, mumbling about dinner being served at seven.

'I shall call for you ladies just before seven,' Daniel said, waiting for Aunt Mathilda and Harriet to turn away before giving Amelia a salacious wink.

She was still pretending to be annoyed with him for his disappearing act in the carriage, but even so she couldn't hide the slight tilt of her lips as she tried to suppress a smile.

Daniel closed the door of his room behind him and flopped down on the bed. He was in a wonderful mood; he loved it when things came together. It would only be a matter of days before he would propose to Amelia and then he would insist on a speedy wedding. With her dowry in his possession he would be able to keep Annabelle at bay a little longer.

The only thing that would make it all better would

be to wrest Edward away from Annabelle once and for all. Over the years he had made repeated attempts to convince his ex-lover to give up their son to his care. He had tried appealing to her better nature, explaining Edward would have a good upbringing with him, and then he had resorted to bribing her. Annabelle, however, was an astute woman. She knew she could extract more from Daniel if she kept hold of their son.

So Daniel had sent a man to check on how his boy was doing, to investigate whether she ever treated his son badly, ever raised her hand to him. His agent had reported back that although she seemed a little indifferent to the boy, he was well looked after and the agent had never seen him suffer at her hands.

Daniel had wrestled with his conscience for months. He hadn't been able to decide whether it would be better to take Edward away from his mother, knowing that it would mean revealing the truth to his son about his illegitimacy, or whether to leave him where he was and shield him from the reality of his birth. Neither was an ideal solution and every day Daniel wondered whether he had made the right choice, but when he faltered and thought about claiming Edward as his own he only had to remember Rupert's tortured soul and he sat back and remained in the shadows. It was devastating for a boy to know he was illegitimate. More devastating than it was to be raised by a rather distant mother. He would not put his son through that. So Edward stayed with his mother and Daniel continued to pay and torture himself over his decision.

He shook himself from his reverie and glanced at the clock. It was quarter to seven and he had to prepare himself for an evening of wooing Amelia. He grinned. Just two weeks ago the idea of courting a young heiress had made him shudder and wish for any number of alternative torments, but now he was rather looking forward to stealing a kiss from Amelia and causing her to blush, all the while convincing her they would be the perfect match.

At ten to seven he knocked quietly on Amelia's door. Far from keeping him waiting like most young women would, Amelia eased open the door immediately, looked surreptitiously up and down the corridor, then pulled him inside.

Daniel grinned—she was making the business of seduction so much easier for him. Before she could say a word he looped an arm around her waist and pulled her in for a kiss.

He loved that she couldn't resist him. Despite having pulled him into her room for a reason, and that reason clearly having nothing to do with seduction, Amelia couldn't bring herself to break off the kiss.

'Did you want to say something, my sweet?' Daniel asked, then kissed her again before she could answer him. She was stiff in his arms but kissed him back with grudging vigour. 'Maybe my lady would like to compliment me on my riding skills?' he suggested, then planted his lips firmly on hers before she could get a syllable out. 'Or maybe my goddess would just like to gaze into my eyes for the few minutes before dinner. I'm happy to oblige.'

This time when he kissed her Amelia managed to pull away, spluttering with indignation.

'Now, now, my precious gem, don't go pretending you didn't enjoy my kisses.'

Amelia was nothing if not fair and she inclined her head, knowing she could not deny that she enjoyed every moment their lips were locked together. After a few seconds she raised her chin and looked at him, her eyes blazing.

'You abandoned me, then you planned to torture me by making me spend the night with that snake.'

Daniel gave her his most leery grin. 'I meant it when I said you could spend the night in my room.'

Amelia didn't even bother to acknowledge his remark.

'I can't spend another day cooped up with her. I'll murder her.'

Daniel didn't voice his opinion that the world would be better off if Amelia did murder Harriet. She was her cousin, after all, and despite their differences Amelia might object to Daniel insulting her kin.

'You could always nestle in front of me on my horse,' Daniel suggested.

'Tomorrow I want to ride.'

Daniel saw she was deadly serious and tried to quash the sickness he felt at seeing Amelia mount a horse. The last time he'd seen her ride she'd ended up being thrown and he'd thought he had lost her.

'Amelia,' Daniel said in what he hoped was a conciliatory tone, 'maybe that's not the best idea.'

She stiffened and he reached out and took her hand.

'I've ridden since I was six years old,' she mumbled. 'Just because you saw me the one time I fell off...'

He raised his eyebrows. Amelia was a good horsewoman, but she was also one of the clumsiest people he knew. He didn't believe she'd only ever fallen from a horse once.

'Well, the one time I fell *badly*,' she corrected.

'Maybe I can be convinced,' Daniel said. 'I am a reasonable man after all.'

Amelia's face lit up. 'What would convince you?'

'A kiss.'

He saw her hesitate and for a second he wondered if she would refuse. She was well within her rights to toss him out of her room and scream for her aunt. Of course the sensible girl didn't. She wanted it as much as he did.

Daniel waited for her to come to him. All their previous kisses he had initiated, but this time he wanted to feel her hands on his jaw, see her lips parting as she swayed in closer to him.

Slowly Amelia moved closer so their bodies were pressed together. She raised a hand to his cheek and traced the angle of his jaw, then she looked into his eyes before she closed the gap between them. Her kiss was feathery light and it sent Daniel almost mad with desire. His lips screamed out for more and every nerve ending was on fire. Amelia brushed her lips against his again before pulling away. The minx was teasing him.

'We will be late for dinner.'

Daniel glanced at the clock on the wall and growled something under his breath no well-bred lady should ever hear.

Chapter Fifteen

Lizzie couldn't sleep. There were too many thoughts running through her head. No, that was a lie, there was just one very large and troubling thought: Daniel.

She couldn't get him out of her mind. All through dinner he'd looked at her with smouldering eyes and barely concealed desire. It made Lizzie burn for him and wish for just one moment alone so she could feel his fingers on her skin.

Kissing him again had been a mistake. She'd been truly annoyed with him for leaving her in the carriage with Harriet and had been determined not to succumb to his teasing flirtation. Then he had challenged her to kiss him and she'd not been able to stop herself. It hadn't been about convincing him to let her ride tomorrow, although that was a welcome bonus, it had been about *her* kissing *him*. In all their other kisses she had been a willing participant, but she had never initiated the kiss. She'd wanted that control, so she'd kissed him. Lizzie knew she could have kissed him all night, but she wanted to show him that he wasn't the only one who could be driven mad with desire, and by the looks he had given her throughout dinner she rather thought she had succeeded.

Lizzie turned over in bed and tried to banish Daniel from her mind. She wondered for the thousandth time whether he did actually like her just a little. Not her supposed fortune, but her.

Knowing she was torturing herself for no good reason, Lizzie got out of bed and pulled her thick nightgown around her body. She needed to clear her head and that wouldn't happen tossing and turning in bed all night.

Quietly she slipped through the door and padded down the hallway. The last of the patrons of the inn had gone home well over an hour ago and Lizzie supposed even the landlord was tucked up in bed by now. Reaching the bottom of the stairs, Lizzie made the decision to venture outside. Despite the mild temperature during the day, the night's air had a bite to it and Lizzie found herself shivering for a few moments. Instead of turning round and going back inside she pulled her nightgown closer around her body and walked to the edge of the yard. There were a couple of upturned barrels positioned looking out over the dark countryside, ideally placed for a weary traveller to rest for a few moments. Lizzie sat down and looked up at the stars, trying to put her problems in perspective. She hadn't even stretched her neck out fully before she felt a hand on her shoulder.

An icy spear of fear pierced her heart as she spun round. Daniel was standing behind her, his face shadowed with rage.

Lizzie shot to her feet.

'Are you mad?' Daniel asked in clipped tones, obviously trying hard to keep the full force of his anger in check.

'I…' Lizzie began.

Daniel held up a hand to stop her. 'You must be mad,' he said. 'For I know you are not stupid.'

'Thank you,' Lizzie said quietly, unsure whether it was meant to be a compliment.

'And only a mad or a stupid woman would leave her room and venture outside a public inn on her own in the middle of the night.'

Lizzie opened her mouth to speak and then abruptly closed it again. He had a point. When she thought about it properly it was rather foolish.

'Do you know what could happen to you?' he asked.

Lizzie sensed he didn't really want her to answer.

'You could be robbed,' Daniel said, holding up a finger for each of his suggestions. 'You could be raped. You could be *murdered*.'

Lizzie tried to look contrite.

'Come inside. Now.'

She didn't argue and allowed him to haul her back inside. Silently they ascended the stairs and Daniel pulled her into her room.

'I can't believe how much danger you put yourself in. It's as though you don't have a single little bit of regard for your own safety.' He was ranting now, albeit quietly.

Lizzie knew she had to stop him. 'I'm sorry,' she said quietly. 'You're right, it was downright stupid.'

That took the wind from his sails.

Daniel ran a hand through his hair and just looked at her. He looked harried and on edge. Lizzie realised he must have been worried for her.

'What were you doing out there?' he asked after a minute.

'I wanted to think. In India I was always outdoors. I can't think being cooped up inside.'

'You need to be careful,' Daniel said, his voice softer now. 'Not everyone is as gentle as you.'

Lizzie nodded and wrapped her arms around herself. Daniel stalked around the room, making the space seem small and crowded by his large presence.

'I shouldn't be here,' Daniel said suddenly, as if only just realising they were in her room together.

Lizzie waited for him to move towards the door, but he didn't even make a pretence at leaving.

'You scared me, Amelia,' he repeated, but more gently this time.

He took a step towards her and grasped her by the top of her arms. Despite the warmth Lizzie shivered.

At that moment she knew something was going to happen between them, something more than the mesmerising kisses they had been sharing already. Daniel's eyes had narrowed ever so slightly as though he had realised what he wanted and was intent on taking it, and Lizzie knew she was powerless to resist his seduction.

'Maybe before I leave I could be granted one kiss, to sustain me during the long walk back to my room.'

Lizzie didn't even have it in her to point out that his room was just across the hall, a mere three feet from door to door.

Before she knew what was happening Daniel had pulled her to the bed and sat down. Lizzie cautiously sat down beside him. She knew she should put a stop to this, she knew she shouldn't let his seduction of her continue. Proper young ladies were not meant to allow gentlemen into their bedchambers, let alone engage in whatever it was that was coming next. She was not going to marry Daniel, he would not have her when he found out who she really was, and that meant any indiscretions could have real consequences for her.

'Daniel,' she whispered, 'we shouldn't.' Not *we can't* or *I don't want to. We shouldn't.* She knew her words were giving him licence to continue.

'Hush, my sweet,' he murmured in her ear, then nibbled on her earlobe.

Lizzie gasped as his tongue traced tiny circles on her velvety skin and she knew she was lost. She'd let this man do anything to her.

Gently Daniel trailed kisses down her neck to her shoulder, then along her collarbone to the base of her throat. Lizzie felt light-headed with desire. She wanted his lips all over her body, his hands touching her in a place no one ever had before.

Daniel paused for a second, as if deciding whether to go any further, then bent his neck and lowered his lips back to her skin. With nimble fingers he undid the top few buttons of her nightgown and pushed the cotton garment down. Nothing more was exposed than would be in a rather risqué dress, but Lizzie felt naked under his gaze.

'You have beautiful skin,' he murmured.

If he'd told her she was beautiful, Lizzie would have known he was lying, but as she looked down at his lips on the skin of her chest she wondered whether maybe she did have beautiful skin.

Daniel's lips paused in their descent as he stopped to undo a few more buttons of her nightgown. Before he pushed it even lower he stopped and looked into her eyes, giving her the opportunity to tell him to stop. Lizzie bit her lip but said nothing. She wanted this, she wanted him. She wanted to feel his lips on her breasts, his hands to explore where no one else had ever been allowed to go. She knew it was wrong and she knew she should stop him, but she didn't want to. Lizzie had always been a realist. She was aware this was the first and last time a man such as Daniel, a man she actually liked, was going to touch her intimately. If her uncle got his way, it would be the cruel Colonel Rocher who would be allowed to use her body whatever way he saw fit. If she refused to marry the colonel, it was likely she would remain a spinster and never feel the touch of a man again. So whatever her future this was her opportunity, and for once in her life she was going to do what she wanted rather than what was right.

Daniel's eyes lit up as Lizzie gave a shaky nod of

her head and he pushed her nightgown fully over her shoulders and down over her breasts. For a second he just looked at her, but before Lizzie could start to feel self-conscious he raised a hand and cupped one breast, and Lizzie lost the power of coherent thought.

Smiling at her moan of pleasure, Daniel started to trace circles around her nipple and Lizzie felt herself arching her back to press her breast into his hand.

'All in good time, my love,' he whispered, then continued his slow journey across her skin.

'More,' Lizzie murmured before she could stop herself, blushing at her forwardness. Daniel just grinned, then obliged.

As he lowered his lips towards her skin Lizzie felt herself holding her breath in anticipation. When his mouth covered her nipple she almost cried out. Gently he began teasing her, nipping and licking and sucking. Somehow Daniel had manoeuvred her back on to the bed and expertly he now straddled her, never moving his mouth more than a couple of inches from her nipple. Lizzie felt her body buck and writhe underneath him. She arched her back and pressed her chest into the air, silently begging for more.

For a second she tensed as Daniel started to slide his hand down her body, but then she was pulled away from every single little concern about what they were doing by his mouth on her other nipple. As he teased her with his mouth his hand found its way under her nightgown and he started to caress the skin on her legs.

Lizzie felt her body tense as his hands drifted closer to her most private place, but gently he coaxed her to relax. She wanted him to touch her and even though she had never experienced anything like this before she had a primal urge that wanted him to enter her and fill her.

The first time he touched her Lizzie's hips bucked. Just a single caress sent waves of sensation all through her body. Smiling possessively, Daniel started to stroke her with slow rhythmic movements of his fingers, then before she knew what was happening he had dipped a finger inside her. Lizzie tensed, the invasion unexpected, but within seconds she felt her instincts take over and her hips start their slow movement up towards him.

Daniel stroked and teased her until Lizzie didn't feel in control of her own body. Her breath was coming in short, sharp gasps and her heart was hammering in her chest. Something was building deep inside her and she knew she needed to release it. Lost in her own little world of pleasure everything else had ceased to exist.

Suddenly the sensation deep inside her burst out and took over her entire body. Lizzie moaned and writhed, clutching at the bedsheets with her hands. She felt as though she was weightless, soaring through the air.

Slowly the pulsations lessened and she felt herself returning to reality. After a minute Daniel rolled off her and scooped her into his arms.

She felt his hardness pressing into the small of her back and a thrill of excitement coursed through her; she had caused that, plain old Lizzie Eastway.

'You are an amazing woman, Amelia,' Daniel said, nuzzling the back of her neck.

Lizzie stiffened but forced herself to relax again. Just tonight she was going to let herself forget who she really was and enjoy the fantasy. She would pretend this was her life.

'Amelia, I've got something to ask you,' Daniel said, the serious tone of his voice making her turn over to look at him. 'Marry me. Be my wife.'

Lizzie felt all the contented glow drain from her body and she crashed back to reality. Slowly, without even realising she was doing it, she started to shake her head in the hope he would take back the words.

He was looking at her in confusion and Lizzie realised she must look a state. All the blood had drained from her face and her mouth hung open in shock. It wasn't that the proposal was unexpected, all the time they had known each other had been leading up to this moment, but Lizzie had foolishly thought she had a bit more time. She couldn't marry him, of course she couldn't, but she didn't want their time together to end.

'Why?' she managed to whisper.

'Why? Because I want to marry you. We'd make a good match and I like you.'

Lizzie felt the tears brimming in her eyes. It wasn't enough. If he'd said he loved her, then maybe they'd have a chance, she would have been able to admit her true identity and maybe, just maybe, he'd still want her.

She shook her head. 'Daniel, I can't, I'm sorry.'

He looked shocked, as if he'd never considered she might turn him down. Lizzie felt miserable. She supposed he thought a plain girl like her would jump at the chance of marrying him. He was right, of course, Lizzie would jump at the chance of marrying him. He was kind and funny and definitely very attractive. A much nicer prospect than Colonel Rocher. The problem was it wasn't she whom he wanted to marry. He had proposed to Amelia—rich, well-connected Amelia.

'You can't?' he asked, picking up on her choice of words.

She shook her head and tried to look away.

'No, Amelia,' he said, turning her back to face him. 'You don't just get to say no with no explanation.'

'I'm sorry, Daniel.'

He looked deep into her eyes for a few seconds, then turned away.

'It wouldn't work. It's not enough.'

'I rushed you. I asked too soon. Forgive me.'

Lizzie nearly broke down and told him the truth, but at the last moment self-preservation stopped her. If she confessed who she really was, or more to the point that she wasn't Amelia Eastway, then she would likely be out on the street with no money and no connections. He wouldn't take her to stay at his estate and the Hunters would have no reason to look out for her, they weren't her relations. Lizzie knew these were all excuses, reasons to put off confessing her deception, but she couldn't help wanting just a little more time as Amelia.

'I'll give you more time,' Daniel said as he stood to leave. 'We'd make a good match, Amelia, you'll see in a few days.'

He left, smiling at her from the doorway. Lizzie blinked back the tears as she smiled back, knowing he would never say the three little words that would mean they could be together; he would never say *I love you* quite simply because he didn't. And without love there was no way he would ever forgive her for her deception.

Chapter Sixteen

Daniel pushed his horse to go faster as the house came into sight. In the pinkish light of dawn it looked beautiful, set atop a small hill with a lake on one side and a small copse of trees on the other. Daniel loved this estate and it saddened him that he had allowed it to become so neglected. It was not derelict by any means, but over the past few years most of his money had been given to Annabelle and the estate had suffered for it. The house, which needed a staff of at least forty, survived with a hard-working and loyal skeleton staff of ten. The grounds were pristine immediately surrounding the house, but neglected as you got further away, testament to how few gardeners and labourers he could afford to employ. Daniel knew one day it was likely he would need to sell off land to keep Annabelle quiet, but he couldn't quite bring himself to abandon his tenants or sell the softly undulating fields he had grown up playing in. One day maybe, but hopefully not yet. Hopefully soon he would also have Amelia's dowry to tide him over.

He desperately wanted to keep the estate intact, to pass on the Burwell legacy as a whole just as his ancestors had. For a few years after Rupert's death, even after both of his parents had passed away, Daniel had avoided the estate, certain that unhappy memories would be dredged up on his return. When he did finally come back to his childhood home he found more happy memories than unhappy. Before Rupert had appeared on the scene Daniel had idolised his father. He was kind and caring and fun to be around. He more than made up for a mother Daniel barely saw, a woman who never once smiled at her husband or child. After Daniel had started at Eton and understood more what was happening with Rupert, he hadn't known how to view his father. On the outside he was the same man, a father who was always waiting to welcome him back from school with open arms, eager to hear about all his achievements and latest schoolmates, but any time Daniel mentioned Rupert he sensed a sadness within his father and now he realised it was regret. After Rupert had killed himself Daniel had partly blamed his parents, wondering how his father could remain so distant. Over time he had understood that his father had only ever been trying to protect everyone whom he loved and in his own way had tried to look after Rupert, too. Daniel could no longer find it in himself to blame his father for being human and making a mistake.

He frowned, coming back to the present. He wasn't sure yet how to secure Amelia as his wife. They had been at his estate for three days and so far he'd seen Amelia for exactly thirty seconds. Once they had arrived, she'd sequestered herself in her room, sending messages at each meal to say she was still recovering from the fire. Daniel could hardly argue with that—the poor girl had almost died—but somehow he didn't believe that was why she was staying in bed. He rather thought it had something more to do with the night they had spent at the inn and his proposal that followed.

Daniel had pretended not to understand her cryptic refusal of his proposition, her saying 'it's not enough'. In reality he knew what she meant. She wanted love, or more specifically she wanted him to love her.

Daniel shook his head in frustration. They liked each other. He made her laugh, he would always be kind to her, he'd allow her to keep whatever interests she had and they certainly were physically compatible. He'd be the model husband, but he could not love her. He'd loved a woman once before and he was still paying for it years on. Amelia might be nothing like Annabelle, but Daniel knew he had no space in his heart for love.

He could have just said it, he supposed, told her that he loved her. She probably would have agreed to his proposal there and then. It felt wrong, though, starting a marriage off with such a deception. Daniel was concealing so much from Amelia already, he didn't want to lie any more than he had to. What was more, Amelia was an astute woman. She'd likely be able to tell if he was lying about something so important.

Daniel knew he could seduce her into marrying him. He had seen how she responded to him, how her resolve faltered as soon as his lips touched hers, but for some reason he didn't want to trick her into intimacy somewhere they would be discovered so the scandal would force her to marry him. He wanted her to want to marry him.

His plan was to court her, make her realise that life with him would be enjoyable, so that when he proposed again she would not hesitate in saying yes. The problem was he had to actually see her to court her and with Amelia shut away in her room that was decidedly difficult.

* * *

He was about a mile away from the house when he saw a figure strolling up the hill towards him. He grinned. It was as if his prayers had been answered. Amelia was walking at a leisurely pace, but she did not seem to display any ill effects from the fire. She hadn't caught sight of him yet and by the pursing of her lips Daniel rather thought she might be humming to herself. He grinned—she wouldn't be able to escape him now.

'Good morning,' Daniel called cheerily as Amelia appeared at the top of the hill.

For a second she looked guilty, as if she had been caught out in her deception.

'Feeling better?'

They both knew Amelia had been perfectly well the past few days but had used the ill effects of the fire as an excuse to avoid him.

'Yes, thank you,' Amelia ground out, looking over her shoulder as if wondering whether she could outrun him.

'I'm glad to hear it. I have been bereft without your company, my dear.'

Amelia looked at him through narrowed eyes but remained silent.

'I have been wasting away with boredom.'

'You cannot waste away with… Oh, never mind.'

She turned back towards the house and Daniel nimbly slid from his horse and took her arm in his.

'Shall we go for a walk?' he asked. 'Enjoy the morning air.'

'You have your horse.'

'You'd prefer to ride?' he asked with a gleam in his eye. 'Snuggled up quite scandalously between my thighs?'

Amelia's cheeks reddened, but she held her ground. 'I would prefer to continue my walk alone.'

'That I do not believe.'

'You think your company is so enjoyable?'

'I think *you* enjoy my company much more than you're willing to admit.'

Amelia opened her mouth to protest but then promptly closed it again. It seemed she couldn't bring herself to lie to him completely.

'How about you grant me ten minutes, and if you're not having fun by then I'll allow you to return to the house on your own?' Daniel offered.

Amelia cocked her head to one side whilst she considered, then nodded gracefully. 'Ten minutes,' she agreed.

'The things we could do in ten minutes,' Daniel mused, leading her gently up the hill and away from the house. 'I don't know where to start.'

'You can't kiss me,' Amelia said suddenly. 'That wasn't part of the deal.'

'We never agreed on that. Indeed, we never stipulated what we could and couldn't do.'

He stopped walking and turned to face Amelia.

'We can do anything at all.'

Amelia swallowed hard as he reached up and brushed a strand of hair from her face.

'Anything in the world.'

For a second they just stood staring into each other's eyes and then their lips were on each other's, frantically searching the other one out. Daniel pulled Amelia into his arms, running his hands down the length of her back and cupping her buttocks.

'The things we could do in ten minutes,' Daniel murmured. Then reluctantly he stepped away, grabbed her by the hand and began to pull her up the hill.

'What about your horse?' Amelia asked, her breathing heavy with exertion.

'He knows how to get home.'

Sure enough his horse had already started trotting back towards the house.

Daniel wanted to stop where they were, sink to the ground with Amelia in his arms and make her his, but he knew that was a bad idea for two reasons. Firstly, he had resolved to show Amelia that they made a good match without seducing her, and secondly, Daniel wanted to stay in control, and he most certainly didn't feel in control when his lips met Amelia's.

So instead of kissing her he pulled her further away from the house and towards the lake. It was romance he needed, something that showed Amelia she was attracted to him emotionally as well as physically. Daniel smiled to himself, the years of seducing less virtuous women were about to pay off; he could use all the lessons he'd learnt wooing merry widows to make it impossible for Amelia to resist him.

'Where are we going?' Amelia said, her breath coming in fast bursts.

'To the lake.' Daniel grinned at her. 'If you grant me longer than ten minutes, I'll let us walk there.'

Amelia looked at him appraisingly, but her pounding heart and screaming muscles must have got the better of her and she nodded.

'Twenty minutes,' she conceded.

'Give me thirty and I promise you won't ever want this morning to end.'

'That's what I'm afraid of,' Amelia murmured under her breath. Daniel knew he wasn't supposed to hear her comment and he pretended that he hadn't, but inside he was celebrating. The way things were going he probably could have her agreeing to marry him in thirty minutes. Not that he was going to push his luck and propose again too soon.

'Isn't it beautiful?' Daniel said as he led her down to the lake. It had trees on its northern shore but otherwise was open to the softly undulating hills.

'It's beautiful,' Amelia agreed.

'And the things you can do in a lake...' Daniel trailed off and wiggled his eyebrows suggestively.

'Such as fishing?' she asked drily.

'It depends what you want to hook on your line. I'm hoping for a little less scaly prey.' It wasn't the finest compliment he'd ever paid a woman, but Amelia didn't seem to take offence. 'Or if fishing isn't your cup of tea we could indulge in a little swimming.'

'Wouldn't it be rather cold?'

'I can think of a few ways to warm you up.' Daniel was thoroughly enjoying himself. It wasn't often women he was pursuing put up even a token resistance.

'I'm not sure Aunt Mathilda would approve,' Amelia said as they reached the water's edge.

'It wasn't her I was planning on taking with me.'

Daniel led Amelia around the perimeter of the lake until they reached a small jetty.

'How about a spot of rowing?' he proposed.

'Is this just a ploy to get me on my own somewhere I can't escape once your thirty minutes are up?' Amelia asked.

'Most certainly,' Daniel said with a grin. 'The question is do you want to escape?'

Amelia didn't answer him but instead gripped his arm and stepped daintily into the small rowing boat. Daniel grabbed the oars and hopped in himself, taking up his position opposite her.

'Now, I know sometimes little mishaps happen when you are around,' Daniel said as he fitted the oars into place and pushed away from the jetty, 'so please refrain from any sudden movements. Even if you're overcome with passion and just *have* to kiss me, please remember we are in a capsizeable boat.'

'Mishaps?' she asked.

'Since I've known you, which isn't all that long, you've demounted me from my horse, flattened me at the bottom of the stairs and got yourself flung from a horse, not to mention caused me to get my eyebrows singed in that fire.'

Amelia leant in as if trying to get a closer look at his eyebrows.

'My valet was mortified,' Daniel said. 'All that time he spends grooming me to perfection and I go and get my eyebrows burnt rescuing a damsel in distress.'

'They're not singed at all,' Amelia declared as she sat back suddenly, causing the boat to rock from side to side. 'And your housekeeper has told me you don't even have a valet.'

Daniel grinned. 'Caught out again by the tales of disloyal staff. But you can't deny the other things happened.'

Amelia grimaced. 'I have been known to be a little less than graceful from time to time.'

Daniel rested the oars in their holders for a minute and leant across and took her hand. 'I think you move with the grace of a swan, albeit a swan that loses its footing every so often.'

Daniel could see Amelia didn't know what to say to his compliment and it struck him that she wasn't used to people saying nice things about her. He'd seen hints of it before when he'd complimented her; Amelia wasn't used to being told she was beautiful or lovely or graceful. All those compliments that should be showered on young ladies had passed her by. He wondered how that had come to be. She was a pretty young thing, although not what society might think the most attractive, she had an irresistible mouth and an adorable smattering of freckles across her nose. He found it hard to believe he was the only one who had ever seen her charms.

Maybe things were different in India, but that was

hard to believe. A young, eligible heiress should be overwhelmed by suitors spouting compliments wherever they lived in the world.

'Amelia, I want to tell you something, but I need you to promise you'll listen to what I have to say.'

She looked as though she was going to protest, to say that of course she always listened, but at the last moment she just nodded.

Daniel leant forward, careful not to rock the small rowing boat, and tilted her chin with his hand so she was looking directly into his eyes.

'I think you're beautiful,' he said sincerely.

Immediately she opened her mouth to protest, but Daniel moved quicker and put a finger against her lips.

'I think you're beautiful,' he repeated. 'I love the shape of your mouth and the tilt of your lips. I love the tiny freckles on your nose. I love how I could get lost in your eyes. And I love how even just the smallest of smiles transforms your face.'

Amelia looked at him with tears glistening in her eyes. Daniel knew no one had ever told her she was beautiful before. He cursed whoever it was in her past that had called her plain or even just neglected to compliment her. A woman needed to feel desirable—every man who had ever succeeded at seducing one knew that—and he'd wager Amelia had never been made to feel desirable before. He just couldn't understand it—did the rest of the world see a different person to him? He almost scoffed now when he thought back to the time he'd convinced himself he would be able to resist Amelia, that physically he wasn't attracted to her. Her appeal had crept up on him and now he found it hard to keep his hands to himself no matter what the situation.

'Do you mean it?' Amelia asked, her voice so quiet it was barely audible.

'I mean it.'

She hesitated as if still trying to find reasons not to believe him. 'I know you are a…man of the world,' she said slowly, 'and such compliments must come easy to you.'

Daniel couldn't help but grin. 'I'm not a monk, Amelia. I've spent my life enjoying the company of lovely women, but it's you I find beautiful.'

She must have seen the truth of it in his eyes for her face lit up with pleasure. Daniel wanted to capture that moment, that look, and keep it for ever.

Chapter Seventeen

Lizzie felt as though she were walking on air. Daniel thought she was beautiful. She'd replayed their conversation over and over again in her mind and she knew he wasn't lying. He'd looked at her with his dazzling blue eyes and he'd made her fall in love with him.

She sighed loudly. Who was she fooling, she'd been falling for him ever since that first kiss. She'd got herself into a right mess. Every day she was falling deeper in love with a man who thought she was somebody else entirely. A man who thought she was beautiful, had told her that he loved her lips and her freckles and her smile, but hadn't actually said he loved her. Which most likely meant that he didn't.

Lizzie was a pragmatist. She knew she'd never been destined for love—in fact, marriage to a decent, kind man had almost been too much to wish for. So Daniel not loving her was not a problem in itself, even if her heart wanted him to utter those three little words. The problem came with her true identity and more specifically her lack of a dowry. Daniel had to be in need of money. Although his estate was beautiful and tended by a small group of loyal staff, there was no hiding the fact that it was in dire need of some money. The furnishings were just a little too worn and the staff overstretched. Daniel needed a wealthy wife and in her he thought he had found one.

He might love her smile and enjoy her company, and maybe even desire her if the episode in the coaching inn was anything to go by, but he was so keen on their marriage because he thought that as well as all those things, she was rich. Which she most decidedly wasn't. Her uncle had never even mentioned a modest dowry, and Lizzie knew that if he did deign to provide something, it would be nothing like Amelia's, nothing like what Daniel was expecting.

So the fact that he thought her beautiful was more a horrible irony than anything else; for years Lizzie had been overlooked, had faded into the background beside her stunning cousin, and now someone had noticed her, had thought she was beautiful, but he needed Amelia's dowry.

'Feeling better?'

Lizzie spun towards Harriet's voice. The young woman was leaning against a pillar in the entrance hall, looking anything but concerned about the state of Lizzie's health.

'Yes, thank you,' Lizzie said, hurrying towards the stairs, hoping she would be able to get to her room before Harriet engaged her in conversation.

'Heard from your cousin recently?'

Lizzie froze, her hand clutching at the banister, her legs suddenly feeling rather weak.

'My cousin?' she asked, trying to keep the tremor from her voice.

'Yes, your cousin, the one who was meant to accompany you here.'

Lizzie allowed herself to breathe again. When Amelia had left her at the docks they had agreed they would pretend Lizzie had been taken ill and was going to recuperate at the house of an old family friend in the country for a while.

'She's recovering slowly,' Lizzie said noncommittally.

'Measles, was it?'

'Mmm-hmm.'

'She'll be excited to hear of her upcoming marriage, I suppose.'

Lizzie just gawked at Harriet. Had she read the letter? But that was impossible. The letter had come straight to her from the housemaid and then it had burnt in the fire.

Something pulled at the edge of Lizzie's memory, some detail that didn't quite add up.

'What do you mean?' she asked.

'Elizabeth's engagement to Colonel Rocher,' Harriet explained calmly.

Lizzie felt the world spinning. Harriet must have read the letter, there was no other way she could know that piece of information.

Suddenly an image flashed into Lizzie's mind—the candle by the window in her room. Surely Harriet hadn't crept in whilst she slept and taken the letter, maybe reading it by the light of the candle? A more horrific thought started to take shape—what if Harriet hadn't put out the candle? Had that been the source of the fire? It would have been a mistake, of course, even Amelia's horrible cousin wouldn't intentionally set fire to Lizzie's room. Even so Lizzie knew she would double-check the lock on her door every night.

Lizzie knew she had two choices: either she could confront Harriet, or she could run away. The old Lizzie would definitely have chosen the latter, she would have scuttled up the stairs and prayed Harriet would leave her alone. Lizzie pushed back her shoulders, lifted her chin and told herself she was a confident and beautiful young woman.

'You read the letter,' she stated.

Harriet's eyes narrowed. 'And what letter would that be?'

'The private letter from my father to me.'

'Something's wrong with you,' Harriet said quietly, moving towards Lizzie with menace in her eyes. 'Something is very wrong and I'm going to find out what.'

'Why do you hate me so much?' Lizzie asked.

Harriet had made her dislike of Lizzie clear from the first day they had met, before they had even got to know each other.

For a moment Lizzie thought Harriet might not reply, but then the young woman's mouth twisted into a sneer.

'What have you got that I don't?' Harriet asked. 'You're not beautiful, you're not funny, you're just rather ordinary, but when you walk into a room you have suitors flocking towards you, just because your father is rich.'

'They're only interested in me because of my dowry, how do you think that makes me feel?'

Harriet snorted. 'You have an earl eager to do anything to make you his wife. Who cares if it's because of your dowry or because you can stand on your head and juggle at the same time. The end result is the same—you become a countess.'

'One day you'll find someone to marry, Harriet,' Lizzie said. 'And you might even love him. Then it won't matter if he's an earl or a duke or a prince.'

'That's easy for you to say, but men will always choose an heiress over someone like me.'

'Is that really why you hate me, Harriet?'

Lizzie watched as Harriet's expression turned into contempt.

'You want to know the real reason?' she spat. 'Why don't you ask your father?'

Lizzie frowned. 'What?'

'The wonderful Colonel Eastway, the clever man who made his fortune in India.'

Lizzie certainly didn't think he was wonderful, but she couldn't tell Harriet that.

'I bet he never spares a thought for all those he stole from.'

'What are you talking about, Harriet?'

Lizzie knew her uncle was ruthless, but she couldn't imagine him a thief.

'We used to be rich, you know,' Harriet said. 'Until your father advised mine on how to invest his money and he lost everything.'

Ah. That would be quite a valid reason for Harriet to dislike her family.

'And then a few years later he makes his fortune in India and doesn't even think about us, about the lives he ruined.'

'I'm sure he never meant to...'

'It doesn't matter what he meant. You're rich and we're poor, all because of the advice of your father. I could have been a great heiress, I could have had hundreds of suitors flocking after me, but instead it's you they're chasing.'

Dramatically Harriet spun around and sailed out of the front door.

Lizzie felt herself slump. Harriet hated her with a vengeance, and she had a feeling she would try to find any way to destroy Lizzie that she could. It wouldn't be long before she found out Lizzie's secret.

Lizzie's hands were trembling and her knees felt weak. All the bravado that had infused her just minutes before had fled and she was left a shuddering wreck.

Slowly she forced herself to climb the stairs and stumble along to her room. Once inside she locked the door, checked it twice, then collapsed on to the bed.

She was worried and not just about her secret becoming public. Of course that was bothering her, she didn't want to be exposed as a liar. Aunt

Mathilda had been so kind to her and her whole relationship with Daniel was built on a lie. She didn't want them to find out, but equally she knew they must. When Amelia had begged her to swap identities with her for a couple of weeks Lizzie had been more than reluctant, but her cousin had squeezed her hand and Lizzie was reminded of all the occasions that Amelia had stood up for her when no one else had. So she'd agreed to Amelia's plan, even though it went against her moral compass. At the time she hadn't known the people she would be lying to, hadn't realised that one day she would become fond of them and lying to them would hurt.

More than that, though, was now the worry about her cousin. It had been well over two weeks since Amelia had left Lizzie at the docks, racing off to find the army officer she had formed an attachment to when he was stationed out in India. She'd promised Lizzie she would be back within two weeks and, although Amelia was flighty and was renowned for losing track of time, Lizzie couldn't believe that her cousin would forget to pen a short note to assure Lizzie she was all right.

The problem was Lizzie didn't even know where to start in looking for her. Amelia had been very cagey about the identity of this officer and so

Lizzie didn't have a name, let alone an address, for the man.

Her whole life was unravelling before her eyes, the lies catching up with her and her future more uncertain than it ever had been before.

A sharp rap on the door made her jump and Lizzie wondered for an instant whether it was Harriet come back to taunt her some more. Eventually she rose, crossed the room and unlocked the door, opening it a sliver to reveal a footman standing outside.

'A letter, madam,' he said, presenting the letter to her on a tray with a bow.

Lizzie took the letter with trembling hands. Surely this wasn't from Amelia—that would be too much of a coincidence.

The writing was unfamiliar and Lizzie ran her fingers over the thick paper before opening it. Carefully she broke the seal and quickly read. It made her smile.

Dearest Amelia,
I enjoyed our outing this morning and thought it was an unparalleled success. Despite spending over an hour in a small rowing boat neither of us ended up in the water—what more could a man ask for from a rendezvous with a beautiful woman? Well, maybe a man could *ask for more, but it certainly wouldn't be proper.*

Seeing as you denied me your company for so many days I feel another outing is warranted, and soon. Meet me at three today for an afternoon of excitement and I guarantee I will be the perfect gentleman. If you want me to be.
Yours,
Daniel

Lizzie couldn't help but smile. Even when her whole world was falling apart Daniel could make her feel both normal and special at the same time.

Daniel. He would know what to do. Not that she could tell him her whole predicament, not yet at least, but she could ask for his assistance in finding Amelia. Then, when she had summoned up the courage, she would tell him the truth about her identity.

Before she could lose her nerve Lizzie rushed out of her room and down the stairs. It was late morning and she assumed Daniel would be in his study, doing whatever it was one had to do to run a country estate.

She knocked, waited for a response, then pushed the heavy wooden door open and entered the room.

Daniel surveyed her from behind a large mahogany desk.

'Is three o'clock too long to wait, my sweet?' he asked.

'Yes, no.' Lizzie forced herself to take a deep breath and crossed the room towards him. 'I need your help.'

Daniel rose, walked around his desk and guided her into an armchair positioned by the window. Lizzie waited for him to take a seat in the second chair, but instead he stood behind her and started trailing his fingers along her shoulders.

'You seem tense, my dear,' he said and began to gently knead her shoulders with his hands.

Momentarily Lizzie felt her body relax and forgot the reason she had come in.

'Maybe I could help with that tension.'

Daniel dropped his lips to the nape of her neck and started to trail kisses across her skin. Lizzie's eyes fluttered as she tried to resist his touch, but after a few seconds she was melting into his body.

'What was it you wanted to ask me, my dear?' Daniel asked as he took the dainty sleeves of her gown and pushed them down her arms.

Lizzie's mind was trying to function, trying to remember what it was she had come here for, but every time she caught a glimpse of her purpose Daniel distracted her with a kiss.

'Did you want to ask me to kiss you?' he murmured in her ear, nibbling the lobe as she felt the desire mounting deep inside her. 'Or did you want me to touch you?' He dipped a finger inside the bodice of her dress, stroking the skin and distracting Lizzie even more.

'I...' Lizzie tried to focus, to bring their meeting back to her agenda.

'Maybe you wanted to ask me to repeat what we did at the coaching inn.'

Lizzie's eyes snapped open and she managed to push Daniel away.

'I need your help,' she said, trying to pull her dress back into place. 'And I need you to be serious.'

As if sensing her distress, Daniel moved away from her and sat down in the armchair opposite.

'How can I be of assistance?' he asked, all trace of joviality gone in an instant.

'I need to find someone,' Lizzie said slowly. 'Someone I'm worried about, someone I haven't heard from for a while.'

Daniel frowned and motioned for her to go on.

'I can't tell you much more...' Lizzie hesitated. 'But if you could recommend someone who could be trusted, who could make confidential enquiries on my behalf?'

She knew it was asking a lot of him.

'Amelia, are you in trouble?' he asked quietly.

She shook her head. 'But I'm concerned someone I care a great deal for may be.'

She saw his composed expression falter for an instant and realised there was a flicker of jealousy. He hid it well, but Daniel was worried she might have feelings for another man.

'A good friend of mine, she was meant to write to me and I haven't heard anything.'

He seemed to relax instantly. 'Can you tell me anything? This woman's name, why you're concerned?'

Lizzie shook her head. 'One day I promise I'll explain, but please don't ask me to yet. I can't betray a promise I made.'

Daniel looked at her for about a minute, as if weighing up her words.

'I know a man who will make discreet enquiries for you,' he said. 'But I urge you to trust me, I will help you no matter what the problem.'

Lizzie reached out and took his hand. 'I will tell you soon, I promise, but I need to find my friend first, to make sure she's all right.'

Daniel nodded. 'I will write a letter to this man and ask him to travel down here at his earliest convenience.'

'Thank you,' Lizzie said, feeling a weight lift off her. She stood, feeling a little awkward with her secret sitting between them. 'Do you still want to meet at three?'

Daniel grinned, immediately back to the carefree young-man persona he presented to the world. 'Of course. I'm mad with anticipation already.'

Lizzie moved to the door but stopped with her hand resting on the door handle. As she turned to bid Daniel farewell her eyes fell upon the open desk drawer Daniel had placed something inside when she came in the room. If she wasn't very much mistaken, it was a portrait. Forcing a smile on her face, Lizzie said goodbye and left Daniel's study, wondering whom he kept a picture of hidden in his desk.

Chapter Eighteen

Daniel drummed his fingers absentmindedly on the banister as he waited for Amelia to emerge from her room and join him for their three o'clock outing. Her request earlier had puzzled him. It was certainly strange, wanting to employ a man to find someone but unable to tell him who.

What was puzzling him more was his reaction to her request. Normally this kind of secrecy had him trying to figure out exactly what was going on, but today, after Amelia's request, he had calmly penned a note to a man he knew would handle the business discreetly for her and got on with his accounts. It wasn't that he was not curious—far from it, he wanted to know the details of Amelia's life—but more that he trusted her. And that revelation was baffling all on its own.

Daniel had been trusting once, but Annabelle and her lies and schemes had killed that trust. Now he was lucky if he didn't view even his oldest and most loyal friends with a shred of suspicion. That was why this business of Amelia's, searching for a lost friend but unable to tell him more, should have him prying into every secret she had, but Daniel didn't feel the need. He trusted her. He trusted her to tell him when she was ready and he trusted her to make the right decision.

It was a liberating feeling, trust. He felt like singing from the rooftops, shouting from the windows. Finally he had found someone he trusted. Making her his wife seemed even more vital now. He liked Amelia, he desired Amelia, but most of all he *trusted* Amelia.

Daniel wondered for a moment whether he should just confess his whole sordid past to Amelia. Over the past week the idea of telling her every last detail, from his brother's suicide to Annabelle's seduction to his illegitimate son and the blackmail he was now caught up in, had seemed very appealing. He didn't like keeping something so important from her and on a couple of occasions he had nearly confessed everything, including the reason he had started courting her. It would be liberating to share the burden of his secrets, especially with the woman he was planning on spending the rest of his life with. Then Daniel thought of the way Amelia's face had lit up when they were in the rowing boat and he'd told her she was beautiful. Bit by bit he could see her self-confidence grow. Amelia was blossoming right before his eyes. If he told her the reason he had been so eager to get to know her was because he needed her fortune to pay his old mistress, she would be crushed, all the confidence she had gained would be wiped out in an instant. One day the time would be right to confide in her, but not yet.

'I hope I'm dressed appropriately,' Amelia said as she descended the stairs. 'You could give me some clue as to what you've got planned for this afternoon.'

Daniel grinned, took her hand and placed it in the crook of his arm.

'How would you have dressed if I'd told you we were off to meet the king?' Daniel teased.

'Not in my third-best dress.'

'I think you look lovely in your third-best dress.'

'Where are we going really?' Amelia asked.

'You'll ruin the surprise.'

Amelia looked at him long enough for him to cave. A man couldn't be expected to hold strong under the weight of her deep brown eyes.

'Just a little clue, then. I'm taking you to do something I wager you've never done before.'

Amelia sucked in her bottom lip as she considered the clue. Daniel knew they were in full view of anyone passing through the hallway, but he still wanted to lean forward and coax her lip out from her mouth.

'Whatever you're thinking, remember we're in public,' Amelia hissed.

'What makes you think I'm having inappropriate thoughts?' Daniel asked, moving closer and slipping his arm around her waist.

'Aren't you always?' Amelia mumbled. Then louder, 'You have that look in your eyes again.'

'What look?' Daniel frowned, he was normally so in control of his expressions.

'That look. The one you get when you're thinking of…being intimate. It's as though you want to eat me.'

Daniel almost choked with surprise. Amelia frowned.

'That's more true than you could ever realise…' he paused '…but I promise to remedy that one day soon.'

He bent his head and quickly nibbled her ear, knowing she wouldn't allow him to kiss her for long in public. It was scandalous enough that they were sneaking off for an afternoon alone together, without Amelia's aunt to chaperon them, but Daniel knew none of his staff would say anything and it didn't matter too much as he was planning on marrying Amelia at the earliest opportunity anyway.

He counted. It took five seconds before Amelia had summoned the willpower to push him away.

'Stop it,' she hissed. 'Anyone could see.'

'So your objection is to any possible witnesses, not to what I was doing?'

Amelia mumbled something under her breath.

'If that's the case, I'll find somewhere more private for us, somewhere we won't be disturbed.'

'I thought we were going out.'

Daniel let out a sigh and pulled away. 'As my lady wishes,' he said, then swooped in for a sneaky kiss.

He led Amelia out through the front door and round the side of the house, then they began the twenty-minute walk across the fields to where Daniel had instructed a groom to set up for their afternoon's activities.

As they got further away from the house Daniel felt Amelia's body begin to relax. He wondered what had her so tense. He'd seen the antagonistic glares Harriet sent Amelia's way, but surely a little cousinly dislike wasn't enough to be making Amelia so jumpy. Maybe it was something to do with this missing friend.

'Are we going shooting?' Amelia asked, her eyes lighting up as she saw the target set up ahead of them.

'We are indeed.'

'Oh, I love shooting.'

Daniel turned to her, momentarily speechless. 'You've shot a pistol before.'

'Pistols, shotguns, my cousin and I used to do target practice all the time in India.'

'Who on earth taught you to shoot?'

Amelia gave him an appraising look. 'We lived surrounded by army officers. There were always plenty of volunteers.'

Daniel bet there were lots of eager young officers trying to impress Amelia with their shooting prowess. He suddenly had a foul taste in his mouth at the thought of another man wrapping his hands around Amelia's, of him moving in behind her to help her with positioning. Of the faceless young officer standing that little bit too close and dipping his head to nuzzle Amelia's neck.

'Was there someone in particular?' he asked, hating the strain he heard in his voice.

Amelia laughed. 'My cousin always had officers fighting to be the one to teach her things. Whoever didn't win her favour would have me as the consolation prize.'

Daniel stopped without warning, tugging on Amelia's arm. 'Then they were fools,' he said. 'Stupid, blind fools.'

Amelia opened her mouth to protest. Before she could get a single syllable out Daniel kissed her. It wasn't gentle or particularly elegant, but he needed to make her understand.

'Fools,' he repeated. 'Any man who doesn't see how irresistible you are is a fool.'

Again Amelia started to protest.

Daniel cupped her face gently and made her look into his eyes.

'What did I tell you earlier?'

For a second Amelia looked blank.

'You're beautiful.'

'Compared to my cousin I'm…'

Daniel stroked her cheek. 'I think that's your problem, my sweet, you compare yourself to this cousin of yours far too much.'

He knew by the look in her eyes it was more true than Amelia cared to admit.

'And I promise you I wouldn't look twice at your cousin with you around.'

'You can't promise that,' Amelia said, frowning again. 'You've never met her. *Everyone* falls in love with her.'

Daniel didn't hear any hint of bitterness in her

voice and he realised Amelia must love her cousin very much.

'I wouldn't even notice her. Not with you there.'

He could see Amelia was struggling to believe him. He wanted to give her the confidence she was sorely lacking, he wanted her to see herself as he did.

Daniel pressed a hand into the small of her back and pulled her close into his body.

'Do you feel what you do to me?' he asked, pressing his hips into hers. 'That's all you, not your cousin, not any other woman. You.'

Amelia seemed momentarily stunned, but even as she regained her senses she didn't pull away.

'You drive me crazy,' Daniel said. 'And one day you will be mine. I can't have it any other way. I want you too much to let you go.'

Gently he released her, only keeping hold of her hand.

'So you're going to give me a good bit of competition,' he said, motioning towards the target.

Amelia just stared for a minute, obviously still processing Daniel's words, before rallying.

'I was the best shot this side of Calcutta,' she said with a grin.

'Then how about a wager?' Daniel said.

'What do you propose?'

'If I win you grant me a whole hour, in private, to show you just how desirable you are.'

Amelia swallowed, allowed her tongue to dart out to moisten her lips, then asked, 'And if I win?'

'I grant you an hour, in private, to do whatever you want with me.'

She laughed and the tension that had been sizzling between them was broken.

'Anything I want?' she asked with a mischievous grin.

'Anything.'

'So if I asked you to clean out a pigsty?'

'I'd be honour bound to do it.'

She seemed to contemplate her options for a moment.

'Deal.'

Daniel took Amelia's proffered hand and shook it. Inside he was singing with joy; Amelia had just agreed to a whole hour of blissful seduction. No matter who won Daniel knew how that hour would end.

He wasn't sure whether he was more pleased about the inevitable marriage that would come after such intimacies, or the intimacies themselves. Of course he hadn't lost sight of his ultimate aim, to marry Amelia and secure her dowry, but as each day passed he was growing more enamoured with the idea of actually being married to her. Waking up every day with Amelia in his bed, talking to her over the breakfast table, then taking her back to bed. He'd never imagined he'd actually want to get married, but every moment he spent with Amelia was convincing him that having a wife he desired as much as her could be no bad thing.

In truth Daniel couldn't believe his luck. For years bad things had happened to him or to those around him. First his brother's death, and then Annabelle's seduction and betrayal. And the event that had hurt him the most; the knowledge he had a son whom he would never be a true father to, a boy he would never swing up on his shoulders, never teach to ride, never tuck into bed.

Finally, with Amelia, his luck had changed. This was the woman he was prepared to marry even if she had a face full of warts and poor personal hygiene, if it had meant obtaining her dowry to keep his son safe. Instead he had found a woman he could barely keep his hands off and someone whose company he enjoyed as well.

When he had scooped Amelia up from the burning room Daniel had been scared he might lose her. His heart had pounded like never before and he'd felt sick inside. Although he'd known Amelia for only a couple of weeks the idea of losing her had made him realise just how much she meant to him.

Amelia picked up a pistol and began to inspect it, feeling its weight in her hands. Expertly she flicked open the barrel and checked bullets before closing it back up.

'Best of six?' she asked.

Daniel ran a finger around his collar and wondered if he was about to be beaten by this surprising woman. Amelia was shy and retiring at first glance. It was only as you got to know her that her hidden depths became apparent.

'Best of six,' he agreed. 'Ladies first.'

Amelia took her time, adjusting her stance first, then lining up the pistol with the centre of the target. After about a minute of fine adjustments she was obviously ready to fire.

Calmly she squeezed the trigger. The bullet hit the target about three inches from the centre. Without moving her feet Amelia made a small correction to the angle of the pistol and fired again. Each successive shot got closer to the centre and the final bullet hit the bullseye just slightly off the very middle.

'Impressive, Miss Eastway,' Daniel said. 'I think I may be surrendering to an hour at your mercy.'

He picked up a pistol, inspected it, took up position and squeezed off his shots.

They both squinted at the target, then stepped towards it. Daniel's shots were all close to the bullseye, with one nearly central.

'I think that's a draw,' Daniel said with a grin.

'What's the tiebreaker?'

'Why have a tiebreaker?' Daniel asked. 'Why don't we have an hour each?'

'An hour each?'

Daniel could see Amelia was trying to say no but couldn't quite bring herself to utter the words. She wanted her hour with him, but she just didn't want to admit it.

'First you will have an hour at my mercy and then we'll swap.'

'Two hours, alone?' Amelia asked, absentmindedly chewing on her bottom lip.

'We did shake on it,' Daniel reminded her.

'We did,' Amelia said.

'Then that's agreed. Tomorrow I will find some way of getting your aunt and cousin out of the house and we shall enjoy two whole uninterrupted hours together.'

He couldn't believe it when Amelia nodded in agreement. He knew she desired him, knew he could make her almost forget her own name with just a single kiss, but he had half expected her to say no, to pull away from him at the last moment and remember all the rules of propriety that would have been drummed into her as she grew up.

By agreeing to these two hours alone she was almost agreeing to the marriage he had proposed before. Daniel knew she couldn't willingly let her virtue be taken and not marry him. It would be madness, especially when he was so keen on the match. He smiled. Tomorrow they would enjoy an afternoon of pleasure and he would gain a fiancée.

Chapter Nineteen

Lizzie knew she was being beyond foolish. She couldn't spend two whole hours alone with Daniel. Whatever was left of her virtue would certainly not remain intact. She knew what a scandal it was just being in the house alone with him, even if they did not see each other, but she couldn't find it in herself to care. She couldn't resist him. Even if she went in with the best of intentions, one of his smouldering looks would have her begging him to make her his.

She would have to tell him the truth. Once he knew who she really was, then it was his decision whether he still wanted her as his wife, but she wouldn't allow him to seduce her and then tell him. Daniel was an honourable man and once he had truly taken her virtue, then he would insist on marriage, even if he didn't want it when he found out her true identity. She would not be the woman who forced him down the aisle.

Lizzie sighed—it had been a nice fantasy. She had been drawn into his world and she had fallen completely and irreversibly in love with Daniel. Lizzie had always assumed she would never fall in love, it seemed like the sort of thing that happened to other people, but here she was completely infatuated with a man who thought she was someone else. What made it worse was that he desired her. Lizzie knew all the compliments he paid her were to advance his cause, but when he looked her in the eye and told her she was beautiful she believed him. Daniel had helped her find her self-confidence.

Glancing at the clock, Lizzie flopped back down on to her bed. Daniel had taken her aside after breakfast and whispered his instructions in her ear. He had arranged for all the ladies to take a trip into Cambridge to do some shopping. At the last minute Lizzie was to cry off sick.

She'd done just as he'd ask, saying her chest was feeling a little sore and that she planned to rest for the afternoon. Harriet had glared at her and Aunt Mathilda had twittered on about it not being right for a young lady to be left alone in a gentleman's house, but Daniel had flashed her his most charming of smiles and made assurances that her niece's reputation would be perfectly safe, so the two women had gone shopping.

Now she just had to wait for Daniel to knock on her door.

Five minutes later she felt she was going mad with nerves. Knowing she couldn't wait much longer, she opened the door and peeked out into the corridor. Lizzie almost shrieked with shock. Standing just outside her door, with his hand raised ready to knock, was Daniel. He held a bunch of flowers in one hand that he must have picked from the garden.

'May I come in?' Daniel asked after a few seconds.

Lizzie's heart was racing, so instead of replying she just nodded. As Daniel entered her bedroom and closed the door behind him the room suddenly felt very small.

'Daniel,' Lizzie said, hearing the tremor in her voice.

'Yes, my sweet.'

'I need to tell you something. Something important.'

Lizzie felt herself backing away as he approached her. She needed to tell him the truth, let him know that she wasn't Miss Amelia Eastway, heiress; she was penniless Elizabeth Eastway.

'I need to tell you something, too,' he purred in her ear.

Lizzie felt her resolve slipping as soon as his lips touched her skin. She wanted this afternoon, wanted to feel his hands all over her body, his lips kissing her. She wanted to know what it felt like to make love to the man she loved. This would be her only opportunity. Once Daniel knew her true identity, he wouldn't be able to marry her; he needed an heiress. A marriage couldn't be built on desire alone and she knew he didn't love her otherwise he would have said so in the coaching inn. So once he knew who she was they would have to go their separate ways, get on with their lives. Lizzie knew she would never love another man; her future was either as the unhappy wife of Colonel Rocher, or as a spinster, maybe an old lady's companion or a governess. This was her one and only opportunity to be intimate with the man she loved.

'I'm not who you think I am,' she said, her conscience overcoming her desire.

'None of us is.'

Before Lizzie could say another word, before she could explain her meaning, Daniel's lips found hers and she was swept away, unable to break off the kiss even if her life depended on it.

Daniel eased her backwards across the room, towards the bed. Lizzie felt his hands on her shoulders, his fingers tracing patterns on her sensitive skin.

He broke the kiss to start to unlace her dress and Lizzie momentarily regained her self-control.

'Daniel, I need to tell you my secret.'

'All in good time. We all have secrets, Amelia, and one day we'll come clean about everything, but not today. I don't care what your secret is, this afternoon you're mine.'

Momentarily Lizzie wondered what secrets Daniel was keeping from her, but the thought was swept out of her brain when Daniel spun her round and started kissing the nape of her neck.

'You have such a lovely neck,' he murmured. 'So graceful.'

His lips trailed lower, kissing her between her shoulder blades as he pushed the material of her dress down her back. Lizzie felt her dress slip over her breasts and instinctively she raised her hands to cover herself. Daniel reached around and took her hands gently in his, placing them back at her sides.

Lizzie knew she had to stop him now and tell him her true identity or she would be swept up in the moment. She looked at his sparkling eyes full of desire and his lips ready to kiss her, and she swallowed the words she had been about to say. She wanted this afternoon, wanted it more than she had ever wanted anything in her life. She needed Daniel to kiss her, to make love to her. Lizzie knew that once this afternoon was over she would have to tell him her true identity and that would likely mean the end of their wonderful relationship, but she wanted to make love with the man she loved just once in her life, even if he never wanted to see her again afterwards. Her mind made up, Lizzie surrendered to Daniel's deft touch.

Expertly he freed her of her dress and as it pooled around her feet Daniel picked her up and lifted her out of it. Lizzie was still wearing her thin cotton chemise, but she felt naked under his gaze.

Slowly Daniel turned her around so they were facing each other and Lizzie watched as he started to tug at his cravat. Quickly he took off the outer layers of his clothes until he was clad only in his shirt and breeches.

Lizzie hesitantly raised a hand and placed it on his chest, feeling the heat of his body through the thin cotton.

'Why don't you take it off?' Daniel suggested.

With fumbling fingers Lizzie tugged the shirt over his head. Daniel reached out, took her hand and placed it on his chest.

'Feel what you do to me,' he said.

Lizzie could feel his heart pounding under her fingers, but she was distracted by the silky smoothness of his skin overlaid by the hairs that covered his chest. Slowly, as if she were in a trance, Lizzie ran her fingers down on to his abdomen and watched as his muscles tensed and tightened at her touch. She stopped about an inch above his waistband, not confident enough to do what she really wanted and dip a finger below the band and explore beneath.

'I want to see you,' Daniel murmured. 'I've wanted to see you since you flattened me in the Prestons' garden.'

Lizzie couldn't help but smile. The night she had made her début seemed so long ago now. That was the night she had first been kissed by Daniel, had first fallen under his spell.

With gentle fingers Daniel gripped the hem of her chemise and started to lift it over her body. All her life Lizzie had felt as if she blended into the background. People never noticed her, in particular men never noticed her, especially when Amelia was standing anywhere close by. Lizzie had grown to accept it and the few times she was noticed she had felt self-conscious and uncomfortable. Right now, with Daniel's eyes burning into her skin, she should feel shy, instead she felt beautiful. She wanted Daniel to lift her chemise, to look upon the body she had been unhappy with for so long, for she knew he would see her curves and her beauty where she saw her flaws.

Involuntarily Lizzie shivered as he exposed her body to the air. Although she felt the blood rush to her cheeks as Daniel's eyes raked over her body, she forced her arms to stay at her sides and not cover herself as she instinctively wanted to.

'You're perfect,' Daniel said.

Lizzie knew it wasn't true, but in that moment she felt perfect in his eyes.

He stepped closer to her, narrowing the gap between them so their bodies were almost touching. Gently Daniel raised a hand and ran his fingers from the base of Lizzie's throat, through the dip between her breasts and over her abdomen. He paused just before he reached the soft hair that covered her most private place, then his fingers continued their journey downwards.

Lizzie was overwhelmed with desire. She wanted him to touch her all over, to kiss her lips and bury himself inside her. With fumbling hands she reached for the waistband of his trousers and started to unclasp the fastening. Daniel groaned as she pushed the material down from his hips and he kissed her deeply.

As if it were no effort at all Daniel scooped Lizzie into his arms and carried her to the bed, laying her down gently before kicking off his trousers. Lizzie's eyes widened as she saw him naked for the first time, but before she could say anything Daniel was straddling her and his lips were once again on hers.

'I want you, Amelia,' Daniel whispered in her ear. 'I want you more than I've ever wanted anyone.'

Lizzie couldn't speak, instead she pulled Daniel closer to her, pressing her hands into his back in an attempt to weld their bodies together.

'All in good time, my love,' Daniel said, nibbling on her ear.

Lizzie felt the blood pulsing round her body as Daniel's lips trailed across her skin, kissing and nipping as they went. He captured one of her breasts in his hand and brought his lips to the nipple, grazing it with his teeth and making Lizzie cry out with the jolt of pleasure it sent through her body.

'I want to spend weeks exploring every inch of your skin,' Daniel whispered as he pulled away for just a second. 'I want to know every curve and every perfect imperfection.'

Lizzie knew she couldn't take much more of his teasing. She wanted him, even though she didn't really know what that meant, she wanted him more than life itself.

'I need you,' she said, her voice sounding breathless and foreign to her own ears.

Daniel ignored her pleas and worked his lips

across her skin to her other breast, circling the nipple with his tongue before taking it into his mouth.

'I need you,' Lizzie repeated.

This time Daniel took notice of her and raised himself up above her, looking down into her eyes.

'After this there is no going back,' he said.

Lizzie knew he was trying to be chivalrous and she also knew he expected to marry her, so this would be no more than a little indiscretion, but still he was offering her a way out. She knew there was a very good chance he wouldn't want her once he knew her true identity, but she couldn't bring herself to stop him. She wanted this so badly, wanted to make love to the man she loved even if it was just the once. This way she would always have the memory of this afternoon, of their lovemaking, even when she was lonely and far away. When she was once again starved for affection it would keep her going when nothing else could.

'I want this,' Lizzie said.

Daniel smiled at her, kissed her deeply on the lips, then pushed inside her. Lizzie found she was tensing, but slowly Daniel coaxed her to relax. His hands were everywhere, stroking and soothing, until Lizzie knew the full length of him was inside her.

As she got used to the unfamiliar sensation of being so full Lizzie felt a warmth spread deep inside her and her body began to react instinctively. Lizzie started to push her hips up towards Daniel, letting out a small moan as he withdrew nearly all the way and groaning with pleasure as he plunged back inside her. As the blood pounded around her body their pace quickened and Lizzie felt a wonderful pressure building deep inside her.

Daniel thrust in and out of her, his eyes never leaving her face, his body completely in tune with her own. Lizzie started to moan; soft whimpers that she had no control over. Her whole body was tensing as if it were about to uncoil. Lizzie's hands gripped the sheets, her fingers turning white from the pressure, then with a final thrust the release came. It was an explosion deep inside her and it was all Lizzie could do to stop herself from screaming with pleasure.

As Lizzie's body tightened she felt Daniel stiffen inside her and with a groan he collapsed on top of her. They lay panting together, their hearts beating in time, for a few minutes, neither able to utter a single word.

After Daniel had caught his breath he rolled off Lizzie and she felt suddenly bereft, but in moments he was behind her, moulding his body to the contours of hers.

'Have I ever told you you're beautiful?' he whispered in her ear.

Lizzie wriggled in closer to him.

'Beautiful and perfect in every single way.'

She didn't care that all her life she'd been called plain, she didn't care that she was always overlooked when men entered the room. Daniel saw her and Daniel thought she was beautiful.

Chapter Twenty

Daniel could lie like this all day. He felt immensely satisfied. He'd wanted Amelia ever since they'd shared that kiss in the Prestons' garden and his desire for her had been building every day since. As he gently kissed her shoulder he smiled. Far from dampening the desire that burned inside him their session of lovemaking had just made him want Amelia even more. Good job she was going to have to agree to be his wife now. He could think of nothing more pleasurable than shutting himself and Amelia in the bedroom for a couple of weeks whilst he fully explored her body and got to know her mind.

Daniel was just letting his eyes droop when there was a sharp rap on the door. Both he and Amelia immediately sat upright in bed, gathering the sheets to cover their naked bodies.

Amelia looked at him with panicked eyes and Daniel leapt out of bed, ready to strongly chastise whoever it was who dared to disturb them. Quickly he pulled on his breeches and flung his shirt over his head, not bothering with the rest of his clothes. With a glance back over his shoulder to check Amelia was completely covered by her sheet, he unlocked the door and opened it a crack.

His butler stood outside. Daniel frowned—there was absolutely no reason for his butler to disturb him in the day anyway, let alone when it was obvious he was breaking every rule of propriety with an innocent young woman.

'I'm sorry, sir,' the butler said, his expression pained. 'You have a visitor.'

Daniel nearly shouted at the man for disturbing him for such a trivial reason, but one look at the man's face told him this was no ordinary visitor. He looked down the corridor and saw a huddle of servants and realised his butler had been nominated to knock on the door and deliver the bad news.

'Who?'

His butler cleared his throat, caught Daniel's eye and whispered, 'A woman and a boy.'

Daniel had to stop himself from staggering backwards. Annabelle was here, in the same house as Amelia. He shot a worried look back over his shoulder at Amelia, who was still huddled in the bed. He wanted to run down the corridor, to snatch his son up into his arms and never let him go again, but he knew Annabelle would never let that happen. As much as he wanted to see his son he needed to get them out of the house, away from Amelia, or all his plans would be ruined.

'Put them in my study,' Daniel said quietly. 'Don't let her talk to anyone.'

His butler immediately hurried off to carry out Daniel's orders and left Daniel alone with Amelia. He shut the door and turned back to the bed.

'What's happening?' Amelia asked, the sheets pulled adorably up to her chin.

'Nothing to worry about,' Daniel said, forcing his voice to sound cheerful. 'Just a bit of urgent business I've got to sort out.'

Amelia looked confused but didn't protest. Quickly Daniel pulled on the rest of his clothes, ran a hand through his tousled hair and pecked Amelia on the cheek. He tried to ignore her mournful expression, not wanting to think what was running through her mind. No doubt she was assuming now he'd taken what he'd wanted he was fleeing and leaving her without her virtue and without a proposition of marriage. Daniel wished he could stay and reassure her, he wanted to gather her in his arms and promise nothing would ever hurt her again, but first he needed to deal with Annabelle.

'I'll be back soon,' he said, dropping another kiss on her forehead. Then he left the room before she could question him about where he was scuttling off to so soon after he'd taken her virginity.

Daniel took a couple of moments to compose himself before he entered his study. Seeing Annabelle always raised his stress levels and he needed to be clear-headed to get her out of the house and as far away from Amelia as quickly as possible.

He opened the door and immediately felt his heart constricting in his chest. Sitting on the floor, playing with a small toy soldier, was his son. Daniel wanted to scoop the boy up in his arms and never let go. He wanted to shower him in kisses and love and get down there on the floor and play soldiers with him until his son fell asleep in his arms.

'My lord,' Annabelle said, dipping into a curtsy and smiling at the look on Daniel's face.

Never before had she brought their son to one of these meetings. She would let Daniel catch glimpses of him at a distance when she wanted to remind him of his obligation to pay her, but she had never brought Edward to see him like this. Daniel took a step towards his son.

'Edward, come to Mother,' Annabelle said, a cruel smile pulling at the edge of her lips.

The little boy obediently picked up his toy soldier

and walked to his mother, smiling shyly at Daniel as he went past. Daniel's heart nearly broke in two. He wanted to be a father to his son, he wanted it more than life itself, but he knew that to protect him Edward could never find out his true identity.

'You're running out of time,' Annabelle said as she motioned for her son to sit down at her feet.

Daniel closed the study door firmly behind him, not taking his eyes off his son for a second.

'I've got what you want,' Daniel said.

Hathaway had loaned him the two hundred pounds before Daniel had left London, the rest he had managed to scrape together.

'I hear you've caught yourself a nice little heiress,' Annabelle said.

Daniel didn't want Annabelle even thinking about Amelia. His ex-lover sullied everything and he knew that no matter what he needed to keep her and Amelia apart.

'Once your circumstances have improved, I'll expect some of that good fortune to come trickling our way.'

Daniel had been afraid she'd increase her demands once he was married. She was a greedy woman who had become used to living in luxury. Daniel knew his son was not badly treated and didn't want for anything, except for perhaps a little more of his mother's attention, but he also knew most of the money he gave Annabelle was not spent on Edward. It went towards her fine dresses, her expensive jewels and her lavish lifestyle.

'There is only a finite amount of money, Annabelle,' Daniel said with a sigh.

'Don't make me do something I'll regret.' She reached down and placed a hand on their son's head.

With the extra attention Edward was distracted from his soldier and looked up at the two adults.

'I'm Edward,' he said to Daniel. 'Who are you?'

'My name's Daniel,' Daniel said, his heart breaking. He hated the thought that his son would never know he was his father, but he knew the shadow of illegitimacy was a worse fate.

'Daniel is one of Mummy's special friends,' Annabelle said.

Edward lost interest then and went back to his soldier. Daniel felt the weight of sadness pressing on his chest, almost crushing him.

'Just give me what you owe now,' Annabelle said, clearly getting bored. 'Then once you come into your fortune we will renegotiate.'

'Don't come to the house again,' Daniel said as he dug out the cash he'd borrowed whilst in London from one of the drawers in his desk.

'Lest your little heiress see us and figure out the real reason you're marrying her?'

Daniel certainly didn't want Amelia ever coming into contact with Annabelle.

'Just send a note and I'll meet you in town.'

Annabelle took the money from his hand, but as Daniel started to pull away she grabbed his wrist, pulling him closer to her.

'We could still be a happy family,' she whispered in his ear.

'I couldn't endure a single hour in your presence, let alone a lifetime,' Daniel hissed back.

Annabelle pulled away, laughing.

'Always so passionate.'

'Just leave,' Daniel instructed, retreating slightly. He watched as Annabelle gathered up their son and for the thousandth time wished the boy was staying with him.

'Remember what you're paying for,' Annabelle said with her hand resting on the door handle.

When Daniel had been young and naïve, and desperately in love with Annabelle, he had told her all about his half-brother. He'd told her of their awkward days at school together when Daniel had not known how to act around Rupert, and he'd told her of their time at university when Daniel tried to reach out to his brother, only to be rejected. He'd also let her see his deepest wounds, the emotional scars left by his brother's suicide and the feelings of guilt he carried around with him every day. Annabelle knew all his secrets and she wasn't afraid to use them to her advantage. She was an intelligent woman and from the very start she had played on Daniel's fears.

Without letting Daniel say goodbye to his son Annabelle opened the door and sailed out of the room, only to stop a few feet into the entrance hall.

'Who are you?' he heard Amelia ask.

The bottom dropped out of Daniel's world.

He considered slamming the door to his study and allowing the two women in his life to fight it out, but Daniel had not allowed himself to shy away from a difficult situation throughout his adult life and he wasn't about to start now.

'She's leaving,' he said bluntly, before Annabelle could even open her mouth to reply.

His ex-lover shot him a glance and then smiled her most dazzling smile. Daniel watched with narrowed eyes as she sashayed through the hall and out the front door. Amelia's eyes were fixed on Annabelle's retreating form as well.

Once the front door had been closed behind Annabelle, Daniel and Amelia stood in silence for over a minute. Daniel could almost see the thoughts as they tumbled through her head. None of them were positive.

'Amelia,' he said, reaching out his hand to her.

She pulled away from him and took a step back.

'You left me in bed alone,' she whispered eventually.

Daniel didn't want to do this out in the hall. He wanted Amelia somewhere private, somewhere he could haul her on to his lap and kiss her until she forgot to be angry. Then he could explain. Looking at her expression, Daniel knew he would get away with nothing short of the whole truth.

'Let me explain,' Daniel said, taking a step back towards his study in the hope she would follow.

'You took my virginity, then you just left me in bed alone.'

Daniel knew that wasn't the whole issue. It had been unacceptable leaving Amelia on her own after they'd made love, but she would have understood if it were a truly urgent matter. Instead she'd emerged to find Daniel had left her to talk to another woman.

'She's your mistress, isn't she?' Amelia asked, her voice unnaturally calm.

Daniel shook his head. He knew things looked bad, but if he could just explain to Amelia, he thought maybe she would understand.

'She's beautiful.'

Daniel couldn't deny Annabelle was stunning. She had the looks so many men desired, the looks he had once found so beguiling. Her hair was a thick shiny mane of dark brown, her eyes were a stunning green and her figure was curvaceous in all the right places. At one time Daniel hadn't been able to resist her, he hadn't been able to say no to any request she made. That was before he'd seen her true nature and now that he knew the evil heart that beat inside her chest she was as attractive to him as an old crone.

'Amelia…' he started but stopped when she held up her hand.

'She's beautiful,' she repeated in a voice that allowed no argument.

Chapter Twenty-One

Lizzie felt the tears welling in her eyes, but she forced them away. She would not cry. She would not let Daniel see her cry. She didn't know what was worse; the fact that she had so naïvely given herself to Daniel when he had another woman waiting downstairs, or that the other woman was so stunningly beautiful Lizzie knew Daniel couldn't be attracted to her when this mysterious goddess was around.

'She was the woman in the park,' Lizzie said suddenly, as the image of Daniel's ashen face popped up in her mind after he had seen the woman and the boy in Hyde Park.

Lizzie understood now why Daniel had looked so alarmed, why he had dragged her out of the park faster than was gentlemanly. This woman was his mistress or his lover and he hadn't wanted them to meet. If they did, Lizzie would never fall for Daniel's sweet talk and assurances that he couldn't resist her, that she was beautiful. Compared to his mistress she was the plainest woman in Britain.

'Stop,' Daniel commanded, finally seeming to pull himself together. 'Whatever thoughts are running through your head, just stop.'

Lizzie couldn't. She pictured them together, laughing at her naïvety, thinking it hilarious that she was falling for Daniel's compliments.

Lizzie didn't resist as Daniel took her hand and pulled her into his study, closing the door firmly behind her.

'She's your mistress, isn't she?' Lizzie asked the question Daniel had ignored earlier.

Daniel raised his hand to cup her cheek, but Lizzie pulled away. She couldn't afford to fall under his spell again. Daniel was a skilled seducer and if she allowed him he'd make her forget what she'd seen and be begging him to kiss her within minutes. She needed a clear head.

'Just tell me the truth.'

Daniel stepped away and she saw his whole body sag. Ever since she had first met him Lizzie had sensed he carried a large burden and maybe now he was about to reveal all to her.

'It's a long story,' Daniel said. 'You'd better sit down.'

For a moment Lizzie thought about refusing, about staying on her feet just out of sheer stubbornness, but she sensed Daniel was telling the truth when he said it was a long story and there was no need for her to be more uncomfortable than she was already.

'First I need to tell you about my brother,' Daniel said, choosing to sit in the armchair opposite hers. He slumped backwards, making no further attempt to touch her.

'I don't see—' Lizzie started to say, but Daniel cut her off.

'I'm not trying to distract you, or to garner any sympathy, but things will be a lot clearer if I tell you about my brother.'

The tone of his voice told Lizzie that he was deadly serious, so instead of protesting she sat back in her chair and tried not to think of the beautiful woman Daniel had left her bed for.

'When I was a boy I thought I was an only child,' Daniel started slowly. 'I dreamed about having a brother, someone to play with, someone to cause mischief with.'

Lizzie had also been an only child, but from a young age she'd had Amelia and they'd been inseparable. She couldn't imagine growing up without a constant companion.

'One day when I was about eight an old woman

came to the house with a boy around my age. My father almost didn't let them in, but the old woman thrust the boy at my father and I can remember him hurrying them into his study.'

Lizzie could almost picture a young version of Daniel watching everything through the banisters, wondering what was going on.

'It turned out my father had sired an illegitimate son. The boy's mother had died during childbirth and his grandmother had raised him.'

'This was Rupert.'

Daniel nodded.

'I found out later that when his grandmother came to the house she knew she was dying. She convinced my father to look after Rupert in her place.'

'You finally had the brother that you wished for.'

Daniel grimaced. 'It wasn't anything like what I'd imagined. My mother refused to have Rupert in the house, so he was sent to live with one of the tenant farmers and his family nearby.'

Lizzie felt sorry for the young boy who had lost his mother and his grandmother and then been rejected by his father, but she knew it was a common enough story. Men the world over fathered illegitimate children they then didn't know what to do with.

'I was forbidden from seeing him,' Daniel said

with a sad shake of his head. 'And back then I idolised my father so much I obeyed him and stayed away.'

She knew only too well the sway of a persuasive guardian. Colonel Eastway had had her toeing the line since she'd moved to India.

'We grew up a few miles apart but never laid eyes on each other after that first day.' Daniel sighed. 'So imagine my surprise when Rupert turned up at Eton a few weeks into the first school term.'

Lizzie had known the boys attended school together from Daniel's forced comments whilst they were in the park a couple of weeks previously, but at the time she hadn't realised the significance.

'He was my brother, my own flesh and blood, but I didn't know him.' Daniel shook his head sadly.

Lizzie could imagine only too well what had happened next. Rupert would have been immediately singled out for ridicule and bullying. Not only was he illegitimate, a fact none of the boys would have allowed him to forget, he had so far been raised with the children of a tenant farmer, not nobility. The mannerisms that would have come so easily for the other boys would not have been obvious to him.

Daniel raked a hand through his hair and Lizzie could see how much the memory of those schooldays upset him even now.

'I should have done more, I should have forced the other boys to accept him.'

Although Lizzie was still furious with Daniel for humiliating her with this other woman, she couldn't help but feel sorry for him. He blamed himself for his brother's death, that was clear for anyone to see, and he blamed the young boy that he had once been for not helping his brother even in the early days.

'I just didn't know how to act around him, so at first I avoided him. Then it became the norm. We were brothers, but we hardly even acknowledged each other when we passed one another on the stairs.'

'Children can be cruel,' Lizzie said, remembering the jibes from the other military children she had received out in India. 'But you have to remember you were only a child yourself, you didn't know what would be the outcome.'

Daniel grimaced. 'I wasn't a child when we went to university.'

Lizzie remembered Daniel telling her before that both boys had attended Cambridge, but Rupert had killed himself at the end of the first term.

'For years Rupert had been targeted for being different, for being illegitimate. As I got older I knew what the other boys were doing was wrong, cruel even, and in the last few years at Eton I quietly tried to stop them teasing Rupert.'

Lizzie could see the memories were almost too much for Daniel to bear, but she knew he thought this was related to his mistress and his desertion of Lizzie today, so she let him continue.

'Then we went to Cambridge. I finally felt like an adult and I finally tried to reach out to Rupert.'

'He didn't want to know you?' Lizzie asked.

Daniel shook his head. 'He refused to see me, cut me off whenever I tried to speak to him.'

Lizzie wanted to reach out and comfort the man she loved, but the face of the beautiful woman Daniel had just deserted her for flashed before her eyes and she stayed where she was. She didn't know how the story of his brother's death related to his explanation of his behaviour that afternoon, but she knew it pained him to discuss his brother, so the very fact that he was telling her all the sordid details of his past meant Lizzie owed it to him to listen.

'I tried for the entire term to apologise to Rupert, to tell him I was sorry for not standing up for him before, but he wouldn't even see me.'

Lizzie could see by his earnest expression that Daniel truly had tried to make up for the mistakes he'd made whilst he'd still been a child.

'The bullying he'd experienced whilst he was at

Eton only got worse at Cambridge. Rupert was always solitary, but he refused to socialise and this ostracised him even more. He became a sort of recluse, only scurrying out to go to lectures.'

Lizzie could imagine Daniel at university, socialising and drinking with his friends, all the time worrying about his reclusive half-brother, who wanted nothing to do with him.

'At the end of the first term I wanted to try one last time to speak to Rupert, to apologise and try to make amends. It was Christmas and I thought maybe we could share a meal and a drink.'

Lizzie could see by the pain behind Daniel's eyes that they were getting close to the crux of the story.

'I went to his rooms and refused to accept his silence, so I barged in, ready to insist we try to be like true brothers.' Daniel pinched the bridge of his nose and took a deep breath before continuing. 'He was just hanging there, lifeless, staring down at me.'

Lizzie gasped. She had never imagined Daniel had found his brother's body. It was a cruel trick of fate and she knew the image of his brother with a rope around his neck would never leave Daniel.

'I'm so sorry,' she murmured, momentarily forgetting she was livid with him and instead just wanting to comfort this man in pain.

Lizzie slipped off her chair and knelt down in

front of Daniel, who was now staring off into space as if seeing his brother's dead body all over again.

Daniel gripped her hand as if it were his only anchor to this earth and Lizzie allowed him to take comfort in her.

'There's more,' Daniel said after a minute.

She could tell by the haunted expression on his face that the story somehow got even worse.

'Rupert left a note. In it he blamed me entirely for his suicide, said I should have helped him, should have been there for him.'

Lizzie could tell Daniel was trying to hold back the tears. It was disconcerting seeing this man, normally so strong and with a smile never far from his face, reduced to a shadow of his normal self.

'He said if I were a true brother he would still be alive.'

Lizzie wanted to reach up and take Daniel in her arms, to reassure him that it wasn't true, but she knew her words would fall on deaf ears. For years Daniel had been blaming himself for his brother's death, for years he had held himself responsible for his brother's actions. She wasn't going to be able to reverse it with a kiss and a few soft words.

Daniel fell silent, his whole body slumping in the chair as if just telling the tale had exhausted him.

Lizzie sat still for a few minutes, completely conflicted. She loved this man, loved him more than she ever thought was possible. She had given herself to him entirely, only to have him betray her. When she had seen him exiting his study with his mistress her heart had broken in two. Lizzie, who had always guarded her heart knowing no man could truly love her, had let Daniel in and immediately he had betrayed her.

Despite that, and despite Lizzie knowing she would never recover from what Daniel had done to her, she wanted to comfort him. She couldn't stay quiet just because she was angry with him. She needed him to know, no matter what he had done to her, his brother's death was not his fault.

'Daniel, you can't blame yourself,' she said slowly. She could tell the words barely registered in his mind. 'Listen to me,' she said sharply. Daniel looked at her, surprised by the sharp note in her voice. 'Blame the boys who bullied him, blame the schoolmasters who didn't discipline those who persecuted him, blame your father for not including him in the family, blame those who actually made his life hell, but do not blame yourself.'

'I could have made it all better.'

Lizzie shrugged. 'You might have been able to make it a little better, but you wouldn't have been able to change everything.'

'A little better may have been enough to stop him killing himself.'

'When you first went to Eton you were just a boy, just a child. You couldn't be expected to know exactly what to do. And later, when you were older, you tried to make amends.'

'Rupert's still dead.'

Lizzie could see these arguments weren't going to work, so she changed tack slightly.

'That boy who was just here, would it be fair of me to blame him for not stopping his mother coming to see you?'

Daniel looked at her as though she had lost her mind.

'Well, would it?'

'He's three years old.'

'Exactly, only a child. He can't be blamed for failing to stop the destructive actions of another. I certainly don't blame him.'

'I was thirteen.'

'Still a child. A child who was trying to navigate an adult's world.'

Daniel shook his head, not accepting this argument, either. Lizzie raised herself up on her knees so she was looking directly into Daniel's eyes.

'This has been eating away at you for years,' she

said. 'And you need to start forgiving yourself or it will destroy you.'

Daniel looked at her bleakly. 'There's more. So much more.'

Chapter Twenty-Two

Daniel could see the hurt and betrayal clearly in Amelia's face even when she was reassuring him that his brother's death wasn't his fault. He needed to make her understand Annabelle was not his mistress, but in doing so he would have to tell her of his much greater secret.

'I continued with my degree at Cambridge,' Daniel said, clutching on to Amelia's hand, worried that any second she would pull away and refuse to hear any more of what he had to say. 'It was as though I were in a trance. I studied, I socialised, but the whole time I felt as though I were living in a nightmare.'

Amelia nodded as if she understood, but Daniel knew that was impossible; he barely remembered what that period had been like himself. Guilt had overshadowed everything he did and he'd been plagued by flashbacks of the moment he'd discovered his brother's body.

'My father died during my last year at university and in a way it was a relief. I didn't have that connection with Rupert any longer. Once I graduated, I threw myself into the business of trying to forget.'

It had been more than a relief when his father had died. When he was a young boy Daniel had idolised his father, but over the years as he had understood what had happened with Rupert, that respect had turned to disdain. His father had refused to take proper responsibility for his actions, allowing his son to live a sort of half-life; he paid for his education but made him live with a tenant farmer family, he never saw Rupert, instead sending his steward to check on his welfare. Since Daniel had become a father himself his opinions had mellowed slightly and he now understood his father had been in an impossible situation. His wife had refused to have his illegitimate son in the house, but he had still wanted to give him a good start in life. Maybe the old man had just been trying to do his best for his entire family and Daniel had seen for himself the regret in his father's eyes whenever he thought about Rupert.

His mother he could never entirely forgive. She had been a distant woman throughout his childhood, almost to the point of being cold. Daniel could never remember her telling him she loved him as he thought mothers were supposed to. He understood how difficult it must have been for her to have the evidence of her husband's infidelity paraded in front of her, but Daniel still couldn't forgive her refusal to even consider allowing Rupert a chance at a normal family life. When Daniel had travelled back home to tell his parents of Rupert's death his father had sobbed—it had been the only time Daniel had ever seen him cry. His mother had sat completely still, no change of expression on her face, no words of remorse. She hadn't even moved to comfort the man she had been married to for more than twenty years.

Daniel returned his mind to the story he was telling Amelia. After he'd graduated he had been wild for a while. He'd neglected his newly inherited estate and all the people who relied on him for their living.

'I spent my days in London, drinking and socialising and enjoying the company of women who promised to make my pain go away.'

He glanced down at Amelia and saw her struggling to keep her composure. Daniel knew he shouldn't talk so candidly of his wild exploits with other women when they had been so intimate only an hour before, but he knew she needed to see the whole picture to understand.

'I was wild and out of control and I didn't care.'

'Something changed you,' Amelia said, understanding. 'Something made you care.'

Daniel could remember the first time he'd set eyes on Annabelle. He'd thought it had been love at first sight as he'd caught her eye across a crowded room.

'I met Annabelle.'

'That was her? The woman who was just here?'

Daniel hated the strained note in Amelia's voice, hated that he had caused her this pain.

'That was Annabelle.'

'You loved her?'

Daniel could see Amelia was close to tears, but he couldn't lie to her now. The only way she might understand why he had kept something so important from her was if she knew the whole sordid story. Even if at first it hurt.

'I fell in love with her. I fell deeply and fast. I thought she was my saviour. I started to care about life again.'

Amelia's hand slipped from his own and in that second Daniel realised she loved him. Amelia loved him. He'd known she cared for him and that she certainly desired him, but until now he hadn't realised that she loved him. Hearing of his infatuation with another woman must be breaking her heart.

'She was the first person I really told the whole story about my brother. The only person other than you.'

Annabelle had seemed like an angel at the time. She'd made him forget his pain, made him focus on something other than his guilt.

'We were of entirely different stations in life, moved in different circles, but I was so deeply under her spell I was convinced I could marry her and everything would work out.'

Amelia slumped backwards a little and Daniel had to stop himself from trying to haul her into his arms. If she resisted him, it would make everything so much worse, so instead he continued with his story.

'I almost proposed to her, I almost made the mistake of asking her to become my wife. That had been her aim all along, of course, to become a countess, to become respectable.'

'She wasn't respectable?' Amelia asked.

Daniel shook his head. 'I was blinded by love at the time, but since I've found out she was quite a notorious courtesan. She'd spent years at the fringes of society waiting for a lovesick idiot to be fooled by her stories and dazzled by her beauty.'

Daniel had just seen a down-on-her-luck, sweet young woman who he had promptly wanted to rescue. She'd told him she loved him, convinced him that despite their differences their love would allow them to be together. Of course, she had never really loved him, Daniel knew that now, she had seen a damaged and vulnerable man and seen an opportunity to become a countess and never have to worry where her next patron was coming from. Annabelle was motivated by money and she had thought that by snaring Daniel she would never have to worry about money again.

'So what happened? Why didn't you propose?'

He grimaced, hating the memory of what had happened. Hating how stupid he'd been.

'I had this grand proposal planned. I was going to take her to the seaside, propose on the beach. I'd even written down what I wanted to say to her, how I'd tell her it didn't matter that she couldn't have children, that she'd always be enough for me.'

'What made you change your mind?'

'It was pure chance really. This man turned up, a real scruffy lowlife. He wouldn't leave Annabelle alone, kept claiming he was her husband. Demanding money to keep quiet.'

It was then everything had started to unwind. Always the consummate actress, Annabelle had shrugged him off and laughed with Daniel about the ravings of a drunken old man, but the doubts had started to creep in. Daniel set his steward to look into the matter and in a few days he had the whole truth.

'Annabelle was a trickster, a con artist. She preyed

on lonely men and took whatever she could from them. In me she saw the loneliest and stupidest of the bunch and thought I was her way out.'

Amelia had stopped pulling away from him and sat in stunned silence.

'I was a fool.'

'What did you do?'

'I confronted her. She tried all her usual tricks— seduction, sweet words of eternal love, even hysterics—but for the first time I could see them for what they really were. I could see her for what she really was.'

Daniel shook his head in disgust, still amazed all these years later that he had been taken in by her. If her husband hadn't turned up when he had, Daniel was sure Annabelle would have gone through with the sham wedding. Daniel would have introduced her to the world as his new countess and he would have had a hard time dismissing her from his life after that.

'Love quickly turned to hate as I realised what a fool she had made of me. I threw her out with just the clothes on her back.'

'There's more, isn't there?' Amelia asked.

Daniel nodded. This was the bit of his past that hurt the most, more than losing his brother, more than his humiliation by the woman he thought he loved.

'I didn't see her for months and slowly I started to get my life back. I have to say one thing for Annabelle, she made me realise what was important. I focused on running my estate, reconnected with loyal old friends.'

He'd also started socialising again, but Amelia didn't need to know that part. She no doubt had heard of his less-than-upstanding reputation, but he didn't need to confirm that he'd started seducing women. Of course, only women who wanted to be seduced. Amelia was the only innocent he'd ever even kissed, but there had been plenty of less virtuous women he'd spent long nights with, always making sure never to get too attached, never to let his heart become involved. Annabelle had broken his trust and broken his heart. He wasn't going to make the same mistake twice.

'Then she contacted me, asked for a meeting. Said it would be to my advantage.'

'Did you go?' Amelia asked, completely engrossed in his story now.

'I went.'

Daniel raked his hand through his hair, remembering every detail of that meeting. The day his life had really changed.

'I told you about my brother so you would understand,' Daniel said.

Amelia looked confused but moved a little closer so she was sitting on the floor right next to his chair again.

'My brother died because he was illegitimate. He was bullied and tormented because of it all his life.'

Amelia's eyes widened with shock as she slowly realised what he was about to tell her.

'Annabelle knew how much Rupert's death had affected me, she knew I was adamant I would not sire an illegitimate child. Before we were intimate for the first time she told me she could never have children.'

Daniel had been a little relieved at the time. Never being able to have children at all seemed better than becoming a father to an illegitimate child. If Annabelle hadn't told him she couldn't have children, he would have made sure they took precautions. As it was he hadn't seen the need.

'I suppose it was all part of her plan, another way to tie me to her.'

Daniel knew now Annabelle had wanted to get pregnant all along. He supposed if her husband hadn't turned up it would have been a reason to hurry along the wedding and secure her future as his wife.

'She fell pregnant?'

'The first I knew about it was when she turned up to our meeting with a baby.'

'Your baby?'

'At first I didn't believe her, but one look at the child and I knew he was mine.'

Amelia was staring off into the distance as if trying to piece together everything he'd told her.

'You had an illegitimate child, your worst nightmare,' she said slowly.

Daniel nodded.

'The boy who was with her.'

'My son, Edward.'

Amelia remained quiet for a few minutes and Daniel sat watching her, allowing her to figure out the chain of events.

'You pay her,' she said finally. 'That's why she was here.'

Daniel could see the frown developing on her face and wondered exactly what she was thinking.

'After everything you've been through,' Amelia said with disbelief, 'you pay her to keep quiet. To shut your own son away, just so society won't think badly of you.'

Amelia shot up from the floor and started backing away from him, as if she couldn't bear to be in his presence.

'You pay her to keep your dirty little secret and to keep your son away.'

Daniel stood and crossed the room in two steps, taking Amelia by the arm so she could not flee any further.

'No,' he said firmly.

'After everything you've been through, after what happened to your brother, still you value the perception of society over the feelings of your son.'

It was the closest to hysterical he had ever seen Amelia. Even when confronted with the sight of Daniel with Annabelle less than an hour after they'd been making love Amelia had remained calmer than she was now.

'You disgust me,' she said, the tears welling in her eyes. 'How could you reject that poor, innocent boy? How could you condemn him to be raised knowing his father is ashamed of him?'

Daniel realised his son's situation must resonate strongly with Amelia. In the short few weeks that he'd known her he'd seen all her insecurities. Someone in her past had made sure she felt inferior, maybe even unwanted. Now she was thinking Daniel had done the same to his own son.

Quickly Daniel released her and crossed to his desk. He opened the top drawer and pulled out a miniature, thrusting it at Amelia. It was of his son as a baby.

'I keep this with me wherever I go,' he said. 'It is the first thing I look at when I wake up and the last thing before I go to sleep. I love my son. I love my son more than life itself.'

'But not enough to claim him.'

Daniel knew he was losing her. Soon Amelia would leave the room in disgust and probably refuse to see him ever again.

'And you were going to make me complicit in this whole sordid mess as well. You were going to use the inheritance to continue to pay Annabelle to hide your son from the world.'

'I don't pay her to hide the truth from the world,' Daniel said slowly, sinking back into his chair.

'Of course you do,' Amelia said.

'I pay her to hide the truth from him.'

Amelia opened her mouth to reply, but as she digested the words she closed it again.

'You pay her to hide the truth from him,' she repeated slowly, as if trying to make sense of his statement.

'At first I tried to get Annabelle to give me custody of Edward, but she refused.'

'As his father you could have just taken him,' Amelia said.

Daniel nodded. 'That is true and often I wish I just had.'

At the time he'd been a mess, not knowing what to do for the best. Annabelle's drunken husband had died earlier in the year, before Edward was born, but Annabelle had told him because she was married when Edward was conceived Daniel would never get his hands on the boy. Technically Edward wasn't even illegitimate, seeing that Annabelle was married, but in the eyes of society, the people who would make the boy's life miserable, he was Daniel's illegitimate son.

'You have to remember Annabelle knew all about my brother. She knew all my deepest fears.'

'She knew you wouldn't want your son growing up to be illegitimate.'

'She said if I took him she'd make sure he knew he was illegitimate, that she would make him notorious.'

'So you had to pay her to keep quiet.'

'Annabelle kept Edward and made it clear that if I ever tried to take him she would ensure he knew he was illegitimate.'

'And she keeps demanding more and more money,' Amelia stated and Daniel could only nod morosely.

Amelia sat down in the chair opposite his again.

'I can't have Edward going through what Rupert

went through. I just can't. I send my steward every few months to check Annabelle is treating Edward well and I pay her.'

'Wouldn't you rather Edward lived with you?'

Daniel raked a hand through his hair and sighed. 'Over the years I've struggled so much with what to do for the best. I love my son, but I couldn't be a good father to him.'

When Annabelle had first turned up with their son in her arms Daniel had wanted to reach out and pluck Edward from her, but something had held him back. He'd thought of Rupert's face every time one of the boys at school made a cruel remark, or how the healthy young boy turned into a withdrawn young man. He hadn't been able to protect his brother from the world, what made him think he could do a better job for his son? Annabelle might not love Edward the way he did, but she had never failed in protecting a loved one the way Daniel had, either.

'She doesn't even let you see him, does she?'

Daniel shook his head. His son was growing up without him and there was nothing he could do about it.

Chapter Twenty-Three

Lizzie felt outraged and sick at the same time. She couldn't believe what this woman was putting Daniel through. She had taken his deepest, darkest secret, his guilt about his brother's death, and she was using it against him. It was despicable.

She knew she had to tread carefully. Daniel's emotions had been battered over the past decade and she wasn't going to be able to undo anything with just a few words, but maybe she could plant some seeds of reason that would slowly blossom.

'Annabelle played on your greatest fear,' Lizzie said slowly. 'She's threatening you with making history repeat itself and having your son suffer as your brother did.'

Daniel nodded, as if he agreed with her summation.

Lizzie knew she needed to be close to Daniel to make him listen to what she was saying. Now he had told his story he had withdrawn into himself and she needed to coax him out again.

Slowly she stood and moved over to his chair, perching on the arm and taking one of his hands in her own.

'I know you had an awful experience with your brother. I know he suffered terribly because of his illegitimacy...' Amelia paused and tried to form her thoughts into some semblance of an order '...but it wouldn't have to be the same way with Edward. Even if he knew he was illegitimate, if he was loved it wouldn't matter.'

Daniel looked at her as though she were mad.

'If you loved him and raised him secure in the knowledge that he was loved, no matter the truth of his birth, his illegitimacy probably wouldn't affect him as much as you worry it would.'

For a moment there was a spark of hope in Daniel's eyes and Lizzie wondered whether she had got through to him. Then the bleak look returned and Daniel shook his head and let out a deep sigh.

Lizzie didn't push the matter. It had taken years for the damage to be done—Daniel wasn't going to realise illegitimacy wasn't the worst thing in the world if you were loved straight away—but maybe she had planted the first seeds of change in his mind.

'I'm sorry I jumped to conclusions about Annabelle,' she said softly.

Daniel smiled grimly. 'What were you supposed to think? I left you minutes after taking your virtue to see another woman.'

'I understand why now.'

'I wanted to get rid of her before you had a chance to run into her.'

Lizzie gently stroked the palm of his hand with her thumb.

'You didn't want me finding out why you needed that dowry so badly.'

Lizzie knew she had to tell him the truth about her identity now. Annabelle's presence might have forced Daniel to tell her his secrets, but he could have fobbed her off with half the truth. Instead he'd trusted her with the full tale, with every one of his secrets. It wouldn't be fair on him to keep hers any longer.

Lizzie knew once she told Daniel she wasn't Amelia Eastway it was likely their relationship would be over. Daniel was a good man, a principled man, and now he had taken her virginity he would probably still insist on marrying her, but it wouldn't be a marriage of love. He'd never said he loved her and once he realised the depth of her deception she would be lucky if he could bear to be in the same room as her. She also knew she couldn't be responsible for Daniel being unable to pay Annabelle. If she left, Daniel would be free to find another heiress and the secret of his son's birth would remain safe.

'You're a good woman,' Daniel said, looking up into her eyes. 'Not many would stick around after they heard what I was mixed up in.'

'I've got a secret of my own,' Lizzie said quietly. She was unable to look Daniel in the eye, knowing as soon as she said it the affection she saw there would vanish.

He smiled at her gently. 'Nothing could be as bad as what I've just told you.'

Lizzie knew it was much, much worse.

She sat silently for a few moments, trying to figure out the best way to tell Daniel she wasn't who he thought she was. Just as she opened her mouth to speak there was a knock on the door.

'Interrupted again,' Daniel said, squeezing her hand. 'I'll get rid of them and then I'm all yours.'

He rose from the chair and crossed the room, opening the door to his study just a crack as if he were the gatekeeper to the world.

Lizzie was struggling to find the right words to tell Daniel her true identity.

Daniel, I lied to you.

Daniel, I'm not who you think I am.

Daniel, I'm impersonating my cousin.

Daniel, I'm a penniless orphan.

She needed to phrase it right so he listened to her whole story. Lizzie couldn't bear the thought of having to run after him, trying to explain her deception.

Daniel quietly closed the door and turned back to face her.

'Your revelation may have to wait a few minutes,' Daniel said, the concern showing clearly on his face.

'What's happened?' Lizzie didn't want any more delays, she wanted to finally tell Daniel who she really was.

'There's a policeman here to see you.'

'To see me?' Lizzie could hear the panic in her own voice.

A hundred different scenarios ran through her mind as she began to panic. It had to be about Amelia. She hadn't heard from her cousin in weeks. Something awful must have happened.

'He's been shown into the Green Room. I'll accompany you. There's nothing to worry about, Amelia, I won't let anything happen to you.'

Lizzie felt his strong hand wrap around hers and for a moment she felt safe and secure. She knew whatever news the policeman brought she would be able to cope with Daniel at her side, but if it was about Amelia her secret would be told for her.

Gently Daniel pulled her to her feet and led her to the door. Just before he opened it and ushered her out into the hall he placed a soft kiss on her lips and looked deeply into her eyes.

'I'll be there the whole time,' he reassured her.

As they entered the Green Room a man in his late forties stood to greet them.

'Henry Golding, Bow Street Runner.'

'I am Burwell. This is Miss Eastway.'

They all sat awkwardly and waited for Mr Golding to explain his presence.

'I'm very sorry to have to disturb you in the country, my lord, but there has been a very serious allegation made against Miss Eastway and we are duty bound to investigate.'

Daniel nodded and glanced at Lizzie. She wondered what the allegation could be.

'I understand you were both present at the unfortunate fire at Mrs Hunter's house in London last week.'

'Miss Eastway was almost killed in that fire,' Daniel said. He edged towards her protectively and Lizzie wondered what this could all be about.

'Quite. Unfortunately there has been an allegation that Miss Eastway started the fire deliberately.'

Lizzie's mouth dropped open with surprise and she saw Daniel's defences rise. He was going to fight this battle for her. It felt wonderful to be protected, to have someone in the world who would stand up for her no matter what. Lizzie knew once Daniel found out her true identity he wouldn't feel the same way, so she allowed herself this one final act from him.

'Impossible,' he said with authority.

Lizzie knew those born into nobility often were self-assured and confident. Daniel had certainly never lacked conviction or assertiveness, but Lizzie had never seen him in full lordly glory until now. His bearing was regal, his expression told of a man you wouldn't want to argue with and the tone of his voice suggested whoever he was conversing with was wrong and he was right.

'You are entitled to your opinion,' Mr Golding said.

'Do not be a fool,' Daniel said quietly.

This time Mr Golding raised an eyebrow but did not back down.

'Miss Eastway is an intelligent young woman. Tell me why she would start a fire in her own bedchamber and almost perish in the flames if it was deliberate?'

Mr Golding had no answer.

'I was the one to pluck Miss Eastway from the

jaws of death and I can assure you there was no way she started the fire.'

'Maybe if Miss Eastway would be so kind as to tell me what she remembers.'

The request was put to Daniel and he almost looked as though he was going to refuse.

'Of course,' Lizzie interjected. 'It would be no trouble.'

Mr Golding sat back and turned to face Lizzie for the first time. She felt the full intensity of his stare and for the first time she began to worry. Mr Golding did not seem like the sort of man to back down from anything, even when faced with an angry earl.

'I had been reading a letter one of the maids had brought up to me before bed.'

'So you had a candle lit?'

'As would everyone in the house at that time of night,' Lizzie gently chastised him. 'It was dark and getting ready for bed without the light of a candle would have been next to impossible.'

Mr Golding nodded and Lizzie felt Daniel shift closer to her protectively.

'I remember blowing out my candle before going to sleep. The next thing I remember is waking up feeling so hot I thought I would melt. I tried to make for the door, but the smoke was so thick I tripped on something and went sprawling on the ground.'

Lizzie had spent the past week trying not to remember the fire. If Daniel hadn't been passing the house, or if he'd even been just a minute later, she would have died.

'That's where I found Miss Eastway,' Daniel said.

Mr Golding nodded. 'There's nothing else of significance you remember?'

The image of the extra candle sitting on the table by the window flashed into Lizzie's mind. She had her suspicions that Harriet had actually sneaked into her room to read the letter. And if she had, had she left a candle burning by the window and the extremely flammable curtains?

Lizzie shook her head. Mentioning the extra candle and her suspicions about Harriet wouldn't help. She didn't know anything for sure and, as much as Harriet disliked Lizzie, Lizzie was sure she would never have set her own house on fire on purpose. Whatever had happened it must have been a terrible accident and nothing more.

'Thank you, Miss Eastway, for clarifying events for me.'

'Tell us about the accusation,' Daniel growled, making Mr Golding edge back in his chair.

'An anonymous letter was received a few days ago detailing the events of the fire. Someone was able to pinpoint exactly where the fire started and stated they saw Miss Eastway deliberately put a candle to the curtains.'

'Any idea who sent the letter?' Daniel asked. 'I'd be looking at them as a suspect if I were you.'

Lizzie was wondering the same thing herself. Someone wanted her to take the blame for Aunt Mathilda's house burning down.

'We don't have any leads on that front.'

Lizzie smiled, trying to distract the men from this train of thought. The only person who would have sent that letter was Harriet and, however misguided Amelia's cousin was, Lizzie didn't want to get her into trouble. She would have a word with Harriet in private and no one else would ever have to know.

'Apart from this anonymous letter, do you have any proof?' Daniel asked.

Mr Golding shifted in his seat.

'We are gathering fresh evidence all the time.'

'But no proof—in fact, nothing to go on except the word of someone who will not identify themselves.'

'A crime has been committed,' Mr Golding said self-righteously. 'And I will make sure whoever is responsible will be suitably punished.'

Mr Golding stood, bowed to Lizzie, inclined his head towards Daniel, then quickly left the room, no doubt to be shown out by Daniel's butler.

'How very strange,' Daniel said, looping his arm

around Lizzie's waist and pulling her closer to him now they were alone.

Lizzie nodded absentmindedly. The day had been a very strange one all round. First she had lost her virginity to the man she loved, then found out he had an illegitimate son, and now she had been accused of arson. There was only one more thing to do today and that was tell Daniel the truth. No doubt that would be the most damaging revelation of the afternoon.

Chapter Twenty-Four

Daniel reached out and touched Amelia's forehead in the spot just between her eyes. That little furrow was back between Amelia's brows, the one she got when she was worrying about something. Daniel felt he could devote his life to making that furrow stay away.

'Daniel, I need to talk to you,' Amelia said.

'I know, you want to tell me your secret.'

He was a little curious about what had her so worried. Daniel knew it wouldn't be anything major. Amelia was a sweet, innocent young thing. She was probably worried because she had let some young soldier kiss her back in India. As the thought came into his head Daniel realised he didn't like the idea of Amelia kissing anyone else. He wanted to be the only one to taste her lips, to make her shiver with anticipation as he drew his mouth across her skin.

'Please, Amelia, I want to listen. Just give me ten minutes, then I'm all yours.'

She looked as though she were going to protest, but even though it was obvious she really wanted to get whatever it was off her chest she couldn't deny him ten minutes.

'It's a beautiful day outside,' Daniel said. 'And I think we could both do with some fresh air. Meet me in the rose garden in ten minutes.'

Without giving her a chance to protest Daniel kissed her quickly on the cheek, rose and walked out of the room. He had a lot to prepare in ten minutes.

Daniel had thought his world was about to implode when Amelia had stood not a few yards from Annabelle. The look in her eyes had been pure devastation. He knew now Amelia loved him, it was obvious in her every look, her every touch, and for her to come across the woman she supposed to be his mistress was devastating. If Daniel had been in her place, he probably would have cursed and shouted and refused to listen to any explanation, but Amelia had kept a lid on her pain and had heard him out.

Even though everything had pointed to Daniel being the worst possible scoundrel, Amelia had believed in him enough to listen to his explanation.

When he'd told her about his brother she had shared his pain, then when he had explained about

Annabelle and Edward she had surprised him yet again. Far from trying to distance herself from his messy private life she had sympathised with him and felt angry with Annabelle on his behalf.

Daniel couldn't believe she was still in his life, she hadn't made her excuses and abandoned him as he'd been certain any woman would when they found out about his son. She knew what he wanted her dowry for and she hadn't once voiced an objection.

He knew he had to get her to agree to marry him. Amelia Eastway was one of a kind and he'd be the biggest fool in the world if he let her slip through his fingers. Now they had made love Daniel was pretty sure she wouldn't refuse him again. There was no real reason to. She loved him and she desired him. Now she even knew his deepest, darkest secret and hadn't gone running for the hills. There was no reason they shouldn't be together.

'William,' Daniel said, once he had sought out one of the footmen, 'I need you to bring a bottle of champagne out to the rose garden in half an hour's time.'

That should give him plenty of time to persuade Amelia to marry him. After she'd got whatever it was that was worrying her so much off her chest, of course.

With his first task accomplished Daniel dashed

upstairs and started rummaging around in his room. He was searching for a token to give to Amelia to seal their engagement. He would take her to get a ring made just for her in the next couple of weeks for the wedding, but he wanted something special to give to her now and he had just the thing in mind.

With five minutes to spare Daniel rushed back downstairs and out into the garden. Thankful there was no sign of Amelia yet, he busied himself picking the most beautiful blooms, checking over his shoulder that the gardener wasn't looking and feeling like a naughty schoolboy for picking roses in his own garden.

When Amelia emerged from the house and walked towards the rose garden Daniel could see the tension on her face and for the first time wondered whether this secret of hers might actually be something serious. He suddenly had a vision of her secretly marrying another man and he felt a sickness start to build in the pit of his stomach.

'Daniel,' Amelia said as he rose to meet her.

Her face was white and drawn and her eyes looked hollow and haunted.

'Before you speak I want to tell you something,' Daniel said.

'Please…' Amelia's voice was quiet and pleading

'...no more delays. I need to tell you the truth about who I am before I lose my nerve.'

Daniel nodded. He didn't want her to speak, he didn't want to know her secret, not if it was something that would keep them apart. As he sat next to her on the stone bench, his thighs pushing against hers, he just wanted to envelop Amelia in his arms and never let her go.

'I love you,' Daniel blurted out.

He hadn't meant to say it, he hadn't even realised he was thinking it, but as soon as the words were out of his mouth Daniel realised he meant them. He loved her. He actually loved her. He didn't know when it had happened, or how, but he did know it was the truth.

'You love me?' Amelia asked, clearly thinking she had misheard.

'I love you.' Daniel cupped her face and looked into her eyes. 'I love you, I love you, I love you.'

Now he'd said it once he couldn't seem to stop.

'I love your kind heart and I love your forgiving nature. I love your beautiful face and I love each and every one of your freckles. I love the way your body fits perfectly with mine and I love how you respond to my kisses. I love each and every little bit of you.'

Daniel was grinning now. He never thought he would fall in love again. After Annabelle's betrayal he had sealed his heart off, keeping everyone at a distance and only allowing himself the shallowest of feelings for anyone. In just a few short weeks Amelia had broken through all of his defences and she'd mended the heart he'd thought was broken for ever.

'I love you, too,' Amelia said, tears forming in her eyes.

'I'm sorry,' he said. 'I'm sorry I interrupted you. I just had to let you know. You go ahead. I won't say another word until you've told me whatever it is you want me to know.'

Daniel sat and watched as Amelia prepared herself to reveal whatever it was that was worrying her so much. He clasped her hand in his, smiling encouragement, all the time replaying Amelia's voice as she said *I love you, too.*

'Daniel, I'm not who you think I am,' she said, repeating what she'd started to tell him before they'd got caught up in their moment of passion.

She took a deep breath and continued. 'I'm not Amelia—'

She was cut off by a loud shout and both she and Daniel jumped up with surprise.

'Impostor, liar, she-devil.'

Daniel pulled her towards him protectively whilst he assessed the threat.

Amelia's cousin Harriet came dashing from the

house and out into the garden. She was still screaming insults with a satisfied look on her face as she reached Daniel and Amelia.

'What the hell is going on?' Daniel asked.

'She is not who she says she is. She's an impostor.'

Daniel looked at Amelia and saw her shrinking before her cousin's words.

'I was trying to tell you,' Amelia whispered.

'Pah! Unlikely,' Harriet said, jabbing a finger none too gently into Amelia's chest. 'Con artists never confess unless they're caught.'

'I was trying to tell you.' This time Amelia looked directly at Daniel with desperation in her eyes.

He almost ordered Harriet back to the house but quickly decided against it. He needed to know what was going on, no more delays, no more interruptions.

'She is not Amelia Eastway,' Harriet said triumphantly. 'We ran into a soldier who had served under Colonel Eastway whilst we were in Cambridge.'

Daniel was listening to Harriet, but he couldn't take his eyes off Amelia. She seemed to shrink before him, folding into herself as if she were seeking a way to disappear.

'This officer remembers Amelia Eastway well. Apparently she is the belle of all the balls, the most beautiful woman he's ever laid eyes on.'

Daniel frowned, wondering what Harriet was getting at.

'Amelia Eastway, the real Amelia Eastway, is a petite blonde with blue eyes,' Harriet finished triumphantly.

Daniel shook his head. It wasn't possible, none of this made sense. If it weren't for the devastated look on Amelia's face, he would have dismissed Harriet's claims and concluded the officer had been mistaken.

'Amelia?'

She shook her head, the tears flowing freely down her cheeks now.

'My name isn't Amelia. It's Lizzie…well, Elizabeth.'

Daniel felt his world rock and he stumbled slightly. The woman standing in front of him wasn't Amelia Eastway. She was a liar, an impostor. The woman he thought he loved didn't even really exist.

'I'm sorry,' she said quietly.

Daniel tried to look at her, but he couldn't bear it. She still had the same face, the same expressions. She looked like the woman he loved, but in reality he didn't know her at all.

'Please let me explain,' she said so quietly he barely heard her.

'More lies?' Harriet asked nastily.

'No.' Lizzie's voice was firm. 'The truth. The whole truth.'

Daniel sank down on to the bench. He'd trusted her. He'd loved her. What a fool he was. For years he had protected himself against this sort of deception and when he finally dropped his guard he had been taken in by a liar again.

'Who are you?' he asked.

'My name is Elizabeth Eastway. I'm Amelia's cousin.'

'Amelia's poor cousin,' Harriet added. 'Not a penny to her name.'

Daniel watched as Lizzie grimaced, but didn't offer any words of comfort. He just wanted the whole story now, to try to understand why she had deceived him.

'I was sent to accompany my cousin Amelia whilst she made her début into society and searched for a suitable husband,' Lizzie said, her eyes pleading with him to understand.

Daniel couldn't give her any reassurance. He felt numb, betrayed, and he wondered if she was now even telling them the truth.

'Amelia had been secretly in correspondence with a young officer who had served out in India a few years ago. She wanted to go visit him. She said they were in love.'

Harriet snorted and Daniel wondered how she could get so much enjoyment out of this.

'Go away, you stupid girl!' Daniel snapped. Harriet looked outraged but turned on her heel and stalked back to the house, a smug expression on her face. 'Continue.' Daniel nodded to Lizzie.

'She begged me to take her place, to pretend to be her, for a few days, a fortnight at most. She said she'd be back before I made my début and no one apart from Aunt Mathilda would ever know.'

Daniel wondered how Lizzie had been persuaded by her cousin to do such a thing.

'I didn't want to do it, but Amelia is very…persuasive. She begged me and I couldn't say no.'

He wondered if the two women had giggled about the deception that had ended up breaking his heart.

'Then Aunt Mathilda insisted I make my début earlier than we'd assumed and I was presented to society as Amelia. I didn't know what to do and I just kept hoping to hear from my cousin, but there was no word.'

Daniel saw the panic etched on her face even now and he realised this was the 'friend' she'd wanted his assistance in finding.

Lizzie turned to him and took a step forward, but she must have seen something on his face that made her pause, because she didn't come any closer.

'I never set out to deceive you. I just didn't know how to stop the lies once they had started.'

Daniel looked into her eyes but couldn't find any words to say. She wasn't his Amelia.

'Harriet is right,' Lizzie said with a sob. 'I don't have a rich father or a significant dowry. Marrying me won't solve your problems.'

Up to that point Daniel hadn't thought about the dowry, he'd been so focused on the fact that Lizzie had lied about who she was he hadn't even realised that she did not have the dowry he'd started courting her for in the first place.

'Was any of it true?' he asked, his voice gruff and catching in his throat.

Lizzie sank to her knees in front of Daniel and took his hand in hers. He tried to pull away, but she held on firmly, gripping him as if he were her only link to the real world.

'I may not be Amelia, but everything else we shared was real. I love you.'

Daniel looked down into her deep brown eyes and felt himself softening, weakening. It would be so easy for him to forgive her, to take her in his arms and pretend none of this mattered, but he knew deep down that he couldn't do it. It wasn't about the dowry, it was the lies. He'd been hurt once by a woman's lies. He wouldn't let himself be hurt again.

'It wasn't real,' Daniel said. 'None of it was real.'

Lizzie recoiled as if she had been slapped, letting his hand slip through her fingers. As her hand fell away Daniel had a moment of panic; he was losing her. He loved her and he was losing her. Then he hardened his heart. He didn't love her, he loved his Amelia, a woman who didn't exist.

'Hate me,' Lizzie whispered. 'Despise me, refuse to ever see me again, but don't tell me none of it was real.'

Daniel thought of all the moments they had shared, the moments that had made him fall in love with her. The kiss in the Prestons' garden, their outings to the park, the night in the coaching inn, their rendezvous around his estate, and earlier that morning the moment she had given herself to him completely.

He wanted to believe it was all real, not engineered by a woman who was trying to entrap him, but he had experienced first-hand what happened when he trusted a woman. He couldn't make the same mistake again.

'Pack your bags. You're leaving first thing in the morning.'

He couldn't bear to look her in the eye as he delivered the words.

Chapter Twenty-Five

Lizzie sat morosely on the side of her bed. The tears had stopped falling sometime in the middle of the night and she now just felt empty and hollow. She hadn't slept at all. Every time she closed her eyes she just saw the look of betrayal on Daniel's face.

She understood why he wanted her gone, but that didn't make the pain any better. Over the past few days as she had been wondering how best to tell Daniel the truth about her identity she had imagined his reaction hundreds of times. Lizzie had known he would be hurt and betrayed, but nothing had prepared her for the look of utter disgust on his face. He had hardly been able to look at her and when he did Lizzie had felt as though she'd been slapped. The familiar gazes of longing and desire of the man she loved had been replaced by the cold stare of someone she didn't know.

Lizzie choked back a sob. He'd told her he loved

her, just before Harriet had turned up and blurted out Lizzie's secret, Daniel had looked into her eyes and told her he loved her. Just a few minutes later it was clear that short-lived love had turned to hate.

Lizzie stood and checked over her meagre belongings. Most of what she had brought to London or purchased whilst living with Aunt Mathilda had been destroyed in the fire. She had one small case of items hastily bought or borrowed, nothing of hers before she had started impersonating Amelia, nothing to make her feel like plain old Lizzie Eastway again.

There was a sharp rap on the door and Lizzie crossed to it quickly, knowing it would be one of the servants, but holding out a flicker of hope that it might be Daniel, willing to give her another chance.

She opened the door. It was William, one of the footmen. Lizzie gave him a small, sad smile as he looked at her awkwardly.

'Time to go, miss,' William said, picking up her light case and carrying it out of the room for her. They descended the stairs in silence and Lizzie was mortified to see Aunt Mathilda and Harriet at the bottom.

'I'm sorry for lying to you,' Lizzie said, stopping in front of Amelia's aunt.

The older woman smiled at her and gently patted

her on the arm. 'My brother-in-law was always writing to say what a handful Amelia was, wilful and persuasive. I've no doubt who made you go along with this,' she said kindly.

Lizzie burst into tears at Aunt Mathilda's understanding and felt all the despair and sadness come bubbling to the surface again as the older woman took Lizzie in her arms. She didn't release her for a few minutes, holding Lizzie as the tears ran down her face and her chest heaved.

When Lizzie had finally composed herself she stepped back and eyed up Harriet. They certainly weren't going to have a tearful hug.

'I always knew there was something wrong about you,' Harriet said smugly. 'Well, you've got what you deserve now.' Harriet looked her up and down with disdain. 'Look at you, you're plain and boring and have nothing that I don't have. Yet you very nearly married an earl.'

Lizzie looked at Harriet sadly. She was spiteful and jealous, but Lizzie couldn't bring herself to hate the young girl.

'Sometimes people can see past the plain and boring and find something that no one else can see,' Lizzie said, thinking of when Daniel had told her he loved her. 'You'll find the person who sees his perfect woman when he looks at you one day, Harriet.'

'Look how well it's turned out for you,' Harriet sneered.

Lizzie turned away. She was never going to make Harriet like her and right now she didn't have the energy or motivation to even try.

'Miss Eastway,' Daniel barked as he emerged from his study.

Lizzie covered her mouth in shock as she turned to face him. Far from being his normal, well-presented self, Daniel looked as though he had spent the night in the gutter. His eyes were bloodshot, his skin pale and his hair sticking up in all directions. Lizzie wanted to run to him, to take him in her arms and make everything right, but she knew she was no longer in the position to comfort him.

'Let's go.'

Lizzie turned and smiled a final farewell to Aunt Mathilda, then docilely followed Daniel out to the waiting carriage.

Daniel stood aside as a groom helped her up into the carriage, as if he couldn't bear to touch her, but then to her surprise he jumped in himself and sat opposite. He must have seen the question in her expression.

'I'm taking you to London,' he said.

Lizzie had expected him to send her alone. He'd made it painfully obvious that he didn't want to spend any more time than was necessary in her company.

'Thank you,' she said quietly.

Daniel looked as though he might soften for a second, but before Lizzie could say anything else he'd banged on the roof and the carriage lurched into motion.

They sat in a horrible, uncomfortable silence. Lizzie looked down at her hands, her feet, out the window, at the roof, anywhere but at Daniel. She couldn't bear to see the pain on his face, pain she had caused.

Lizzie had known her deception would hurt Daniel, she'd known it ever since he'd began pursuing her, but she had never realised quite how much it would shatter his world until his revelation about Annabelle. He'd been hurt badly before, so much so he had never really trusted another person. That was why he had a reputation as a rake, never bedding the same woman for more than a few weeks. He didn't want anyone to get close in case he got hurt again.

At first Lizzie knew she was nothing more to him than a means to keep his son's illegitimacy a secret and protect the young boy, but as time had passed she liked to think his affection had grown. She knew for sure that he had desired her from the very start, from that magical night in the Prestons' garden, which seemed so long ago now. When he had come to her in the night at the coaching inn he'd done it with seduction in mind, but when they had finally made love Lizzie knew it was because of deeper feelings for her.

She'd never expected love from him, especially after his revelations about Annabelle and her schemes, but yesterday, just before Harriet had come screeching into the garden, he had declared his love.

Lizzie took the memory of him uttering those words and wrapped herself in it. For a few moments at least someone had loved her. Despite what Daniel said about not really knowing her, Lizzie had been herself the entire time. If Daniel loved anyone it was Lizzie, not Amelia. He just knew her by the wrong name.

She was certain those few minutes would for ever stick in her mind. Daniel had declared his love for her, something she had been craving for so long, and then her world had shattered with the revelation of her lie.

Lizzie had known Daniel would be hurt and upset, that he would be angry at her for lying to him for so long, but she hadn't been prepared for the force of his emotions. Now he could barely bring himself to look at her. It was as though her very presence brought him pain.

For a moment she wondered whether he had never really loved her at all, whether it had all been part of the plan to get her to marry him and get his hands on her dowry to protect his son. She could tell his thoughts were never far away from the boy and how to protect him from the world. She let out a small sigh, not noticing when Daniel's eyes flicked to her face and quickly looked away again. Lizzie had to give him more credit than that. He would not lie to her about love. Although losing her dowry would be a big blow, Daniel was more hurt about her betrayal of his trust.

She glanced at him across the carriage. It would be so easy to reach out and take his hand in her own, to beg him to forgive her, but Lizzie knew she didn't deserve forgiveness. She had let him believe she was Amelia, even when he had revealed his darkest secrets to her. Although she had tried to tell him a few times she had always allowed the interruptions that postponed her revelation.

Sitting up straighter, Lizzie decided she couldn't keep quiet. There was something she needed to say to Daniel. She might not deserve his forgiveness, she might not deserve to ever see him again, but she would never be able to look herself in the eye if she didn't try to make him understand one thing.

'Daniel,' she said softly.

Immediately his eyes snapped to her face. For a long moment they both sat there, looking at each other and wondering if there was any way back from this mess.

'I want to say something and I need you to listen,' Lizzie said.

He looked as though he were about to protest already, so Lizzie quickly continued.

'It's not about me, or our relationship. I know I have irrevocably damaged your trust in me and that we don't have a future.'

She wondered if the pain she saw in Daniel's face was reflected in her own. She certainly felt as though her heart was being ripped out.

'I need to say something about Annabelle. About Edward.'

For a moment she wondered if he would snap at her, whether he would tell her Edward was no longer any of her business, but after a long thirty seconds he inclined his head as if he were willing to at least listen.

'Love can conquer anything,' Lizzie said quietly. 'You may think the worst thing in the world for Edward would be living with the knowledge of his illegitimacy, but trust me, a child would rather be illegitimate and loved than legitimate and unloved.'

Lizzie thought back to all the moments in her childhood where she'd wished she had a parent to love her. The moments when Amelia ran to her father and he'd looked down at her, proud and caring, and Lizzie had stood back, trying to hold in the tears. Even the little moments, when she had finally mastered a piano piece, or when she fell and scraped her knee, Lizzie knew every part of her life would have been better with someone to love her.

'When I was a child my parents died. I went to live with my uncle. No one loved me. No one cared if I succeeded or failed. I would have much preferred to be illegitimate but had a parent's love.'

'Being illegitimate killed my brother,' Daniel said stubbornly.

Lizzie shook her head. 'Being alone killed your brother. Your father didn't welcome him, accept him into the heart of the family. Your brother had no one to love him.'

They fell silent. Lizzie knew Daniel wanted his son so badly it was tearing him apart. She could see by the pain in his eyes every time Edward's name was mentioned that he couldn't stand missing out on his son's life.

'Love can conquer anything,' Lizzie repeated.

Chapter Twenty-Six

They had spent most of the journey in silence. Daniel hated to see Lizzie so withdrawn and fragile, but he couldn't bring himself to do anything about it. Every time he thought about reaching out to her his brain screamed that she'd lied to him and there was nothing stopping her from lying again.

After their talk about Edward some of Lizzie's words kept circling round in his head. *Love can conquer anything.* He wondered if it were true. For the first time in years, for the first time since Annabelle had started to blackmail him, Daniel felt a surge of hope. Maybe Lizzie was right, maybe Daniel could still be part of his son's life.

He thought back to Rupert's suffering and he realised that on that front at least Lizzie's words were true. Rupert hadn't had anyone to love him. He'd been bullied about his illegitimacy, but if their father had accepted him and showered him in love, the bullies' words would probably have just slid right off Rupert rather than taking hold and festering.

One thing he could give his son was love. He loved that little boy so much and he barely even knew him. The thought of being the one to raise him, the one to kiss him goodnight and tuck him safely into bed, was almost intoxicating. He wondered whether he could have all that and still protect Edward.

He wanted to ask Lizzie to talk more about it, to explain how love conquered anything. He wanted to listen as she convinced him he could claim his son and not ruin the young boy's life. Daniel glanced across the carriage to where Lizzie sat, staring morosely at her hands.

Before he could find the words the carriage lurched to a stop. Daniel peered out of the window into the dusk. It had been a long afternoon of travelling. He had wanted to get as far as possible on their journey back to London and to avoid the coaching inn they had stayed at only a few nights previously at all costs. He didn't need the memories of his time there with Lizzie, things were painful enough without reliving that night together.

Daniel opened the door and hopped down from the carriage, stretching his leg and back muscles, which were stiff from the long day spent cooped up in the carriage. Once he had regained his normal range of movement, he turned round and automatically held out his hand to assist Lizzie from the carriage. As their hands met Daniel felt a jolt coursing through his body. Even though he despised how she had deceived him his body still responded to her. He craved the touch of her skin against his, the taste of her lips on his own. He wanted her even now, even when he knew they had no future together.

Once on the ground, Lizzie quickly pulled her hand away as if aware of the tension between them the contact had caused.

Daniel turned and walked into the inn, not waiting to see if Lizzie followed him.

'Two rooms, please, for myself and my sister,' he said as the landlord appeared.

Daniel knew travelling alone with Lizzie was scandalous enough. The pretence that she was his sister would at least shield her from a little of the gossip generated in these places.

'Two rooms? Ah.'

Daniel's heart sank. There wasn't another inn for miles and he didn't think the horses would make it that far without rest.

'We have one very nice room, perhaps you and your sister would not mind sharing,' the landlord said.

'We need two rooms.'

'I'm very sorry, sir, but we're completely full. It's uncommonly busy.'

Daniel took a deep breath and reminded himself that it wasn't the innkeeper's fault that there was only one room. A few days ago he would have relished the prospect of spending a whole night with Lizzie so close. Now he couldn't think of anything more tortuous.

'We'll take the room,' he said. 'And dinner.'

'Of course, sir.' The landlord looked very relieved Daniel wasn't going to make more of a fuss. 'I can serve you dinner in the private dining room in half an hour.'

The landlord led them up to the room, showed them in and then quickly retreated before Daniel could change his mind about sharing with Lizzie.

'I can sleep elsewhere,' Lizzie said, her voice barely more than a whisper.

Daniel turned to look at her. 'And where exactly do you propose to sleep?'

'In the carriage?' Lizzie suggested. 'Or maybe the barn.'

Daniel shook his head. 'I may not be pursuing you as my wife any longer, but I refuse to let you put yourself at risk whilst in my company. We will both sleep here tonight.' As he said it Daniel eyed up the small bed and had to suppress a groan. 'I'll sleep in the chair.' The very upright, uncomfortable-looking chair.

Lizzie opened her mouth to protest again, but Daniel silenced her with a look. He might be furious with her, but he wasn't about to let a lady sleep in a chair whilst he was in a bed.

Daniel flopped down into the hard chair and tried to make himself comfortable. He grimaced; it was going to be a very long, sleepless night.

Lizzie walked over to the window and looked out, allowing Daniel to study her back. He had so much he wanted to ask her, so many questions whirling round his head, but he couldn't bring himself to utter a single query. He knew if he started asking her to explain he would be on the slippery slope to forgiveness, leaving himself open to being hurt again.

'Shall we go down for dinner?' Lizzie asked after twenty long, silent minutes.

Daniel roused himself, levering his body from the hard chair and following Lizzie out of the room.

They sat in silence whilst they waited for dinner. Daniel could see Lizzie darting glances in his direction every few seconds as if she wanted to ask him something but didn't know how.

'What is it, Miss Eastway?' Daniel asked eventually after their mutton had been set down in front of them.

Lizzie pushed her food around her plate and tried a mouthful. She grimaced but chewed and swallowed before answering him.

'What happens when we get to London?' she asked eventually.

Daniel tasted some of the dinner himself. It was grim—the mutton overcooked, the vegetables soggy and the potatoes hard.

'I will deliver you to some of your relatives.'

Lizzie nodded as if this were a sensible plan, although by the way she pursed her lips Daniel could see she thought there might be a flaw in his idea.

'Which relatives will you deliver me to?' Lizzie asked.

Daniel shrugged. 'Whomever you'd like to go and stay with.'

He was getting distracted by her lips. They kept pursing and relaxing, and once he even thought he saw the flicker of her tongue darting out.

'Maybe if you would be so kind as to take me to a reputable guest house,' Lizzie suggested.

Daniel looked at her properly for the first time since they'd sat down for dinner and realised there was real fear in her eyes.

'What's wrong with your relatives?' he asked sharply.

'I don't have any. Amelia and my uncle are my only living relatives.'

Daniel cursed under his breath. He might want to try to distance himself from Lizzie so he could start thinking clearly again, but he couldn't abandon her in the middle of London all on her own.

'You didn't think to mention this earlier?' he asked.

'You didn't want to share your plans with me.'

He knew she was right and this was one thing he couldn't blame her for, but Daniel felt annoyed all the same. He'd envisioned dropping her off with some elderly aunt, then going and reassessing his life. The truth was he couldn't think with Lizzie near him. He hated that she'd lied to him, hated that he had allowed himself to be deceived again, but he couldn't bring himself to hate her. He wanted to, but the feelings just weren't there. In fact, he still felt rather protective towards her and there was something deeper, something he didn't care to examine yet.

When he had found out that Annabelle had lied to him all those years ago, Daniel had immediately realised everything they had shared was part of that lie, but somehow with Lizzie things felt different.

He was beginning to wonder whether she did care for him, love him even, and her deception had just got out of hand.

Looking across the table at her, Daniel wanted to forgive her, he wanted to sweep her into his arms and tell her everything would work out, but he knew he couldn't let his heart rule his head. He needed distance, some time to assess the situation, some time away from Lizzie.

'I do not want to be a burden on you any longer,' Lizzie said quietly. 'If you would be so kind as to recommend suitable accommodation, you will never see me again.' There was a choke in her voice as she spoke and Daniel knew she was hurting, too.

'We will figure it out tomorrow,' he said wearily, running a hand through his hair.

Lizzie nodded and went back to pushing her food around her plate, every so often taking a mouthful and grimacing at the taste.

They finished dinner in silence and returned to the room. Daniel eyed up the chair he was going to be spending a very uncomfortable night in and decided he needed some air.

'I'm going for a walk,' he said. 'I'll be back in half an hour. I suggest you are in your nightclothes and in bed by then.'

The last thing he needed was to be in the room

whilst Lizzie undressed. Hearing the rustles and imagining what she was taking off would weaken his resolve and he couldn't be sure he wouldn't sweep her on to the bed and ravish her, despite not knowing how he felt about her any longer.

He slipped out of the room and out of the inn, determined to clear his head before returning to where Lizzie, the woman he'd thought he loved, was sleeping.

Chapter Twenty-Seven

There was no way Lizzie was going to sleep. Her body might be exhausted, but her mind was whirring with activity. She knew she should be making plans for the future, deciding what it was she wanted to do with her life, but Daniel, and the life she could have had with him, kept returning to her thoughts.

She turned over in bed and buried her face in the pillow, letting out a muffled scream. She wished she didn't feel so alone. If only Amelia was here, her one confidante. Lizzie knew Amelia would tell her to fight for Daniel, to make him realise what he was throwing away, but Lizzie wasn't her cousin. No matter what she had been pretending in the past few weeks Lizzie wasn't brave or outgoing or flirtatious.

As she saw it she had two options and neither of them involved the man she loved. Either she could consign herself to a life of misery and return to India to become Colonel Rocher's badly treated wife, or she could strike out on her own. The second option was riskier, but Lizzie knew that after experiencing freedom and love these past few weeks she couldn't willingly give herself up to a man who wouldn't love her and would probably beat her. Before she came to England she would have married Colonel Rocher without argument, but over the past couple of weeks she had found a confidence and self-respect she had never realised was buried deep inside her.

Lizzie heard the door open quietly as Daniel slipped into the room. She kept her eyes closed and her breathing steady. For a moment she wondered if he would come to her, slip into the bed beside her and tell her everything would be all right. She wanted his forgiveness so badly, but she knew it couldn't ever happen. Other men might forgive her deception, but Daniel had been hurt in the worst possible way before, and now she knew he could never forgive her.

Lizzie also knew that if he forgave her, if he agreed they could have a life together, then he would be giving up what he viewed as his son's protection, all for her. That sort of responsibility was too much and she wouldn't be able to bear it if little Edward got hurt because of her.

She listened as he kicked off his boots and sank into the chair. Daniel shifted position every few seconds and Lizzie knew he must be uncomfortable. Another thing for her to feel bad about.

'We can share the bed,' Lizzie said quietly. 'I promise I won't even touch you.'

Daniel grunted and Lizzie wondered if he expected her to seduce him in the middle of the night. As if she would know how.

'I'm fine,' he said. 'Go to sleep.'

Lizzie lay staring up at the ceiling for a few minutes, listening to him shift his body trying to get comfortable.

'Please. The bed is big enough for two. There's no point in depriving yourself of sleep on top of everything else.'

Silence. Five seconds passed, then ten. Lizzie could tell he was weighing the options up in his head. He could spend the night in the chair and start the morning sleep-deprived and aching, or he could share the bed with the woman who had lied about who she was.

Eventually he stood and walked over to the bed.

'I'll sleep on top of the covers,' he said.

Lizzie waited for Daniel to lie down, but he seemed to hesitate.

'I promise I won't touch you,' she repeated sadly.

'It's not you I'm worried about.'

Slowly he got on to the bed, careful not to touch

her at all. Although there was a thick blanket and a couple of sheets separating them, Lizzie could still feel the heat of his body radiating through the layers. She thought back to the last time they had shared a bed together, when she had given herself completely to the man she loved. He'd caressed every inch of her body then, now he was taking pains not to touch her at all.

Tears welled in her eyes and silently Lizzie let them fall down her cheeks and into the pillow. She didn't know how she had messed everything up so much, but she would not take Daniel down with her. She loved him, even though he was rejecting her, and the best thing for him would be to be free of her. Tomorrow she would disappear out of his life and allow him to forget her. He would be free to find another woman, a real heiress, to marry and secure his son's future with.

'Tell me,' Daniel said hoarsely, 'was any of it real?'

Yesterday, when Lizzie had told him of her true identity and the web of lies she had spun to protect her cousin, he had immediately assumed she was a trickster, a seducer, a woman like Annabelle, out to take him for all he had. Lizzie had tried to make him see it was only her identity she had lied about, not her feelings for him, but she knew Daniel hadn't been able to separate the truth from the deception.

Lizzie turned over in the bed to face Daniel in the dark. She couldn't see his face, or his expression, but she knew every feature as well as if it had been etched on her brain. Slowly she reached out a hand and touched his cheek.

'I loved you from the moment we met in the Prestons' garden,' Lizzie said. 'I've never met anyone like you. I've never met anyone who has noticed me.'

She held her breath, knowing this was a pivotal moment. Daniel was angry at her, he felt betrayed, but he was still here beside her. He could have sent her back to London with a maid as a chaperon. In fact, it would have been less scandalous to do so. Instead here he was, lying in bed beside her.

Lizzie felt her jaw clenching with tension and her free hand balling into a fist. This was the moment, their one chance at happiness. If Daniel could bring himself to forgive her, or even just begin to understand that she had never meant to hurt him, they might have a future. She hardly dared to hope. She loved Daniel and over the past couple of weeks she had come to realise that she deserved love. Daniel had made her realise that. He'd pulled her from the shadows and made her appreciate herself, even made her feel beautiful.

'I love you,' she repeated.

The silence stretched out before her and slowly

Lizzie let her hand drop from Daniel's cheek. She'd laid herself bare, told him that she loved him, and he'd responded with silence.

She didn't blame him, she'd broken his trust, but that didn't make his rejection hurt any less.

Lizzie bit her lip to stop herself from sobbing and turned back over in bed so she was facing the wall. She heard every breath Daniel took and part of her was still hoping he would reach out and pull her body towards him, wrap her in his arms and tell her everything would work out.

They lay side by side without touching for what seemed like hours. Every muscle in Lizzie's body was tense and she knew if Daniel just touched her with a single finger she would fall happily into his arms.

He didn't touch her. The minutes ticked by and slowly his breathing steadied and deepened. Lizzie didn't sleep at all. Her mind was active, planning for the days ahead, and her heart was mourning the loss of the man she loved.

Lizzie had lain there through the darkest part of the night and waited until the grey light of dawn started to filter in through the thin curtains. As the first birds began to chirp she carefully got out of bed and pulled on her dress.

She couldn't be there when Daniel woke up. Another day of him being barely able to look at her would destroy what was left of her heart. She had to get away, allow both of them to make a fresh start.

Quickly Lizzie collected all of her meagre belongings into her small bag. She hesitated by the door and looked back at Daniel. He was sleeping peacefully, all the worry from the past few days wiped from his face. Lizzie couldn't help herself, silently she crossed back over to the bed and kissed him softly on the lips. He didn't stir, but as Lizzie pulled away he smiled in his sleep.

Before she could talk herself out of her decision, Lizzie turned away and left the room. Once outside she rested her forehead against the wall and made herself breathe. She was making the right choice, this way both she and Daniel got a fresh start. If she stayed and allowed him to take her to London, the whole situation would get more and more complicated. Now she had accepted they could not be together Lizzie had to move on. It might be heartbreaking, but it was possible.

Once she had calmed her nerves and silenced the voices of doubt in her head, Lizzie descended the stairs and went into the bar. The landlord was already up, cleaning the mess left by his patrons the night before. He nodded a greeting to Lizzie but didn't say anything as she exited the inn.

The night before, just after dinner, Lizzie had discreetly asked the landlord when the first stagecoach to London passed by. If it was on time, it should stop outside in a few minutes' time.

Lizzie waited by the side of the road, every so often glancing up at the window of the room she had shared so briefly with Daniel.

Chapter Twenty-Eight

Daniel stirred and stretched as the light filtering through the thin curtains reached his eyes. He felt warm and contented and as if he could stay in bed all day. He was still half-asleep and instinctively reached out across the bed. He could smell Lizzie and for one moment he forgot everything that had gone before and just wanted her in his arms.

The other side of the bed was cold. With a groan Daniel forced open his eyes and surveyed the room, expecting to see Lizzie sitting in the hard chair trying to ignore the half-clothed man in her bed. The chair was empty and Daniel sat up quickly with a curse. The events of the past few days came rushing back, culminating in Lizzie's declaration of love the night before. The declaration he had said nothing in reply to.

Daniel jumped out of bed, stumbling slightly as his muscles raced to keep up with his brain. Quickly he surveyed the room—all of Lizzie's belongings had gone. She hadn't had much with her, but the small bag with her change of clothes and few personal items wasn't anywhere to be seen.

Within two minutes Daniel had thrown on the rest of his clothes, ran a hand through his hair and pulled on his boots. He certainly didn't look as presentable as an earl should, but he wouldn't offend anyone out here in the country.

'Have you seen the woman I was with?' Daniel asked as he strode into the bar.

The landlord had just finished tidying up from the night before and was sitting at one of the small tables eating a meal of bread and cheese.

'Left early this morning,' the landlord said, getting to his feet as Daniel entered the room.

'She left?' He couldn't quite believe what he was hearing. He'd expected her to be holed up in one of the private rooms, trying to stay as far away from him as possible.

'Asked about the first stagecoach to pass and went outside to meet it.'

Daniel shook his head in disbelief. She couldn't be gone, she just couldn't. There were so many things he wanted to say to her, so many things not yet resolved.

He hurried outside and looked around the deserted

yard. There wasn't even a stable boy in sight. Daniel ran out to the road, wondering if he would find her sitting on a rock, waiting for him to come and rescue her, but she wasn't there.

Daniel felt a pressure begin to build around his heart. He couldn't have lost her, not yet. He might not know what his feelings for her were any more, but he did know he didn't want her leaving his life quite so abruptly.

Making his way back to the inn, Daniel didn't go back inside immediately, instead heading towards the stables. A young lad was just opening the door, rubbing his bleary eyes, as Daniel arrived.

'Saddle one of my horses,' Daniel said. 'Have it ready to go in five minutes.'

He cursed at not having any of his fast horses with him. The beasts used to pull the carriage they had travelled in yesterday were good strong animals, but they weren't particularly fast. He needed to catch the stagecoach before it reached London, otherwise he knew Lizzie would disappear for ever in the vast city.

Whilst the stable boy went about getting one of the horses saddled and ready to go Daniel returned to the inn, collected his belongings and paid the landlord, asking him to keep the rest of his horses and the carriage safe until his return. Hopefully with Lizzie in tow.

* * *

It was less than fifteen minutes later that Daniel was on the road, pushing his horse hard through the flat countryside. He rode like a man possessed, all the time trying not to analyse why he was quite so upset.

Daniel knew this was all his fault. He had set out to take Lizzie to London to get some space away from her. He found it difficult to think straight when she was around. He didn't know whether he could trust her, didn't know whether her small lie had just got out of control, or whether there was a deeper deception going on.

When he'd found out she was lying to him about her identity his mind had instantly darted back to when he had discovered Annabelle's deception. The irrational part of him had screamed that he'd been conned again, allowed another woman to fool him and trick him into giving her his heart. Daniel had immediately tried to protect himself in the only way he knew how; he'd closed himself off.

Last night when Lizzie had said she loved him his resolve had cracked a little. Maybe Lizzie wasn't like Annabelle, maybe she was just a good woman caught up in a lie that had got out of hand. He'd looked into her eyes and seen sincerity and hope and he'd wanted to trust her, but some little part of him had held back.

Now he was in turmoil. He knew he still loved her, but he wasn't sure that he could forgive her. After everything he had been through in the past, honesty was important to him, maybe too important for him and Lizzie to have a future.

Daniel just didn't know. He needed time to sort through his feelings and work out whether Lizzie was right, whether love could conquer anything. He needed time, but he also needed Lizzie waiting for him at the end, which if he didn't catch the stagecoach soon would never happen.

He tried not to think of how he would feel if he never saw her again, but as he forced his mind on to other areas he began to imagine Lizzie alone in the world, vulnerable and at the mercy of strangers. Daniel needed to find her. Whether he could forgive her or not, he would never be able to forgive himself if something bad happened to her.

He rode hard for three hours without a break. He could tell the horse was tiring and that soon he would have to stop for water. Just as Daniel was about to despair that he had lost Lizzie for ever he saw a cloud of dust up ahead.

Quickly he spurred his horse on for one last gallop and within five minutes had caught up with the stagecoach.

Daniel approached carefully, knowing the last thing he needed was to be mistaken for a highwayman and shot by an overeager driver.

'Good morning,' Daniel said as he drew up alongside the horses and the driver.

'Morning,' the driver greeted him gruffly.

'I'm so sorry to bother you, but I'm looking for my runaway sister. I think she might be on board.'

The driver looked Daniel over carefully. Daniel cursed his rumpled clothes and wild hair, knowing he probably looked more like a highwayman than a gentleman.

'Sorry, sir, can't stop the coach in the middle of nowhere. More than my job's worth.'

Daniel knew it was no use arguing. The man had his instructions and wasn't likely to disobey them if there was even the smallest possibility Daniel was there to rob his passengers.

'Where's your next stop?' Daniel asked.

'Coaching inn about an hour away.'

Daniel glanced down at his flagging horse and wondered if the beast could make it another hour. Now they were going at a slower speed it had recovered, but Daniel knew another hour would probably be pushing it.

'I've got a purse full of money that's all yours if you stop.'

Daniel reached into a pocket and withdrew the purse, jangling it temptingly.

The driver looked conflicted. Daniel knew there would be more money in the purse than the driver made in a year, but equally he wouldn't want to be blamed for a robbery if this was all a hoax.

In the end the greed won out and the driver pulled sharply on the reins bringing the horses to a walk and then finally to a stop. Daniel tossed him the purse and quickly dismounted, crossing to the coach in two long strides and flinging open the door.

'Lizzie?' It was gloomy inside but Daniel could see immediately Lizzie wasn't in there.

'Did you pick a young woman up at the Bull Inn?' Daniel asked, turning back to the driver.

'No, sir.'

Daniel cursed as he slammed the door shut. He'd lost her. If she wasn't on this stagecoach, he had no idea where she was. Maybe she was on an earlier stagecoach, maybe a passing carriage had picked her up, or maybe she had decided to walk into the village back near the Bull Inn. Whatever the explanation, Daniel knew he wouldn't ever pick up Lizzie's trail in time now.

He watched as the stagecoach pulled away and felt the despair mounting inside him. Lizzie was lost to him and before he could figure out exactly how he felt about her.

Daniel snorted. That was a lie. He knew exactly how he felt about her: he loved her. What he didn't know was whether he could bring himself to trust her enough to spend his life with her.

Turning back the way he'd come, Daniel let his horse walk at its own pace. There had been an inn just a few miles away and he should be able to get a fresh horse there. Then he would return to his estate and begin the search for Lizzie whilst he tried to work out whether he had a future with the woman he loved.

Chapter Twenty-Nine

It had been nearly two weeks since Lizzie had last set eyes on Daniel, two weeks of misery and fear and hunger. She'd had only a little money when they'd left Cambridgeshire and Lizzie knew it wouldn't last her very long. After a ticket on the stagecoach, a bite to eat and nearly two weeks' accommodation in a rat-infested dive the money was almost gone.

Lizzie had wept that first night. She'd wept for the life she had lost and she'd wept for the hellhole she now found herself in, but, ever practical, Lizzie had allowed herself only one night of self-indulgence.

Standing at the mouth of the alley, Lizzie glanced around her. She'd never imagined she would have to frequent such a neighbourhood, but the past few weeks had taught her she could survive anything. With a deep breath Lizzie walked into the darkness and knocked on a door halfway down the alley.

After a minute the door opened and a small man peered up at her from the gloom within.

'I was told you might be able to help me,' Lizzie said, trying to keep the tremor from her voice.

'What have you got?'

Lizzie ran her fingers over the bracelet on her wrist. It was delicate, a thin gold chain, simple but elegant.

'How much for this?' she asked, unclasping the bracelet and holding it out to the small man.

She tried to ignore the feeling of betrayal. This was all she had of her mother, the only thing she had to remind her of the woman she could barely remember. Lizzie knew her mother would understand, that she would want Lizzie to put her survival over her sentimentality, but it didn't make parting with the last link to her parents any easier.

'I'll give you ten shillings for it.'

Lizzie bit her lip. She knew it was worth more, but equally she didn't know where else she would go to sell it. Cautiously she nodded her head.

She waited whilst the man counted out her money and handed it over, then gave him the bracelet, telling herself it would be worth it.

Lizzie exited quickly before she could change her mind, squinting as she emerged out into the light from the gloomy interior.

With her ten shillings hidden away from any pick-pockets Lizzie made her way through the streets of London towards the office she had been visiting every day for the past week. Today she would find a position, hopefully as a governess, but she would even take something as a housekeeper. Lizzie knew ten shillings wouldn't last her very long and, without knowing where Amelia was, she had no friends or contacts in England whatsoever. Well, except for Daniel, and there was no way she could contact him—she'd promised herself a clean break, and even just seeing him once would make her resolve shatter.

'Miss Eastway,' the woman in the ladies' employment agency said with a sigh as Lizzie pushed open the door.

'Good morning, Miss Farnham,' Lizzie greeted the bespectacled woman, ignoring the sigh. 'I've come to see whether you have any new vacancies today.'

Miss Farnham looked down at the sheets of paper on her desk and Lizzie felt a surge of hope. She just needed one chance, one person to employ her, and she would be safe. Lizzie didn't even want to think what might happen if she didn't find a job before her money ran out completely.

'Do you have your letters of reference yet?' Miss Farnham asked.

Lizzie took a deep breath and considered her reply. The only big lie she had told in her lifetime was pretending to be Amelia and look where that had got her: standing in a shabby office in the middle of a strange city with no money, no prospects and a broken heart.

She had two options: she could tell the truth and most likely face starvation and spending nights on the street, or she could tell her second big lie of her lifetime.

'They came in this morning,' Lizzie said, hoping the guilt she felt didn't show on her face.

Lizzie dug out the two letters and handed them over, hoping Miss Farnham wouldn't look too closely.

The older woman unfolded the first letter and began reading. She nodded in approval and repeated the process with the second.

Of course the letters were forgeries. Lizzie had sat up for hours the night before, trying to think what to say in her references. She'd been complimentary, but not too gushing, stating that she was a good, hard worker who kept to herself.

'This should make things easier,' Miss Farnham

said and smiled for the first time since Lizzie had walked into her office a few days ago.

'Are there any positions available?' Lizzie repeated the question she had asked every day.

Miss Farnham cleared her throat and started searching through the papers in front of her. Lizzie found herself holding her breath.

'There is one thing, the notice came in yesterday afternoon.'

Lizzie waited whilst the older woman found the job she was talking about.

'The only problem is it's a long way away.'

Lizzie would travel as far as she needed as long as it meant there was a job at the end of the journey.

'The position is as governess to two young girls down in Devon.'

Devon. Just about as far from Cambridgeshire as you could get.

'They're looking for someone to start as soon as possible.'

Perfect, Lizzie thought. Even if Devon seemed worlds away.

'The only problem is you will of course have to pay your fare to get down there. The mistress of the house has very kindly said she will reimburse whomever we send once they have taken up the position, but you will have to shoulder the cost up front.'

Lizzie thought of the ten shillings she had hidden in her purse. Surely the fare to Devon wouldn't be more than that.

'It might be a little less costly to find a ship,' Miss Farnham said kindly. 'That way you don't have to pay for your board as well.'

After the passage from India Lizzie had hoped not to have to go on another sea voyage for a long time, but she supposed a journey along the south coast of England would be better than the long voyage half-way around the world.

'I'll book myself a passage immediately,' Lizzie said.

'Good. Take your letters of recommendation and report to this address.' Miss Farnham wrote out an address in Devon and handed it over to Lizzie. 'Good luck, Miss Eastway.'

Lizzie left the small office with a smile on her face. She might never see the man she loved again, but at least she had a job. For the first time in her life she was in charge, she was the one making the decisions. Ever since she could remember Lizzie had obeyed her uncle's every instruction, but not this time. She would not return to India to a life of misery as Colonel Rocher's wife. Maybe a few months ago she would have surrendered to her uncle's wishes, but not now. The past month with Daniel had taught her a lot, but the main thing was self-respect. For the first time in her life Lizzie felt as though she mattered and her opinions mattered, too. She deserved to be happy as much as anyone else and if no one else would fight for her happiness, then she would.

As she walked briskly towards the docks Lizzie couldn't help thinking about Daniel. She wondered what he was doing and whether he missed her. Every time she pictured his smiling face Lizzie felt the pain of leaving him all over again, but she knew it had been the right decision. If she'd stayed, he would have tried to protect her out of a misguided sense of chivalry and Lizzie would have fallen in love with him more and more every day. She doubted Daniel would ever be able to forgive her properly, not after he had been so betrayed by Annabelle, and if she stayed in his life he might come to resent her. Lizzie didn't want him resenting her. She had her memories and she had her new-found self-respect. That would have to be enough.

Lizzie entered the docks and pulled the shawl she had draped across her shoulders tight across her chest. It was the middle of the day and the docks were swarming with people, but she still felt a little nervous coming into such a man's world unchaperoned.

She made her way to the cramped little office of the shipping company that had transported her and Amelia from India to England over a month before. She didn't know the first thing about arranging a passage to Devon, but this seemed a good place to start.

'Good morning,' she said as she entered the office.

A harried-looking clerk glanced up at her with surprise before holding a finger up and returning his attention to the papers in front of him. After a minute he finished what he was doing and looked up again.

'Are you lost?'

Lizzie shook her head, feeling completely out of her depth.

'I need to book a passage to Devon,' she said, trying to smile, but feeling too nervous to manage much more than a grimace.

'We don't sail to Devon. We have routes to France, Spain, India. Nothing to Devon.'

Lizzie sensed the clerk was about to return his attention to the papers in front of him so spoke quickly.

'I've never booked a passage on a ship before,' she said, giving the clerk her sweetest smile. 'I don't suppose you could recommend a reputable company who do sail to Devon?'

The clerk sighed but grabbed a piece of paper and hurriedly wrote something down.

'Salters and Son. Their office is about five hundred feet to your left. They won't scam you and there will likely be other passengers on board.'

'Thank you,' Lizzie said gratefully, taking the slip of paper in one hand. The clerk had already bent his head and returned to his work.

Lizzie walked further down the docks until she saw the battered sign of Salters and Son above a small office almost identical to the one she had just been in.

'Good morning,' a clerk greeted her as she pushed through the door.

'I'd like to book a passage on a ship to Devon,' Lizzie said.

'Our next ship sails tomorrow.'

Before she could talk herself out of the idea Lizzie handed over her money and booked herself a small cabin.

Tomorrow. It was so soon. Whilst in London, although alone, Lizzie knew there were people nearby whom she at least recognised. Acquaintances who would come to her aid if she were in real peril. Once she set sail for Devon, she would be truly alone.

Daniel would be almost a whole country away and there would be no chance of ever seeing him across a room or catching a glimpse of him in a crowd. Lizzie told herself this was what she needed, a completely fresh start, but as she walked out of the shipping office she couldn't help but feel as though she was making a mistake.

Chapter Thirty

Daniel bent down and placed a kiss on top of Edward's head, unable to stop himself from grinning as he did so.

'Daddy, what's a monkey?'

They were sitting in Daniel's study on a rainy afternoon looking at books together. Edward, being just three years old, liked the big old illustrated encyclopaedias with pictures of creatures and sights from around the world.

'A monkey is an animal that lives in the jungle,' Daniel explained slowly. Over the past week he had got used to adapting his language for the young boy, although he was careful not to talk down to him. Even at the tender age of three Edward got offended if Daniel oversimplified things.

'Monkeys swing through the trees and they make this noise.'

Daniel did his best impression of a monkey. Edward was immediately on his feet jumping around after his father, imitating him.

They collapsed breathless after a minute and Daniel enjoyed the feeling of holding his son in his arms.

Once he'd lost Lizzie's trail, Daniel had been frantic. He knew he had to find her, he wouldn't be able to forgive himself if something bad happened to her, and in his mind there was no doubt that it would; she was a pretty young woman without any money.

Luckily the man he had summoned to help Lizzie search for her cousin had been waiting for him when he returned to his estate. Immediately he had instructed the agent to begin searching for Lizzie, and not to stop until he found her. Daniel only hoped he wouldn't be too late.

What he was going to say to her once they were reunited was another matter entirely.

Whatever he decided, he certainly needed to thank her. For days after she had disappeared from the coaching inn Daniel had not been able to stop replaying her words in his head. *Love can conquer anything.*

He'd remembered their conversations about Edward and how she had been convinced a father's love was more important than thinking oneself of legitimate birth. Hour after hour Daniel had tried to figure out if she was right, then eventually he had acted.

Daniel had summoned a lawyer, taken the lawyer to Annabelle, and half an hour later had returned home with his son. The law was made by men and it favoured men, but in this instance Daniel didn't care about the inequality or unfairness of it. Edward was now in his custody, and there was nothing Annabelle could do about it. In the end Daniel had asked his lawyer to draw up a contract that gave Annabelle a small yearly sum of money if she did not try to publicise the scandal. He had also granted her the right to visit their son, as long as the visit was prearranged, and suggested he help her find lodgings in the local area so she could still be part of Edward's life.

'Daddy, can I have a dog?' Edward asked, his nose buried back in the illustrated encyclopaedia.

Daniel glanced at the entry his son was looking at and smiled. On the page was a picture of an Old English sheepdog, complete with shaggy coat and lolling tongue. The dog would outsize his son at least threefold, but Daniel had a sneaking suspicion this was part of the appeal.

'We'll see. Let's get you settled in here first of all and then we can think about a dog.'

A dog wasn't a bad idea, Daniel thought. It would

be a companion to keep his son company as he settled into his new home, someone to explore with and
get him over the transition period. Edward had not
had too much trouble since he had left his mother,
but sometimes at bedtime Daniel saw a scared little
boy tucked up in bed and he wanted to do anything
to help Edward feel completely at home and relaxed.

'I was bitten by a dog,' Edward said as he traced
the picture of the sheepdog in the book. 'But I still
want one.'

Daniel ruffled his son's hair affectionately and
wondered how to go about buying an Old English
sheepdog puppy. A friend for Edward to grow up
with.

'Did it hurt when the dog bit you?' Daniel asked.

Edward looked up at him with wide eyes and nodded.

'You're a brave boy.' Daniel bent down and placed
another kiss on his son's head.

'Mama wanted to have it killed,' Edward said,
pulling a face. 'But I cried until she said no.'

'You forgave it,' Daniel said, 'even though it hurt
you.'

Edward looked at Daniel with his lips pursed and
a question in his eyes.

'What does that mean?'

'To forgive someone?'

Edward nodded, looking up at Daniel as if his father had the answers to all the questions in the world. Daniel felt a rush of love for his son and had to take a deep breath before replying; this was the first of many lessons he was going to be able to teach his son.

'To forgive someone is when you show you don't feel angry or upset after someone has hurt you or done something wrong.'

Edward smiled up at his father.

'So I forgave the dog for biting me?'

'Exactly.'

'And you forgave Mama for keeping you away from me?'

Daniel knew he had to be the bigger man here. His son didn't need to feel anger towards either of his parents.

'That wasn't her fault. It wasn't anyone's fault, so there is nothing to forgive.'

Daniel watched as Edward went back to looking at the illustration of the dog. He knew he could never forgive Annabelle for keeping him and Edward apart for all these years, even if he told his son there was no one to blame, and he was having a hard time forgiving himself for thinking the scandal of illegitimacy would be worse for Edward than having a real father. He had Lizzie to thank for making him realise it.

Lizzie, kind and caring Lizzie. The woman who had got caught up in her own lie and hadn't been able to find a way out. Perhaps all this time he had been too harsh on her. He had made mistakes. In fact, his entire way of thinking the past three years was mistaken, but his little boy, who was only three years old, had forgiven him and allowed them to move on. Maybe he could do the same with Lizzie.

As soon as the notion came to him Daniel knew it was the right thing to do. He loved Lizzie, and it wasn't a love based on lust as it had been with Annabelle. Certainly he desired Lizzie, but his feelings ran much deeper than that. He craved her company, wanted to share every exciting event and every mundane moment with her. He missed her low-pitched laugh and her quiet appreciation of the world.

Daniel couldn't help but smile. He loved her, he loved Lizzie Eastway, and it didn't matter that she didn't have the name he'd first known her by. If it meant spending his life with her, Daniel would be content to call her by a different name each week, as long as her surname was Blackburn for eternity.

He needed to find her and tell her how he felt. He'd been a fool pushing her away and there was a very real possibility he'd lost her for good. Daniel was afraid she might have boarded the first ship for India, intent on fleeing the country after he had rejected her. If she was halfway across the world by now, he knew the chances of getting her back were slim, but he also knew he wouldn't be able to rest until she was back in his arms.

Daniel knew he shouldn't have pushed her away, especially when they had lain side by side together in the coaching inn and Lizzie had told him that she loved him. She'd bared her soul and reached out to him and he had rejected her. Daniel would certainly not blame her if she had fled the country after that incident. He would make it up to her, he would spend a lifetime declaring his love for her, as long as he could get her back in his arms where she belonged.

Daniel was also acutely aware that she had forgiven him for his deception. She had listened to his story about Annabelle and his son, and she had sympathised with him. There had been no anger and no blame. Lizzie had forgiven him immediately, but when she had needed him to understand why she had lied he'd pushed her away.

'You look sad, Daddy,' Edward said as he glanced up from the book.

Daniel wondered how much to tell his son and

knew he should be honest with the boy. Even at just three years old Edward was a perceptive boy.

'I'm thinking about a friend of mine who I should have forgiven a while ago.'

'Why does that make you sad?'

'I don't know where she is to tell her I forgive her and I'm sorry for not telling her sooner.'

'Then she can forgive you, too.'

Daniel hoped so. He didn't know what he would do if Lizzie had sailed back to India, but he knew he'd be completely devastated if she was still in the country and rejected him once he found her.

'I hope she can forgive me,' Daniel said quietly.

Edward lost interest in the conversation and started flicking the pages of the book through his fingers, giggling as he got faster and faster.

Daniel hoped Frampton, the agent he had sent to search for Lizzie, returned with some news soon. He couldn't bear not knowing what had happened to her. He didn't know if she had any money or any contacts or if she was sleeping rough on the streets. The idea of her spending her nights alone in London sent shivers of fear to his heart.

He was also worrying about Golding, the Bow Street Runner who had visited his estate a few weeks before to question Lizzie about the fire. The man had been back, demanding to see Lizzie, even storming in when Daniel had told him she was no longer there. Mr Golding had informed him that he had a warrant for her arrest and wanted to question her further. Daniel just hoped he found Lizzie before Mr Golding did. The accusations against her were ludicrous, but the thought of Lizzie even just having to defend herself in front of a magistrate made him feel sick.

As Daniel watched Edward flicking the pages of his book there was a knock on the door. Quietly his butler entered and looked at Daniel meaningfully.

'Mr Frampton is here to see you, my lord.'

Daniel felt his heart start to pound in his chest. He hoped Frampton had found Lizzie, but just a small part of him worried that the agent would come bearing bad news.

'Show him in.'

Daniel rose from the floor and sat behind his desk, hauling Edward up on to his lap and handing him a small wooden toy soldier to keep him occupied whilst Daniel spoke to the agent.

Frampton entered and Daniel motioned for the tall man to take a seat opposite him.

'Tell me,' he said, his voice hoarse with trepidation.

'I've found her,' Frampton said.

Daniel felt every muscle in his body relax a fraction as the relief washed over him.

'I rode all afternoon to tell you, otherwise it might be too late. Miss Eastway is due to sail for Devon tomorrow morning. She's taking up a position as a governess.'

'Tomorrow morning?' Daniel repeated. It wasn't long enough. He might be able to reach London if he rode all evening and into the night, but he only had to have a small mishap and Lizzie would have already sailed.

Daniel gritted his teeth. It didn't matter. He would follow her all the way to Devon if that was what it took. He wasn't going to lose the woman he loved.

'Westwood,' he called loudly.

The elderly butler stuck his head round the door a few seconds later.

'Tell the grooms to ready a horse. I need to ride to London immediately.'

As usual Westwood didn't blink as he issued the strange order, but just shuffled out of the room to do as Daniel bid.

'I'll write down the ship and location of the dock Miss Eastway is sailing from,' Frampton said, and Daniel handed him a pen and paper so he could do so.

Quickly Daniel pocketed the slip of paper and

handed over Frampton's fee, waiting until the agent had left the room before turning to his son.

'I need to go to London to sort things out with that friend I was telling you about,' Daniel said to his son.

'Can I come?'

Daniel shook his head. 'I'll take you to London soon, but I need to ride very, very fast so I can speak to this friend before she sails away to the other end of the country. You'll be safe here with Nanny Jones.'

He wondered if his son would protest, but Edward thought about Daniel's words for a moment, then shrugged and went back to playing with the toy soldier.

Fifteen minutes later Daniel was ready to go. He gave Edward one last kiss and hug before handing him over to his nanny, then he mounted his horse and galloped down the long sweeping drive. He had to get to Lizzie before she left for Devon, he had to tell her he loved her. He couldn't bear to be without her any longer.

Chapter Thirty-One

Lizzie stood on the deck of the ship and looked out over London. Although she had spent only a short couple of weeks in the city she felt sad to be leaving. This was where she had met Daniel and this was where many of her memories of their time together were based. In Devon she would have no reminders of the walks they took together in the park, or the balls they danced at or the afternoon rides on horseback. There would be nothing to remind her of Daniel except her own bruised heart.

She knew she should be focusing on her new life and grateful that she had found a position as governess. Certainly this life would be better than the alternative: a loveless marriage to a man at least two times her age who was rumoured to beat his wives. At least this way she would be free to make her own decisions.

Despite all this Lizzie couldn't help thinking of

Daniel and the life they could have had together. She would have been happy spending her days by his side and her nights in his bed. If only she had never lied to him, or at least confessed the truth much earlier, then she would be in his arms instead of about to sail down to Devon to start a whole new life.

'We're just loading the last of the cargo,' the captain of the ship said as he came to join Lizzie at the rail. 'And then we'll be off.'

Lizzie nodded and smiled absently at the captain, too caught up in her own thoughts to make small talk. She knew she was watching for Daniel, that some romantic part of her was hoping that he would gallop up on his horse and sweep her into his arms. He'd declare that he forgave her and realised that he couldn't live without her.

The horizon remained empty.

Lizzie sighed and turned away from the rail, leaning back against the wood and angling her face up into the sun. It was a warm day, nowhere near as warm as it used to be in India, but she could at least enjoy the feel of the sun on her face. Life was about small pleasures now.

'Running away, Miss Eastway?'

Lizzie jumped with fright, her eyes snapping open at the sound of the man's voice. Mr Golding, the Bow Street Runner who had questioned her about the fire at Aunt Mathilda's house, was standing in front of her.

'No,' she said, clutching her hands together to stop them from shaking. 'I have a job as a governess waiting for me down in Devon.'

'And is this as Miss Elizabeth Eastway or Miss Amelia Eastway?'

Ah. So he'd found out about her lie concerning her identity.

'Elizabeth,' she said quietly.

'I'm afraid that will have to wait. I am arresting you for starting the fire on May the twenty-third at Mrs Hunter's London home. I will take you to prison to await further questioning by the magistrate.'

Lizzie felt her knees go weak and she clutched at the rail behind her to steady herself.

'I didn't do anything,' she said, beseeching the man to believe her.

'Funny, most criminals say the same thing.'

'I didn't do anything.'

'You can tell the magistrate your side of the story, but for now you're coming with me.'

He grabbed her none too gently by the upper arm and guided her across the deck and down the gangplank. The captain of the ship watched as she went, but did not intervene.

As her feet touched solid ground Lizzie wondered

if she should try to escape. She was all alone, a woman who had no friends to vouch for her, someone who had lied about who she was. Why would the magistrate believe what she had to say?

'Don't even think about trying to escape,' Mr Golding said, hauling her up into a waiting carriage. 'I will shackle you if you give me any trouble.'

Lizzie sank back into the seat of the carriage and tried not to cry. For the past week she had thought her life couldn't get any worse; she'd destroyed her relationship with the man she loved and had been living in a rat-infested boarding house with barely any money for food. Now she wished she could go back, wished she was anywhere but here.

They sat in silence throughout the journey through the city. Lizzie occasionally glanced out the window, wondering whether this was the last time she would see the sights of London, whether she would be waking up tomorrow in a fetid cell.

After well over an hour of travelling the coach drew to a halt and Mr Golding got out. He motioned for Lizzie to follow him, and as soon as her feet touched the ground she was flanked by two other men who grasped her firmly by the upper arms.

Instinctively Lizzie started to struggle. She had nowhere to run and no one to seek help from, but her survival instincts told her she should try to escape nonetheless.

'No point trying to get away, miss,' Mr Golding said sternly. 'Not a single soul has escaped from custody in the twenty years I've been working for the magistrate.'

Lizzie forced her body to obey and allowed the two guards to guide her towards the imposing building in front of her.

'This is a prison,' Lizzie said, her words coming out in a panicky voice.

'That's right.'

'But I haven't done anything wrong.'

'That's your opinion, miss.'

'You haven't got any proof, any evidence. You can't just throw me in prison.'

'You'll be kept in our custody until you are taken in front of the magistrate to face trial, as is usual in a case like this…' Mr Golding paused as if wondering whether to say anything more. 'And we do have evidence, Miss Eastway, plenty of it. We don't just go around arresting people on a whim.'

Lizzie shuddered as she was led through the imposing archway. A small man dressed in tatty clothes and with almost entirely black teeth unlocked the gate as they passed through, then closed it behind them with a loud clang.

'Elizabeth Eastway,' Mr Golding said. 'Awaiting trial under Magistrate Kirby.'

'Welcome to Trinity Prison,' the man with the awful teeth said with a horrible grin. 'I can take her from here.'

As much as Lizzie hated Mr Golding right now she dreaded more being left to the mercy of this scruffy prison guard. Mr Golding just nodded, turned and walked away, waiting at the gate for it to be reopened and then disappearing out of sight.

Lizzie felt a wave of panic wash over her. She was all alone in prison with no one to help her.

'Follow me, miss,' the guard said. 'Smith's my name, and I'll make sure you're well looked after.'

Lizzie had no choice but to follow Smith through another set of gates and into the prison proper.

'I'm guessing you've never been in prison before,' Smith said cheerily. 'Don't fret, miss, I'll steer you right.'

They walked down a dingy corridor lined with damp bricks, passed through another gate and then reached the cells. Lizzie could smell them before she could see them: a foul mixture of human excrement, unwashed bodies and despair.

'We've got half our cells for people awaiting trial with the magistrate,' Smith said. 'The other half are long-stayers.'

They walked past door after door of thick wood, all with a grille at eye level for the guards to see in. Lizzie didn't dare look into any of the cells, she was frightened enough. If she peered inside, she might lose control completely.

'This is you, miss, got the cell to yourself at the moment.'

Smith led her into a small, dark room. There was no window, no natural light at all, just the dim illumination from the candles that lined the passageway outside.

'Right, let's get down to business,' Smith said. 'We provide water, food you have to pay for. Have you got any money on you?'

Lizzie had just the few small coins she had received in change from when she had booked her passage on the ship. She handed them over.

'Good, I'll make a note of how much you've got, subtract the cost of your meals. By the looks of it you'll have enough to pay for three days' worth of food.'

Lizzie swallowed. She didn't know how long she was likely to be held before trial, but three days' worth of food didn't sound like very much.

'If I were you, I'd use some of the money to send a message to a friend, tell them you're here and ask them to top up your account.'

Lizzie didn't know who she could ask. The only people she knew were Aunt Mathilda, whose house she was accused of burning down, and Daniel. Daniel had made it very clear what he thought of her the last time they'd been together, but deep down she knew he wouldn't hesitate to help her when she was in need. She would just have to swallow her pride and ask him for help.

'Could I write a note?' Lizzie asked.

'I'll bring you a pen and paper later—it'll come out of your account, of course.'

Lizzie nodded. The rate things were going, she wouldn't even get a meal tonight.

'Don't worry, miss. Magistrate Kirby doesn't keep prisoners hanging around. You'll get to stand trial within the week.'

A whole week in this place. Lizzie didn't know if she could bear it. As Smith left, locking the thick wooden door behind him, Lizzie sank to the floor in despair. If she was found guilty, she would be spending a lot more than a week in prison. She wasn't sure what the penalty for arson was, but she was sure it would be severe, most punishments set by law were.

Lizzie rested her forehead on her knees and started to cry. She didn't know how any of this had happened—surely Mr Golding couldn't have any real evidence that she started the fire, quite simply because she didn't. Lizzie had known Harriet hated her, even after she had found out Lizzie wasn't Amelia, the real target of her hatred, but surely she wouldn't allow her lie to go this far?

With the tears running down her cheeks Lizzie allowed herself to sob loudly. In the past few weeks she had lost the man she loved and she had lost her freedom. She dreaded to think what she might lose next.

Chapter Thirty-Two

Daniel wove his horse through the crowds, all the time conscious that if he didn't make it to the ship before it set sail Lizzie would be out of his reach for even longer. He pushed onwards, passing ship after ship moored at the dock, hardly taking in the frenzied activity as the crews loaded and unloaded whole hulls of cargo.

He pulled his horse up in front of the *Lady of the Sea* and quickly dismounted, flipping a coin to a passing young lad to hold the reins for him until he returned. Quickly he hurried up the gangplank and grabbed the first man he saw.

'You've got a passenger, a lady, where is she?'

The man looked surprised and shook his head. 'Best you speak to the captain.'

He pointed the captain out and Daniel strode over to him.

'I'm looking for a passenger of yours, a Miss East-way,' Daniel said, wasting no time.

The captain looked him up and down, taking in his finely tailored, but currently dishevelled, clothes.

'Who are you?'

'The Earl of Burwell.'

The captain stood a little straighter and swallowed nervously.

'Miss Eastway was due to be sailing with us,' he said in a tone that made Daniel immediately worried. 'She even boarded the ship about an hour ago. Unfortunately a man came looking for her, had a warrant for her arrest.'

Daniel closed his eyes. He'd known they hadn't seen the last of Mr Golding.

'Where did he take her?'

The captain shrugged apologetically. 'I didn't ask.'

Daniel thought for a minute, trying to work out what patch of London Mr Golding must cover and therefore which magistrate he needed to find.

'Thank you,' he said as he dashed from the ship, grabbed his horse and retraced his route along the dock.

Three hours later Daniel was in the foulest mood he had ever experienced. He'd finally found Magistrate Kirby, and the pompous fat man had refused to listen to reason. Daniel had suggested Lizzie be released to his custody until the trial. The magistrate had refused. Daniel had suggested the magistrate drop the case and get on with dealing with real criminals. The magistrate had refused. Daniel had suggested the magistrate should be stripped of his position and thrown into prison himself for letting such a ridiculous case come to court. The magistrate had thrown him out.

Now Daniel was standing in the prison courtyard talking to a much more reasonable man, a guard called Smith. At least he knew how to accept a bribe.

'She's settling in fine, my lord,' Smith said. 'Although she doesn't have much money for food or the like.'

Daniel brought out a few more silver coins and flipped them to Smith.

'See she gets everything she needs.'

'Do you want to see her?'

Daniel nodded. As much as he hated the idea of seeing Lizzie in this awful place, he knew her reality of being locked up here was so much worse. He wanted to comfort her, hold her in his arms and tell her everything was all right.

'Follow me.'

Daniel followed the guard through a few sturdy gates, down a dank corridor and past at least twenty identical cells before they stopped in front of a locked door.

'I can give you ten minutes, no more,' Smith said.

Daniel didn't argue. As much as he wanted to stay and comfort Lizzie, he really needed to be out in the world, finding out exactly what 'evidence' Golding thought he had and how he could quash it in court.

Smith opened the door and Daniel stepped into the cell. It was so dark inside at first he thought it was empty, but then he saw the figure curled up in the corner and he realised it was Lizzie.

Two eyes looked at him warily.

'Daniel?' Lizzie's voice quavered as if she couldn't quite believe it was him.

Daniel stepped towards her, but before he could reach her Lizzie was on her feet and throwing herself into his arms.

'It's all right, you're safe,' Daniel murmured into her hair as she clung to him and sobbed.

'I didn't know if you would come,' Lizzie managed to gasp in between the tears.

'Of course I would.'

'But it's only been an hour since I sent the letter.'

Daniel frowned. 'What letter?'

'The letter telling you I was in here.'

'I never got your letter. I came looking for you.

The captain of the *Lady of the Sea* told me you'd been arrested.'

He could see the spark of hope flare in her eyes, but then she looked at him warily. The last time they had been together he'd rejected her. He could tell a small part of Lizzie dared to hope his presence here meant everything was forgiven, that he had realised he couldn't live without her, but she wasn't about to risk her heart again so readily. This time Daniel would have to speak first.

'I rode all night,' he said.

Daniel knew he was dishevelled, his hair and his clothes were a mess and he had thick stubble covering his chin.

'I've been searching for you ever since that night in the coaching inn,' Daniel said.

Lizzie pulled back and looked up at him. Although the more pressing problem was Lizzie's incarceration, Daniel had to make her see that he loved her. Now it mattered more than ever. He wanted her to know that he would fight for her freedom, that he loved her more than life itself.

'I had to get away,' Lizzie said. 'After...' She swallowed and changed tack. 'I needed to get away.'

'I was a fool, a complete and utter fool.' Daniel took another step towards her and captured her hand in his own. 'I should have told you I loved you then.

I should have shouted it from the rooftops and sung it in the streets.'

Daniel hated that he had to do this with Lizzie locked in prison, but he felt as though he had waited long enough to tell her he loved her. He didn't want her going a single moment longer thinking he was angry with her, or that he didn't want to spend his life with her.

'I was angry and I felt betrayed. I was too caught up in the past to see you never meant to hurt me. To see that you weren't like Annabelle.'

Lizzie's eyes flared with hope and Daniel wanted to gather her in his arms and kiss her until the end of time, but he knew their time together was limited, so instead he pressed on.

'I know you never meant to hurt me, that the lie just spun out of control, but at the time I couldn't get past the fact that you'd lied to me just as Annabelle had, to see that it was nothing alike. Yours was a simple mistake that got out of hand. It was never malicious.'

'It was never malicious,' Lizzie repeated.

'I'm sorry I didn't see all this sooner,' Daniel said, stepping closer and putting an arm around her waist. 'I was blind and stupid and I should never have let you go.'

If he hadn't let her go, she probably wouldn't be

locked up now. He would have been able to protect her from Golding. If she was safely tucked away at his estate, the odious man would never have got to her. Daniel knew he would carry that guilt for the rest of his life, but right now he had to focus on securing Lizzie's freedom.

'I'm sorry I lied to you,' Lizzie said, allowing Daniel to pull her in closer so their bodies were almost touching.

'I understand now. You did it because someone you loved asked you to.'

'I thought it would be a harmless little deception, that I would be back to being plain old Lizzie Eastway before I met anyone.'

'Not old and certainly not plain,' Daniel said, making Lizzie smile despite their surroundings.

'Then when I did meet you I kept putting off telling you who I really was. I tried a few times, but my heart wasn't in it, I was too afraid of losing you.'

Daniel grimaced. 'You thought I only wanted you for your dowry.'

Lizzie nodded. 'Well, Amelia's dowry. Mine is non-existent.'

'I have to admit that was the reason I started to pursue you, but it wasn't long before I realised the woman I planned to marry for financial reasons was the woman who drove me half-mad with desire.'

'Only half-mad?'

Daniel grinned. 'We can work on that as soon as I get you home.'

Lizzie's face fell as she remembered where they were and why she was locked away.

'I'm scared, Daniel.'

'Of course you are.' He placed two fingers under her chin and tilted her head backwards so she was looking up into his eyes. 'Lizzie, I promise you that I'm going to get you out of here. I won't rest until you're back home with me.'

For a moment she just looked at him, then she nodded. Daniel felt the weight of the responsibility as she placed her trust in him.

'I wish I was home with you now,' Lizzie said and Daniel saw the tears starting to fall down her cheeks again.

'I wish that, too.'

He held her in silence for a minute or two, wrapping his arms around her and pressing her close to his body. He wished he could swap places with her, go through this ordeal for her, but he knew he couldn't. The best he could do was quash whatever evidence Golding thought he had against Lizzie.

Suddenly Lizzie pulled away.

'Daniel,' she said seriously, 'you do realise if

we are together you won't have the money to pay Annabelle.'

Daniel felt his heart constrict as he realised how much she loved him. Even now, when her future was uncertain at best, she was still thinking of him and his son.

'I got some good advice on that front,' he said, pulling her close again .

'What happened?'

'A very wise woman told me love could conquer anything and it got me thinking. I summoned a lawyer and paid a visit to the mother of my son, and she soon came round to my way of thinking.'

Even in the darkness Daniel could see Lizzie's eyes flare with hope.

'Edward is now living with me and he knows I am his father.'

Lizzie sprang forward and started smothering Daniel's face with kisses. He loved how selfless she was. Even whilst her life was so grim she was pleased he had worked things out with his son.

'And Annabelle?' she asked after a few minutes.

'It was all very civil with the lawyer present. Of course, as Edward's father I have more parental rights anyway, but the lawyer drew up a contract, which means Annabelle no longer has any hold over me.' Daniel shrugged and broke into a smile. 'I told her she could visit Edward sometimes and I'm going to help her find lodgings nearby. I think it's important that Edward still sees her from time to time.'

'Is Edward coping without his mother?' Lizzie asked.

'He's blossoming. It'll take time, of course, but we've got years to show him we love him.'

'You mean...'

Slowly he looked into her eyes and brought her hand to his lips, placing a kiss on her knuckles. This wasn't how he ever imagined himself proposing, but he wanted Lizzie to realise he was there for her. He wanted her to know he would fight until the bitter end for her freedom, all because he loved her.

'Lizzie, will you make me a very happy man and be my wife?'

'Are you sure, even after all of this?'

'I'm sure.'

He kissed her, gently and reverently, trying to make her see that none of this mattered. He didn't care that she'd lied to him about who she was and he didn't care that she was accused of arson, all he cared about was securing her freedom and spending the rest of his life showing her how much he loved her.

'You still haven't answered me,' he said.

'Yes.'

Daniel allowed himself a moment of pure happiness, then he hardened his resolve as he focused on the task ahead of him.

'One minute.' Smith's voice came through the door.

'Be strong, Lizzie,' Daniel said, grasping her hand tightly. 'I'll get you out of here, I promise.'

'It's Harriet,' Lizzie said. 'I'm sure she's the one who accused me. She hates my uncle for losing all of her family's money. This is her revenge.'

Daniel nodded, knowing he would find Harriet and drag her to court if that was what it took.

'Before you know it we'll be back home and I'll never let you from my sight again.

The heavy door swung open and Daniel pulled Lizzie towards him for one last kiss. As he walked out the door he saw her sink to the floor and he seriously contemplated sweeping back into the cell, gathering her in his arms and fighting his way out, but he knew that wasn't the way to help her. He needed to prove the accusations were false and he couldn't do that if he was locked up, too.

Chapter Thirty-Three

Lizzie tried to stand up straight and hold her head high, but it was difficult when you were dressed in clothes covered in grime and hadn't had a wash for days. The jeering crowds didn't help much, either.

As Mr Golding led her into the courtroom Lizzie desperately looked around for Daniel. She knew he would have been working tirelessly to try to secure her freedom, but part of her was panicking he might not have had enough time. Rather than the week Smith had predicted, Lizzie had been held in the prison for only two days before being summoned to court.

Mr Golding pushed her to a bench at the front of the court, where she sat, her shackled hands resting in her lap, beside the other people standing trial.

Every few minutes she looked around the room, hoping for a glimpse of the man she loved. Part of her still couldn't believe they were actually engaged and once or twice she had wondered if Daniel visiting her in her cell had been a dream, but then she had remembered how he'd held her and how he'd kissed her and she knew he'd been there.

The room fell quiet as the magistrate entered and Lizzie swallowed nervously. He was an imposing man with a shock of grey hair and a huge double chin that wobbled every time he moved. He looked down at the people sitting on the bench in shackles with disdain and Lizzie knew immediately he was likely to be a harsh judge.

Forty minutes later and Lizzie was physically trembling. Three of her fellow shackled prisoners had been led away, all openly sobbing. Two were going to be transported for stealing, one had received a harsh prison sentence for pickpocketing and all this had been decided on within forty minutes.

Before her incarceration Lizzie hadn't thought much about the law and the punishments meted out to the accused. In India every now and then she had witnessed a scaffold being erected, but her uncle had always ushered them off in the other direction, eager to shield his precious Amelia from anything unsavoury.

Now she wished she knew if these sham trials were the norm. The accused were barely allowed a defence. The evidence would be set out before the magistrate, the magistrate would ask if anyone had anything to say to defend the criminal and so far no one had spoken up, then he would proclaim their guilt and sentence them harshly.

'Elizabeth Eastway,' the magistrate called.

Lizzie felt her knees wobble as she was hauled to her feet.

'You are accused of arson. Burning down one Mrs Hunter's house. The penalty if you should be found guilty is death.'

Lizzie felt her head start to spin. Surely this wasn't real. She felt as though she should wake up from a nightmare any moment.

'Mr Golding, please present your evidence.'

Mr Golding stepped forward, handing a piece of paper to the magistrate. The magistrate dipped his head and read slowly.

'I have here a signed statement from one Miss Harriet Hunter swearing that she saw you light the fire that destroyed her mother's house.'

Lizzie shook her head. She'd known Harriet didn't like her, but she never thought she would go to these lengths to hurt her.

Mr Golding handed the magistrate another piece of paper.

'I have another signed statement from a housemaid, Rosie Thomas, stating that she saw you with a candle the night in question.'

Hardly a crime, to be carrying a candle on a dark night, but Lizzie knew it just helped the magistrate seal her fate.

'Does anyone have anything to say to defend Miss Eastway?' the magistrate asked.

Silence. Lizzie looked around frantically. If Daniel didn't speak up now, she was going to die. She scanned the faces in the crowd, desperately pleading with someone to say something, to defend her.

Nothing. Just silence. The magistrate looked down at her severely.

'I'm innocent,' Lizzie said, finding her voice. 'All you have is the word of a spiteful young girl against mine. If you convict me on the lies of one person, you are making a mockery of the justice system.'

The magistrate rose to his feet, his face turning an unhealthy purple colour with rage.

'You may not speak,' he bellowed.

'And why not?' Lizzie asked, trying to keep the tremor from her voice. 'You are about to sentence me for a crime I did not commit. Why may I not defend myself?'

The magistrate spluttered. He was clearly not used to having educated people in his court and certainly not accustomed to being spoken back to.

'I will hold you in contempt of court,' he shouted.

'And what will you do?' Lizzie asked. 'Hang me twice?'

The silence that followed stretched out for what seemed like eternity and was only broken when the doors to the courtroom burst open.

'What now?' the magistrate yelled, turning to face the newcomers.

Daniel strode down the steps, dragging a crying Harriet behind him.

'Get out of my court,' the magistrate ordered.

'I am the Earl of Burwell and if any of you lay a hand upon me I will see to it you are never employed again,' Daniel said as a couple of guards moved towards him.

'I don't care who you are. Here I am in charge.'

Daniel turned to the magistrate with an icy stare and Lizzie felt her heart pound in her chest. He had come back for her. He was here to rescue her, remove her from this awful nightmare and make sure nothing like this ever happened again. She felt all the courage she had summoned to speak up for herself blossom under his gaze and she knew they would be leaving the courtroom together.

'Your case rests on the testimony of Harriet Hunter,' Daniel said, not wasting any time. 'Well, here she is, all ready to tell you she lied.'

None too gently he shoved Harriet forward towards the magistrate.

'This is not how things are done,' the magistrate bellowed. 'Get out of my court.'

'Are you saying you will not listen to evidence that proves this woman's innocence?' Daniel asked calmly. 'That sounds pretty illegal to me. I was sure your remit was to weigh the evidence from *both* sides.'

The magistrate said nothing, so Daniel stepped forward and prodded Harriet.

'Tell the court your name.'

'Harriet Hunter,' Harriet said miserably.

Lizzie wondered what Daniel had threatened Harriet with to get her here.

'And tell the court about your awful lie.'

Harriet looked up at the magistrate and glanced sideways at Lizzie, then she crumbled.

'I'm sorry,' she said. 'I lied. Lizzie didn't start the fire. It was an accident, a terrible accident.'

The magistrate stared for a second, then, finding a new target for his anger, rose to his full height.

'You mean to tell me you lied in a sworn statement?'

Harriet nodded morosely, refusing to meet anyone's eye.

'You have committed an awful—'

'Oh, do shut up.' Daniel cut the magistrate off. 'Now let me tell you what is going to happen.'

Lizzie watched as the man she loved went about securing her freedom. Since her parents had died she had never really had anyone fight for her, but now she had Daniel. She knew he would do anything to keep her safe and that knowledge made her feel like a queen.

'You are going to release my fiancée, the future Countess of Burwell, immediately, and you are going to apologise for treating her quite so abominably. Then I am going to leave with Miss Eastway and Miss Hunter and I will spend the next few days considering who to tell about your dubious views on the law. If I were you, I wouldn't expect to be a magistrate for much longer.'

The magistrate sank back down in his chair, the fight leaving him, and motioned for one of the guards to unlock Lizzie's shackles. As soon as she was free she ran to Daniel and threw herself into his arms.

'Let's get out of here before he regains his composure,' Daniel whispered.

Lizzie felt him slip an arm around her waist protectively and hustle her outside and up into a waiting carriage. He directed Harriet to another carriage before climbing up and sitting beside Lizzie.

Lizzie felt her body go weak and she collapsed into Daniel.

'You're safe now,' he whispered as he gathered her into his arms and pulled her on to his lap. 'I'm never going to let you go again.'

'I thought you weren't going to make it,' Lizzie said as she gripped Daniel's hand.

Daniel grimaced. 'I thought I would have more time, but Kirby seemed in a hurry to sentence you.'

'How did you persuade Harriet to come?'

'I didn't. I just told her mother what she had done. After that Harriet didn't have a choice. Mrs Hunter does care for you rather a lot, you know.'

Lizzie nodded. Aunt Mathilda was a kind woman who had forgiven Lizzie's lies immediately. Of course she wouldn't let Harriet's malice send her to the gallows.

'I care for you rather a lot, too.'

Lizzie smiled as Daniel bent down and covered her lips with his own. He kissed her deeply, as if trying to tell her he would never let her go again.

'In fact, I love you.'

Lizzie felt all the worry and upset from the past few days wash away with his words. He loved her. The man she loved, loved her back.

'I love you, too.'

'Now let's get you home.'

Epilogue

Lizzie placed her hands over her eyes and started counting slowly. Behind her she heard scuffling and laughing as Daniel and Edward dashed out of the room.

'Six, seven, eight...'

Lizzie couldn't believe how lucky she was. Just a few months ago she had been plain Lizzie East-way, a young woman with no self-confidence and no hopes of love. Now she was Lizzie Blackburn, Countess of Burwell, a wife, a lover and, tentatively, a mother to Edward, too.

'Twenty, twenty-one, twenty-two...'

In all the long years she had lived under her uncle's roof Lizzie had never even dared to dream her life might turn out like this. She was happy. Her days were filled with love and laughter and fun, and her nights were filled with passion.

'Thirty-five, thirty-six, thirty-seven...'

Lizzie's heart still pounded in her chest when she caught Daniel looking at her with his dazzling blue eyes and desire written all over his face. She loved it when he stole a kiss from her when they were out and about, loved the fact that he still couldn't keep his hands off her.

'Fifty, fifty-one, fifty-two...'

Her time spent in prison now seemed like a bad dream. All the awful memories had been replaced by moments of love and laughter with her new little family. Of course, there had been gossip. Daniel was the only earl with a wife who had nearly been sent to the gallows, but as with everything the gossip settled down with time.

'Fifty-nine, sixty, sixty-one...'

They'd been lucky with the wedding, too. Daniel had used his connections and Lizzie had found herself walking down the aisle in a private ceremony just two weeks after Daniel had proposed. Her only regret was her cousin Amelia hadn't been there for the wedding. The agent Daniel had tasked with finding her hadn't managed to track her down in time, but this afternoon Amelia was coming to visit. In her last letter she had hinted that she had some news of her own, but wouldn't tell Lizzie what it was. Knowing Amelia, Lizzie guessed that she'd probably impulsively joined the circus or become an opera singer. Nevertheless, Lizzie couldn't wait to see her cousin and find out where she'd been all this time.

'Sixty-five, sixty-six, sixty-seven...'

Lizzie sometimes thought of the life she could have had if Daniel hadn't come after her. She would be a governess in Devon, not much more than a servant, with no one to hold her close at night, no one to wake her with a morning kiss. Or the life she could be living as Colonel Rocher's wife, bruised and battered, her spirit beaten out of her. Or, even worse, she could be awaiting execution for a crime she hadn't committed. All her life Lizzie had assumed she would never experience true love and here she was, more infatuated with her husband every single day.

'Seventy-nine, eighty, eighty-one...'

Of course, there had also been a bit of a scandal when Lizzie's true identity had been revealed and the *ton* had realised she was not the heiress she had presented herself to be. In truth, Daniel had shielded her from the worst of the gossip, both about her time in prison and her lies about her identity, and Lizzie hadn't really cared anyway. She was married to the man she loved and a positive side to the whole situation was that the gossips were talking about her and Daniel rather than little Edward. Her notoriety was protecting him from being the centre of attention.

'Eighty-five, eighty-six, eighty-seven...'

Lizzie stroked her stomach through her dress and wondered if she would be allowed just one more miracle. Daniel was a wonderful father to Edward and she knew he wanted more children, and with the amount of time they spent in the bedroom Lizzie knew if she were lucky it would happen soon. She wanted to give Daniel another child, a little brother or sister for Edward, and although it was far too early to tell, Lizzie had a good feeling about this month. Her monthly courses were just a few days late, but maybe, just maybe, this was the start of a whole new adventure with her little family.

'Ninety-eight, ninety-nine, one hundred. Ready or not, here I come.'

Lizzie spun around and walked out of the room. With Edward being just three years old he wasn't all that good at hide-and-seek, but on rainy mornings like this one he could play for hours, hiding in rather obvious places and squealing with delight as either Daniel or Lizzie found him.

Lizzie walked slowly through the hallway, looking for telltale feet sticking out from under pieces of furniture or a small giggle as Edward couldn't contain his excitement. She made her way into the dining room and stopped just through the doorway.

'I wonder if anyone is hiding in here?' she mused loudly.

She started circling the table, moving round to where a pair of legs were sticking out at the other end.

Carefully she bent down and grabbed both legs by the ankle.

'Oof,' Daniel said. 'You found me. You're far too good at this game.'

He half slid out, flipped over so he was lying on his back, then instead of standing up he looped an arm around Lizzie's waist and pulled her down on top of him.

'We're meant to be searching for our son,' Lizzie said as he kissed the tip of her nose.

'Stop wriggling, woman.' Daniel held her more firmly against him and after a few seconds Lizzie stopped trying to get up.

'He'll enjoy the suspense and thinking he's really foxed you this time.'

Lizzie glanced over her shoulder. Anyone could walk in the room and find them on the floor, half underneath the table and giggling like naughty children.

Daniel waited until she turned her head back

towards him, then kissed her quickly on the lips. Lizzie felt her body melting into Daniel's and all her token resistance faded away as he ran his hands firmly down the length of her back and cupped her bottom before giving it a squeeze.

'Maybe we'll have time to disappear to the bedroom before your cousin arrives once Edward gets tired of hide-and-seek,' Daniel whispered, his breath tickling Lizzie's ear.

Lizzie couldn't help but smile. 'You think Edward is ever going to get bored of that game?'

Before Daniel could protest Lizzie pushed herself upwards and stood, looking down at her husband.

'Help an old man off the ground.'

'You shouldn't hide in places you can't get out of,' Lizzie said with a grin, repeating Daniel's words to Edward from an hour previously when the boy had found himself stuck in the fireplace.

Daniel heaved himself off the floor with an exaggerated groan, then darted forward and swept Lizzie up into his arms with ease. Lizzie liked the feel of Daniel holding her, knowing that she was completely safe and loved.

'Right, we've got a scallywag to find,' Daniel announced, walking out of the dining room still carrying Lizzie.

'Put me down,' Lizzie said with a laugh, knowing Daniel would do nothing of the sort.

'No. Now, where can that son of ours be?'

'I think he's in the library,' Lizzie said loudly.

They heard a giggle coming from Daniel's study. Quietly Daniel crept inside, still carrying Lizzie in his arms. Without making a sound he set Lizzie down on the carpet and together they approached the small pair of legs sticking out from under Daniel's desk.

Lizzie felt overcome with love for her perfect little family. She loved her husband and she loved Edward, the boy she was beginning to think of as her son.

'Got you,' Daniel said as he grabbed his son's legs.

Edward giggled and wriggled out from under the desk. Immediately he threw himself into Daniel's arms and Lizzie felt her heart swell. In the past few weeks she had watched as Edward started to trust his father more and more. Soon it would be as if they'd never spent the first few years of his life apart.

'Again, again,' Edward shouted as he dashed off out of the room.

Daniel turned to Lizzie and caught her hand before she could leave the room to hide.

'I love that little boy,' he said quietly, 'and I love you.'

* * * * *